PENNY PIECES

We went down to a little patch of green by the river, a bench among some bushes, hidden even though I could hear people talking a few feet away. 'Isn't there anywhere better?'

'Don't worry, love, I always do it here.' I swallowed hard, thinking of him sitting there, masturbating with his great dirty cock in his hand, thinking about the bums and boobs of the girls he watched on the streets. His hand scooped a good seven inches of thick cock. Its smell was heavy in the air; really strong. It was actually frightening me, and I wanted to delay the awful moment I took the grotesque thing in front of me in my hand.

'What's your name?'

'Richie,' he answered, taking hold of his ghastly cock and pushing it towards me. 'Ain't I got a nice one?'

My fingers touched the hot damp skin, closing on the hard shaft. My hand looked tiny and pale on his cock, my slim fingers and manicured nails making an obscene contrast to the way it stuck up from his grubby old trousers. I couldn't take my eyes off it; watching myself masturbate a filthy old tramp.

GW00566910

PENNY PIECES

Penny Birch

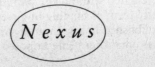

This book is a work of fiction.
In real life, make sure you practise safe sex.

First published in 2001 by
Nexus
Thames Wharf Studios
Rainville Road
London W6 9HA

www.nexus-books.co.uk

Typeset by TW Typesetting, Plymouth, Devon

Printed and bound by
Cox & Wyman Ltd, Reading, Berks

ISBN 0 352 33631 5

Contents

Penny Pieces *is a collection of short stories, opening and ending with filthy dirty essays from me, the rest told by characters from my books. Anybody who has read my stories before will know that these are going to be pretty naughty; anybody who hasn't either has a treat in store or a big shock coming . . .*

1

Six Faces of Correction – Penny Birch

Being spanked is a pretty emotional experience for a girl, and that doesn't go away, no matter how many times it happens. I've lost all count of the number of times I've been spanked, but it is still strong and I still crave more. Pleasure is the overriding feeling for me, but that doesn't mean it doesn't hurt, both physically and mentally. The moment when my panties come down still fills me with an overwhelming sense of shame and exposure, and I'm not acting when I kick and squeal. Sometimes I even cry. Spanking hurts even when the victim is enjoying it, even when it is the thing she most wants, and some people seem to forget that. I want my arm twisted or my hair pulled to hold me in place; I want my bottom exposed and my cheeks spread to show off my pussy and bumhole; I want to be spanked until I howl. My emotions are real, and I hope that knowing that will be part of what makes my tormentor demand her pussy licked or his cock attended to once I've been thoroughly punished.

Punishment is the key, the idea being that however much I may want my spanking I am being given it because I deserve it. My first spanking actually came from my Aunt Elaine and was done strictly to punish me. She has no idea that afterwards I took myself to orgasm with a hairbrush in my pussy and a toothbrush up my bum. If she had known she'd have been horrified. Part of the thrill had come from the fact that I really had had no say in the matter, and ever since then the idea of having my control taken away from me has been important in my spanking fantasies.

In reality I'm a stickler for respect and consent, and nobody gets me across their knee unless I want them to. Fantasy is different, and I often think about how it would be if people would just take charge of me occasionally and give me a thoroughly good spanking and all the powerful emotions that come with it. Better still would be if I didn't know how much I was going to enjoy it, an experience I've never had, because by the time Aunt Elaine got to my bottom I already knew I needed a spanking.

It might have been different though, in so many lovely ways, which I often fantasise over. I always like to imagine my mind in a welter of confusing emotions, but with one uppermost, whatever it might be. Pain is popular, and the anticipation of pain. To get the best out of it I'd have to know I was going to be spanked well in advance of the event. That way I'd be really nervous, with butterflies in my stomach and a desperation to go to the loo. I'd probably be in tears before the first smack fell, long before. It would have been at college, only I'd have been even more innocent and insecure than I really was, which was plenty. Maybe I wouldn't even have understood the effect that an ever so slightly chubby bottom squeezed into a pair of snugly fitting jeans can have on men.

Generally I prefer girls, but for a spanking to really hurt it must come from a man; some great, hulking brute twice my weight with hands like hams. The rowing coach would have been perfect, a huge man running slightly to fat when I'd known him, well over six foot and probably weighing sixteen or seventeen stone. Mr Griffin had been his name. He'd had no respect for women at all, and I remember him pulling one of the female cox's ponytails so that she stumbled into the Thames, then laughing as she came up choking and spluttering. It might have been me . . .

I was furious as I pulled myself out of the water. I was blushing too, my face red with embarrassment as they all laughed at me. To make it worse my clothes were soaked, with my top plastered to my breasts so that every contour showed. My nipples had gone hard from the chill of the river and were sticking out really blatantly. Mr Griffin cracked a joke about them, asking me if I'd been putting rabbit pellets down my bra.

By the time I'd managed to scrabble onto the towpath my wet shorts were half way down around my bum, showing even more. As I pulled them up the crew were laughing so hard some of them were having trouble standing up, and Mr Griffin was slapping his legs with delight. Even a curate who'd been walking by the river couldn't keep his face straight.

I ran into the boat hut with their laughter and cruel comments following me. In the Ladies' changing room my anger overtook my embarrassment and by the time I had dressed I was determined to give Mr Griffin a piece of my mind. He was in his office, whistling to himself as he filled in our times in the book. I already knew what I was going to say, but as he looked up my words died in my mouth. My courage failed me completely, and I ended up babbling something about our chances at Henley. His answer was matter of fact, and my ducking wasn't mentioned, as if the way he had humiliated me in front of the crew was totally unimportant.

My revenge was pretty childish, but I just couldn't bear to let him get away with it. That evening I walked down to the river with some vague ideas about getting into his office and making a few clever changes to his paper work. I knew where he kept the key and was just forging his signature on an order for thirty litres of bright pink paint when he walked in. He cut short my flood of apologies and excuses with one word and told me that I was to come to training an hour early the next day. Then came the shock. He told me, straight out. He was going to take me across his knee, pull down my shorts and panties, then spank me on my bare bottom, hard.

I was terrified, and I begged, raved and threatened, but to no avail. I was caught, and we both knew it. He didn't even try to hide the fact that he was going to get a kick out of punishing me, and that made it worse. I could imagine him, the sweat starting on his red face as my buttocks danced under his hand, his laughter changing to a dirty chuckle as his cock hardened against my belly.

All the way back from the river I had an awful sick feeling in my stomach, thinking of the pain and indignity I was going to suffer the next day. I hate pain, and now I was going to have my bottom smacked. I was sure I wouldn't be able to take it, that I would scream and cry and make a really undignified display of myself. With my bottom bare that meant showing off my pussy, even my bumhole. He'd see it all, and I made a mental note to shower properly before going. It was no good asking him to let me keep my shorts up for the sake of decency either. I'd heard the dirty, lecherous tone in his voice when he said they would need to be taken down.

I didn't eat that evening, or do any work. It was impossible, with my mind running over and over on how stupid I'd been and what I'd let myself in for. I couldn't sleep either, but lay there thinking of how much the spanking was going to hurt and what it was going to feel like having a man pull down my panties to punish me. In the end I pulled the bedclothes down and rolled onto my front. With my nightie up I eased my panties down and lay still with my bare bottom uppermost, trying vainly to overcome my fear of being in the same position over Mr Griffin's lap.

In the end I slept, and woke rolled up in the embryo position, still with my panties around my thighs. I'd dreamed about my punishment, and it was awful to wake up and find that it was still to come. I dressed and forced myself to go into the canteen for breakfast. Lectures passed in a blur and by lunchtime the sick feeling in my stomach had returned so strongly that I couldn't face food. I sat in the library after lunch, pretending to read *Nature* while my stomach fluttered and my buttocks twitched in anticipation of my coming pain.

Training was at four o'clock, which meant getting to him by three. There was a lecture at one, during which I found my eyes going to the clock above the whiteboard every few seconds. Two o'clock came and I hurried back to the hall. I showered thoroughly, making sure I was clean. I even powdered afterwards and inspected myself in the mirror, bent forwards with my cheeks held open to make sure that every little crevice was spick and span. It felt ridiculous, preparing my bottom for spanking, as if I wanted Mr Griffin to be impressed, but I just couldn't bear the thought of not being perfectly clean. Looking at my spread bottom from the rear, with my hairy pussy and the wrinkly pink flesh of my vulva and bumhole showing really brought home what was happening to me. Mr Griffin was going to see it, all of it, and he was going to slap the little round bottom-cheeks, slap them pink.

Dressing was just as bad. The last thing I wanted to do was make a sexy show for him, but that didn't stop me putting on fresh white panties and my tightest green rowing shorts. I even put on a new sports bra, in doing so accepting that my breasts were likely to be coming out at some stage of the proceedings. A white and green top, plimsolls and white socks completed my outfit. The white and green were university colours, as if we'd been racing instead of training. I looked smart and sporty, but once again I was cursing myself for getting dressed up for a man who was going to beat me.

I was on the edge of tears as I walked down to the river, with a heavy lump in my throat and the butterflies going crazy in my stomach. Excuses kept occurring to me, ways to get out of it, from saying I was on my period to setting fire to the boathouse. None were practical, and I found myself knocking on his office door with my heart in my mouth and a weak feeling in my bladder.

Mr Griffin greeted me with an oily, lecherous grin. Both of us glanced at the clock, which showed five minutes to three. He frowned, perhaps wishing he had longer to play with my body, while I was glad that the crew would probably turn up before he could go too far.

As he pushed his chair back from the desk and gave his lap a meaningful pat I found myself on automatic. I'd thought of lots of things to say, protests, pleas, even clever quips, but they went unsaid. Instead I walked around the desk and laid myself meekly across his lap, as if I actually deserved what was coming to me.

He chuckled as I got into position, wrapped an arm around my waist and pulled me close in to his body. I could feel the warmth of his legs and the bulge of his cock through his trousers, just as I had imagined it. His right leg came up, lifting my bottom, his grip tightened and his hand closed in the waistband of my shorts.

I didn't struggle. I didn't protest. My emotions were just too strong, too overwhelming; my embarrassment, my horror of the coming exposure, but most of all my fear of the coming pain. All I could do was hang my head in shame and let the bastard pull down my clothes.

He didn't do it. He hauled them up instead, tugging my shorts tight into my crease to spill the cheeks out at either side and pull the material hard against my pussy. It left him plenty to spank, and although my position was incredibly humiliating, at least my most private bits were covered. My relief lasted about a second and then he had pulled the other way and it was down, all of it, little green shorts, tight white panties, the lot. I gasped in shock as my bottom was laid bare, then again as he cocked his leg up higher still and my bum-cheeks came open.

My bumhole was showing, I just knew it. I'd expected him to want to see it, but the reality was far, far worse than anything I had imagined. I was bare, my cheeks were wide and I could feel the cool air on my anal skin and the warmth of his leg against my pussy. It was too much, and I burst into tears, only to have every other emotion blown away by pain as his huge hand came down across my bare bottom with all the force of his arm.

It hurt. It hurt so much that I lost all control of my body. I was shaking my head, gasping, sobbing and screaming for mercy. My fists were beating on his legs, my hair was flying around my head. I was kicking my legs and bucking my body under his arm, no longer caring about the lewd display of my anus and vagina. Nothing mattered but the agonising swats on my bottom, smack after smack, falling in a fast, relentless rhythm to the tune of my squeals.

I'd started crying from shame, but now I was really blubbering, with the tears making a wet patch on the concrete floor beneath my head. He knew, but he just laughed and went right on spanking, not even pausing as he tightened his grip around my waist. There was nothing I could do, only kick and wriggle and howl out my agony until I was dizzy with it and thought I would faint.

I didn't think it could possibly get any worse, but as he once more shifted my body on his lap I found my pussy spread hard on his leg. The slaps began to jam my clit against him. I was going to come, I couldn't help it. I was going to come, and he'd think I was turned on. I was, and I yelled out as it happened, begging for more, begging for it harder, unable to help myself while all the while a little voice in the back of my head was screaming that I didn't want it, that it was the worst possible thing.

After I'd come I slumped across his lap. Mr Griffin laughed and went on with my spanking. He knew it had happened and he thought it was funny, which was the final indignity. Not that it mattered, because he soon had me kicking again by transferring his attention to the backs of my legs. There was a brief pause as my shorts and panties were pulled right down and off, which I did nothing to resist. He went back to work, methodically slapping my legs to the same state as my bottom, indifferent to my continued squealing and blubbering until once more I thought I would faint from the pain.

The spanking stopped as suddenly as it had begun, leaving me gasping for breath. My buttocks were stinging dreadfully, throbbing too, and so hot. My bottom was up and my legs were wide, showing everything, but I no longer cared. I'd been beaten by him, beaten into submission and I felt as if he had every right to see my most intimate parts.

I did it myself. I don't know why, it just seemed as if I had to. His cock was hard against my tummy, and even as he let go of my waist and I slumped to the ground in a kneeling position my hands were going to his fly. He opened his knees and I shuffled forwards, popping the button of his trousers as I did so. His zip came down and I looked up to find surprise on his face, also lust. Still not knowing why I was doing it I took hold of my top and pulled it up, my sports bra with it, exposing my breasts to him. He smiled, a dirty, knowing leer, then closed his eyes in bliss as I pulled open the front of his underpants and took his stiff cock in my hand.

My bottom was stuck out as I masturbated him, hot and red, beaten and goose-pimpled, my cheeks wide to show my pussy and bumhole behind. Half of me wanted his cock inside me, slid up between my reddened buttocks, maybe even in my bottom-hole. I knew I'd do it, and I began to jerk frantically at his erection, desperate to make him come before my resolve snapped and I took him in my hole.

I think it would have happened if he hadn't grabbed me by the hair and forced my head against his penis. He ordered me to suck, snarling out the command, only to come in my face as my lips touched the bulbous head of his cock. I tried to pull away and got an eyeful of semen for my trouble. He milked the rest out over my neck and breasts, soiling my top and wiping his slimy cock-head in my face. Even as he slumped back I was running for the Ladies where I locked myself in a cubicle, sat my hot bottom down on the lavatory seat and masturbated myself dizzy . . .

In reality, of course, I'd have threatened to report him for sexual harassment and I'd never have got my spanking. Getting the most out of sex often means swallowing my pride, and that's never more true than when it comes to taking punishment.

Spankings should be painful for the victim, but from a psychological point of view the pain isn't really necessary at all. What matters most is that the girl knows she has been punished, that she suffers all the humiliation and indignity of having her bottom bared and smacked. The idea of spanking as a degrading punishment is so deeply ingrained in society that the very knowledge that it has been done is enough to keep me on edge long after the pain has faded. The stinging goes, the marks go, but a spanked girl is a spanked girl, forever.

To feel that way before it had actually happened would be to really dread it, worse still if the girl knew that she would find it sexually exciting despite herself. I suppose a strict feminist with hidden spanking fantasies would be in the worst position, regarding it as unthinkable yet wanting it at the same time. Her overriding emotion would be humiliation.

Again, a man ought to give the virgin spanking, a man who represents the complete opposite of how she feels a man should be. He'd be a chauvinist pig for starters, a sexist and proud of it, also arrogant. He'd be small too, shorter than her and weedy, so that she couldn't pretend to herself that she'd been forced or that she'd only done it because he was physically attractive.

If I wasn't so obstinate and critical of popular fads I might have gone that way myself. Without the initial spanking from Aunt Elaine I might even have made it through university unspanked, coming out with my dirty little fantasies a hidden and embarrassing secret. As I'm only five foot two, the man to take me in hand would have to be the next thing to a midget, but I suppose a jockey might have had the right attributes. Jockeys mean horses and stables, some of my favourite things while, if I had embraced one trendy philosophy, then why not others . . .

It was a simple protest, just the six of us determined to demonstrate our right to roam on open land. Culver Down was nearly a thousand acres of chalk grassland and beech wood, and it was grossly unjust that it should be out of bounds to the public. Besides, all it was used for was exercising racehorses belonging to some city fat cat.

The Down was deserted when we arrived, and after the mild thrill of crossing a gate with a PRIVATE NO TRESPASSERS sign on it the whole thing began to be a bit of an anticlimax. We reached the ridge without incident, and it was there I made my mistake. I needed to pee, and the only cover was a beech hangar a couple of hundred yards back down the slope. Telling the others I'd catch them up, I nipped back. In among the trees I whipped down my jeans and panties, let it all out and was just tidying myself up when I heard voices raised in anger from up the slope. Looking up, I found the others in a confrontation with several men on horseback. I started towards them, only to see my friends turn tail and run, leaving me alone.

My courage failed me and I turned back. I was on open down and I knew they'd seen me, but I hoped that a hasty retreat would satisfy them. It did, most of them, but one detached himself from the group, a small man on a beautiful bay horse. I began to panic and ran, which was stupid against a racehorse, and they caught up with me on the far side of the beech hangar. He ordered me to stop and then dismounted, grinning.

He was a little man, in black and yellow check racing colours, obviously a jockey – actually shorter than me, but with all the cocksure arrogance that I hate in men. My friends were nowhere to be seen and the beech hangar hid the group he had been with, so I was more than a little apprehensive as he walked towards me, slapping his riding-whip against his boot. I was expecting a lecture, but he never said a word, just caught me by the hand, jerked me off balance and brought his whip down across the seat of my jeans. It was such a shock, and stung like fire. I yelped, outraged, demanding how he dared to do such a thing. He just laughed at me. I tried to pull away, but he held firm and gave me another cut, across my thighs.

A ridiculous little tableau started, with him at the centre, holding my wrist as I jumped and squeaked to cuts of his whip. It hurt crazily and I got into a whole series of ridiculous postures in my efforts to keep my bottom away from him, which only resulted in me getting my beating mainly on my legs. The pain wasn't the worst thing, though, but the humiliation of being whacked. Me, a grown-up, liberated woman being punished by a man, and instead of taking it with anger and dignity I was squeaking

11

with pain and getting into silly postures to avoid more. The trouble was, my reaction was just the same as it always was in the ridiculous fantasies of being spanked by a dominant male that I tried so hard to repress.

My hidden spanking fantasies had been the last thing on my mind, and it was the shock of having them brought so suddenly to the surface that betrayed me. Instead of just pain, the cuts started to feel warm, and to my utter horror I began to feel the urge to stick out my bottom and take it. I was going scarlet with blushes and he must have realised why, because he laughed, then pulled hard, twisting my wrist. I came off balance and in no time had been forced to my knees with my arm up high behind my back. He pushed down and my bottom came up, then the beating started again, now full across my bottom.

I was still squealing, panting too, my head burning with humiliation because I was excited by what was happening to me when I should have been furious. It hurt all right, and I was close to tears from the pain, with the vicious little whip smacking down across my seat, over and over again. In the end I did burst into tears, not from pain, but from the utter, unbearable humiliation of being punished by a man and finding it arousing. At the sight of my tears he stopped, threw down the whip and called me a baby. As his hand came down under my tummy and began to feel for my jeans button he said that if I was going to act like a baby then I would be spanked like a baby, on the bare bottom.

That was the final straw. I was beaten, all my defiance was gone, and even if he'd let go of my arm I'd have stayed put and let him do it. The tears were streaming from my eyes and I was shaking my head in broken dismay, but at the other end I was lifting my middle, making it easier for him as he popped my button and eased down my zip. His hand left my tummy and went to the waistband of my jeans. They were pulled down, jeans and panties too, tugged off my bottom to the tune of my sobbing and left down around my thighs. Then it was all showing, my full bare moon red with whip cuts, my pussy moist and glistening, my bumhole puckered and tight, my muscles twitching. I was bare, and I should have been angry, and I wasn't, and despite the agony of my humiliation I found a sigh of pleasure escaping my lips.

He began to spank me, his fingertips slapping against my cheeks to make the skin tingle and warm. It wasn't a punishment any more, and we both knew it, although he kept my arm twisted tight into the small of my back. He knew how to spank a girl for sex, warming my bottom until I was panting with pleasure and my pussy felt swollen and fat. I was ready for entry and I knew he could see it, with my hole moist and juicy between my rosy pink bum-cheeks.

If he'd just had me at least I'd have been left with some pride, knowing that I hadn't been able to do anything about it. Instead he asked, politely, pointing out that I was obviously turned on and promising not to get me pregnant. I was sobbing hard and trying to stop myself from saying it, but it came out anyway, a soft, feeble mew of a 'yes'.

He went right on spanking, covering my bottom with the little tingly pats, just hard enough to bring the blood to the surface. My arm was released and I went forwards, onto all fours with my back pulled in to lift and spread my bottom for entry. I cocked my knees apart, stretching my lowered panties taut, and at that the spanking finally stopped. As he pushed down his jodhpurs I was pulling up my blouse and bra, releasing my breasts to the warm sunlight. He got behind me as I went back on all fours. His hands came under my front to cup my dangling breasts, and he mounted me.

He was prodding at my hole, most of his weight on my back as his cock bumped between my smacked cheeks. Twice his erection slid down the crease of my pussy, rubbing my clit. Twice it nudged my bumhole and for one horrible moment I thought I was going to be buggered. Then it found my pussy and slid up, all the way up, filling me with hot, hard cock. He began to fuck me; his front was slapping on my beaten bottom, sending me to a heaven of beaten, submissive ecstasy I had never thought possible.

The tears were still running down my cheeks, but I couldn't deny it. I was a slut, the sort of girl who got off on being dominated by men, the sort I'd always despised. I was what I'd once heard described as a fuckpuppy.

It lasted a long time, his cock moving in me, faster and faster, until I was panting and mewling out my pleasure. He was good; he didn't come up me, although I couldn't have stopped him. Instead he pulled out at the last minute and came over my smacked cheeks, then rubbed it in with the head of his cock, smearing hot semen onto my skin. I was masturbating by then, with my fingers on my pussy, my self-respect gone completely as I came in front of him. The orgasm was superb, the best, far beyond anything I'd had before, but when it was over I just slumped down, lying still in the grass with my naked red bottom uppermost, the cheeks glistening with semen.

As he stepped away he laughed and I turned to see what he was doing. The horse had defecated, and he was scooping up a big double handful of steaming dung, which was obviously meant for me. I tried to get up, but my legs had gone. I was kneeling as he reached me and then it was too late. He dumped the lot into my lowered jeans, grabbed the sides and pulled them smartly up. I felt the dung squelch against my bottom and up between my legs and for the first time found my voice to call him a bastard. He just laughed, and I didn't resist as he did up my jeans to hold it in and rubbed a handful in my face for good measure. Only then did I get my lecture about not trespassing. Finally he made me pose for a last swat across the now lumpy seat of my jeans and I was sent off the land with several pounds of horse-shit hanging heavy in my panties in addition to my spanked bottom . . .

I wish, but in practise very few men are capable of understanding my need for sexual humiliation, let alone getting it right without having to be told what to do. Wanting to be humiliated is even more politically incorrect than wanting to be spanked. Over the last decade sado-masochism has slowly become more acceptable, particularly male submission, as it's a great way for women to show that they can be sexual and in control. Unfortunately it does nothing for me. It is just about OK for a girl to demand the right to be spanked and enjoy it, but the last two fantasies are not going to be appearing in any women's magazines just yet.

So how should a girl go about getting spanked? It's no good bullying some milksop of a 'new man' boyfriend into it, because it just wouldn't be the same. Once or twice, at university, I tried to tease men into doing it, but it never worked. They'd get wound up, but instead of turning me across their knees for the spanking I so badly wanted they would get angry or go off and sulk. Even then, teasing someone isn't really politically correct, because it's unacceptable to comment on most of the things people are sensitive about.

One exception is fat. Criticising somebody for being overweight is seen as acceptable, even desirable, in a way that criticising somebody's race or creed hasn't been for years. Ideally it would be another woman, because I love plump, cuddly girls. The spanking would be pretty well pure pleasure, dominated by a sense of mischief for the way I'd got it . . .

I'd picked Rosa out as a spanker from the way she spoke. She used it to put men down if they made remarks about her weight, threatening to sit on them and spank them in front of their friends. It worked, not only because men found the threat so embarrassing, but because all but the strongest knew that she could probably actually do it.

Rosa was huge, six foot in her bare feet and over twenty stone. She was fat by any standards, with gigantic breasts, rolls at her waist and a big, lush bottom. There was a lot of muscle too, and we'd all seen her arm-wrestle the number eight in the university boat and come within an ace of winning. As is usually the way, most of the men who'd teased her had been the insecure ones, and by the beginning of our second term they'd stopped, fearful of being given the public spanking she had so often threatened. Personally, the idea set my nipples hard and sent a shiver the full length of my spine every time I thought of it.

The idea of it happening scared me, especially if it was done in front of other people, but I couldn't help myself. I started to tease her, silly little jokes about chairs collapsing under her or her bicycle tyres popping when she rode it. She didn't seem to mind at first, but the warning glitter soon appeared in her eyes. When she finally threatened to spank me I went back to my room and masturbated, face down on my bed with my bare bottom pushed up, eyes closed and imagining I was over her lap, being punished for my insolence.

It was a wonderful orgasm, building slowly in my head and travelling down my back until it burst. After that I got worse, deliberately tormenting her, all the while with a mischievous thrill inside me and my stomach knotting in a mixture of delightful anticipation and fear. Her threats became sterner, also more detailed, including how she was going to pull down my panties in front of everyone. The more she threatened the more I teased, until I'm sure she realised that I was actually desperate for it.

I'd always pictured it happening in the labs, perhaps in the coffee area with me across her knee on one of the big comfy seats, pants down and kicking while my colleagues looked on in horrified fascination. They'd have stopped it, but by then I'd have been spanked and I'd have the experience to masturbate over for ever and ever. As it was, Rosa had no intention of doing anything so risky, nor so likely to be broken up before she could get her full satisfaction out of my bottom.

She caught me in my room, one hot afternoon while I was finishing an essay and hardly anyone else was in the hall. I was lying on my bed, reading a paper and thinking vaguely about getting up for a pee when a knock sounded at the door. She came in without waiting for me to respond and my heart went straight into my throat. In her hand was a hairbrush, a big, wooden-handled affair that might have been designed for smacking naughty girls' bottoms.

16

I barely got a yip of alarm out and she was on me, pushing me down onto the bed and climbing on to straddle me with her enormous thighs. As her weight settled onto my back I was left gasping, also completely helpless. She began to talk, telling me that she was fed up with my insults and was going to punish me. I struggled and begged, just for show. The thrill of being in her power and the anticipation of my coming spanking was rising rapidly and it was hard to hold back my giggles.

She took down my pants, which was so, so wonderful. All I had on was a little floaty dress and a pair of cotton knickers, and she stripped me with quick, matter-of-fact motions, lifting my dress by the hem and peeling down my knickers. With my bum bare in front of her it was impossible not to let out a sigh, but I don't think she even noticed. The next thing she did was even better, pointing out that despite my tiny figure anyone with a bottom as fleshy as mine should think twice before laughing at others.

There was a pause while she let the helplessness and indignity of my position sink in, and then she laid the hairbrush purposefully across my buttocks. I pulled my pillow to my chest and gritted my teeth, knowing it was going to hurt however much it might turn me on, then braced myself as she gave my bottom two gentle pats and set to work.

God, it hurt! I'd expected her to use her hand, not to bring a hairbrush, and from the first blow I was kicking and squealing and yelling for mercy. The racket I was making was enough to raise the dead, never mind reach other students through the paper-thin walls, and she stopped abruptly. I experienced a strong flush of disappointment as she lifted her bottom off my back, but she hadn't finished. Reaching up under her dress and lifting one leg then the other, she pulled off her knickers, a big, dark blue pair like old-fashioned school pants. She settled her bottom back onto me and reached round, ordering me to open my mouth. I did it, taking her huge panties into my mouth, right in, until I was choking on them with just a little tag of blue cotton hanging out between my lips. The taste of her sex was thick in my mouth too, adding to my excitement.

With me safely gagged she went back to the beating. As before I lost control immediately, only now I couldn't utter a sound and I could only breathe by panting desperately through my nose. She laughed as she beat me, commenting on the appearance of my bottom and reminding me of all the cruel things I had said about her. My bottom was on fire and I knew I'd be bruised, but I didn't care, it was lovely, and for all the pain it was exactly what I needed. I was sure she knew I was excited, and as pleasure rose through the pain I started to push up my bottom.

She shifted her weight and that was when I realised that I was in real trouble. The problem was my bladder, which was pretty full – in fact painfully full – while the pain of the spanking was making it hard to keep control. I was going to wet myself, which wasn't part of the plan at all. My struggles abruptly became genuine, and as I jerked the gag from my mouth I was begging her to stop, demanding to be allowed to pee and promising that she could punish me any way she liked once my bladder was empty.

Rosa just laughed, wriggled her big bottom in my back and went right on spanking. I tried to get up, using all my strength in an effort to roll her off my back, but I might as well have tried to move a mountain. It was pointless – she wasn't going to stop – and as the feeling in my bladder rose to a stabbing, agonising pain that put my burning bottom to shame, I just let go. I did it with a choking, miserable gasp as the pee burst from my hole. It went in my knickers and over my thighs, spraying about wildly as I bucked and writhed with the pain of my spanking.

I was screaming out my emotions, cursing her and calling her a fat bitch and worse as the contents of my bladder emptied out onto my clean bed. She only spanked the harder, laughing as she beat me and my pee sprayed out and splashed over my hot bottom. My panties were soaked, my dress too, and plenty must have gone on her. She didn't seem to care, spanking gleefully away and

18

bouncing on my back to knock the breath from my body and squeeze out the last few drops of urine onto the bed.

The spanking stopped with the flow of piddle, leaving us both panting and wet. The bed was soaking, my belly and pubes pressed to the wet coverlet, my lowered panties dripping with it. She had done what she came to do and I expected her to go, leaving me to shamefaced masturbation in a puddle of my own pee. I knew I'd do it, because the sense of mischief had returned, dirty and compelling, making me want to be just as rude as I possibly could be.

She didn't go, she didn't even get up, and she wasn't talking any more either. In guilty silence she pulled open my bottom-cheeks and I let her do it, not even protesting when the hairbrush handle went between my legs and up inside me. Maybe she'd meant to leave me like that, spanked with a hairbrush protruding from my vagina, maybe not, because she didn't leave it but began to fuck me slowly. I pushed my bum up, sighing my compliance to our guilty, dirty sex. Her hand slid down between my thighs, cupping my sex, her palm starting work on my clitoris.

I was brought to orgasm like that, wriggling, spanked and helpless on my wet bed, in absolute ecstasy as she fucked me and frigged me. As I came I called out her name, then sank down, apologising brokenly for all the names I'd called her and thanking her for the punishment. In response she finally climbed off my back, took me tenderly in her strong, heavy arms and pulled my head down between her massive thighs . . .

Actually, I could never be such a little bitch, it's just not in my nature. Mischief is, although it is seldom my principal emotion during spankings. The sense of being rude goes with it, of doing something improper, something I've been brought up to regard as unthinkable. Well, no, something that I should regard as unthinkable. In fact, I think about that sort of thing a lot. Panty-wetting is like that. If you look at it from a completely objective point of view it's really not such a big deal. It doesn't hurt, and while it may

19

be uncomfortable it's really no worse than slipping in the mud. Try telling that to any girl who's ever wet her panties!

What makes it strong is the social disapprobation, and that's something that excites me a lot. Exhibitionism is the same, rude and daring, although with less of the delicious shame that panty-wetting brings. Ideally, of course, a girl who wets her knickers ought to feel guilty for such disgusting behaviour and expect a just punishment, during which her overriding emotion will be contrition.

An old-fashioned disciplinarian would argue that contrition is always the right attitude for a girl to bring to a punishment. After all, she has done wrong and she should expect to be chastised. If that chastisement happens to involve the exposure and beating of her bottom, then that is simply because it is the most practical way to punish an erring girl. The idea that it might turn him on? Ridiculous!

Gross hypocrisy, of course, and nowadays any girl who wets her panties is more likely to expect sympathy than a spanking, and to get it. Victorian double standards are not for me, and I loathe people who preach against promiscuity and so forth, then get caught with their pants down on top of their secretaries. Still, sometimes I do feel I deserve a beating for my behaviour, and it might be nice to be caught by someone who not only didn't know that I like it but expected me to think that they didn't either. Nor should they think that it was something they should do despite the risks, but something they felt they had a perfect right to do . . .

I was perfectly aware that if I went into town I was supposed to cover up; after all, the holiday reps had drummed it into our heads firmly enough. My argument was that if I was prepared to accept their culture, then so should they be prepared to accept mine. Besides, I was a tourist, and without tourism the town would have been little more than a cluster of run-down huts.

So I put on a knee-length yellow sundress, sandals and a wide-brimmed hat. Looking at myself in the mirror, I decided that no reasonable person could possibly consider me indecent. There was no cleavage showing, and no thigh,

20

while the loose material barely hinted at the outlines of my panties and bra. Anyway, if they didn't want to see they didn't have to look.

I got to the market with no more than an occasional disapproving glance. Not many people were about in the midday heat, and most of those were women. I felt sorry for them in their robes and veils, covered from head to toe. It seemed obscene that women should be so cowed in the modern world. I imagined their envy and respect for my freedom and it made me feel proud that I had come out in defiance of the conventions forced on them by the men.

At least I felt that way until one of them spat on the ground as I passed. The act was like a signal. Two women began to follow me, then a man, never touching but always close, so that I had to go deeper into the market. I tried to move down an alley, only to find it blocked by two men, lounging idly against the walls, their expressions making it quite clear that they were not going to let me past.

I was getting scared, and began to stammer out protestations, even threats, pointing out that I was a tourist and had a perfect right to be there and to dress as I pleased. If they understood they took no notice, but continued to move slowly forwards, allowing me to move only towards the centre of the market. I reached it to find every exit blocked, as if it had all been worked out in advance. Maybe sixty or seventy people were there, standing around the little raised platform at the centre of the market square. Their faces were hostile, aggressive, the sort of expression that in England would have been reserved for somebody who'd done something really offensive, like kicking a dog.

Maybe they just wanted to scare me, maybe worse, but fortunately I was rescued. The man was an official of some sort, maybe a priest, in long black robes and a hat that I would have found comic in any less threatening situation. He told the crowd to disperse and they obeyed with respectful inclinations of their heads. I was already babbling out my gratitude when he spoke to me in perfect English, telling me to come with him. I obeyed, far too scared to do anything else.

21

We walked some little way up the hill, to the old town, under an arch of weathered yellow stone and through a door. Beyond was a courtyard, cool and green in the shade of some tree with feathery leaves and with a fountain in the middle. I was feeling pretty awkward, also stupid, and had been mumbling out apologies and trying to explain that I hadn't understood the strength of feeling about women's clothes among the locals. I expected sympathy, perhaps tempered by mild disapproval or a wry amusement at my ignorance. What I got was a lecture, explaining the full idiocy of what I had done, rebuking me for both disrespect and immorality.

I remonstrated at first, trying to make my point but aware that there was a lot of truth in what he was saying. By the end I had hung my head and been shuffling my toes, feeling more stupid than ever and also pretty contrite. Even then, when he said I ought to be punished I didn't think he actually meant it, only to be brought up short as he called back into the house and a woman emerged, holding a stick.

It was about three feet long, knobbly and dark brown in patches, as if stained with sweat. The function was all too obvious. He took it and I found myself backing away and shaking my head, absolutely horror-struck that he could think for a moment that I would allow myself to be beaten with it. Unfortunately, not only did I realise that getting back safely to the hotel might well depend on my accepting the punishment, but a nagging little voice in the back of my head was telling me that I actually deserved it.

He told me, quite calmly, that I was to receive fifty strokes, across my buttocks. I tried to explain that I was English and that that sort of thing just didn't happen. Actually, having taken spankings from various people, I don't suppose I sounded very convincing. Most of them had been for fun, though, and what he proposed was no spanking, but a full-bodied caning. I stopped babbling when my backwards progress met the edge of the fountain. He was looking at me, saying nothing, the horrible cane held in one hand and resting on the palm of the other. I

opened my mouth to speak, then shut it and nodded
dumbly.

He made me strip, not just so he could get at my bum,
but stark naked. As I disrobed he watched, his eyes totally
dispassionate as I exposed first my underwear, then my
breasts and lastly my bottom and sex. Even my sandals
and hat had to go, leaving me feeling very small, very
stupid and very naked. Ready, I bent over the edge of the
fountain, sticking my bottom out and biting my lip as I
tried to tell myself that it wasn't going to hurt all that
much. He finished his lecture while I held my humiliating
position, and at the end asked me if I understood that I
deserved what was about to happen. I said I did, and
although there was still some defiance in me I knew at
heart that I deserved what was coming to me.

As for thinking that it wasn't going to hurt all that
much, that was just plain silly. It was agony, each stroke
biting into my naked bottom-flesh like a cut, making me
cry out and dance my feet in my pain. The first time I stood
up and was going to say something, only to close my
mouth as our eyes met and get back over the fountain with
my bottom stuck out for more. By ten I was still jumping
and rubbing my bottom between strokes and I'd started to
cry, but when I looked back in the hope of sympathy all I
got was a look that suggested my response to be more
pathetic than anything.

I took them all, fifty cuts across my bare bottom,
dancing and mewling, jumping and squealing, crying and
even farting, but sticking my poor whacked bottom out
after every one. As I'd guessed, I was pretty turned on by
the end, beaten into a submissive high, not too different
from the ones my boyfriends had got me into by the firm
application of their palms to my buttocks. This was
stronger, though, the result of a beating far harder than I'd
ever have let anyone give me voluntarily. My bottom was
burning, the skin a mass of purple welts, but my legs had
come apart and my pussy was ready.

Frankly, I expected to be fucked from the rear, for all
his pretence that he was just giving me some necessary

23

discipline. I knew he was excited, because there was a conspicuous bulge in the front of his robes. When he said I could get up I stayed posed and gave him a look, wide-eyed, tear-stained and biting my lip. It was too much for him. He told me I was whore in a tone that conveyed as much disgust as arousal, then pulled up his robes. Underneath he was bare, with big balls and a thick, stubby erection poking out of a mass of black hair.

He came behind me, muttering something about it being unclean to fuck me, and the next thing I knew his cock was pressing to my bumhole. I was slick with sweat and it wasn't my first time, so in it went, jammed up my bottom to the sound of my gasps and grunts. He took me by the hips and buggered me, puffing and swearing as he thrust himself against my bruised bottom. It was rough and he was knocking the breath from my body, while I was so shocked by the sudden invasion of my rectum that it only occurred to me to reach back and masturbate too late. He came, deep up me, grunting like a pig as he emptied his semen into my bowels, then pulling out to leave me oozing and dripping from my anus.

I should have come, but when he called me a whore again I found I couldn't do it. He went to wash his cock and I dressed, wondering how I was going to get back to the hotel. In the end he took me, holding my elbow all the way, for all the world as if I was being taken into custody. In the lobby he called for the manager and gave him a sharp word which I didn't understand. Released, I ran for my room, stripped naked once more and brought myself off with my poor whacked, buggered bottom stuck out towards the bathroom mirror . . .

Not that I'd be so stupid in the first place, but still. I love the idea of getting turned on despite myself, especially by something that I also find painful or humiliating, preferably both. Unfortunately, I know my own dirty little mind too well, and I never really get caught by surprise.

I used to imagine that with experience I'd get cool and laid-back, but being spanked doesn't hurt any less as I get older and I still get flustered and nervous when I'm due to be punished. Sometimes I feel I'd like to be cool, one of these girls who can strip off with impunity and take a good whacking with a happy smile on her face. It really gets to sadists when they can't break a girl, and I'd love to leave some arrogant young man red-faced and panting with a broken cane trailing from his hand while I kneel in serene submission, beaten like hell but still poised and calm.

Generally I'm squealing like a stuck pig after the first smack, and I always break pretty quickly, often bursting into tears. Just once I'd like to be the cool one, with my mind quite composed as I was punished, only I imagine it might mean getting more than I bargained for . . .

I think they expected me to be scared when they said they were going to punish me. When I stuck my bottom out and told them to get on with it they were pretty surprised. It had been a running joke for the whole week, all four of them teasing me and trying to make me blush or get cross. It hadn't worked. After all, it was the end of the season and I'd spent the last three winters working as a chalet girl, so I was used to putting men in their places.

Not that it meant I wasn't going to let them do it. I quite fancied a spanking, then sex with all four of them, together, or one at a time if they couldn't handle showing their cocks in front of each other. They were funny really, so eager and boastful, but if they weren't virgins then they weren't far off it: typical public school boys in fact.

I had to coax them a bit and let them get a few beers down before they'd actually do anything, but once they realised I was genuinely game they were keen enough. One told me to get on the table, still joking, and if I'd refused that would have been that. I didn't refuse, but climbed up and got into my best pose for spanking, in a crawling position with my bum up and my back pulled in. For a while they just stared, and then one of the bolder ones told me to pull down my pants.

He may have meant my ski-pants, not my panties, but I decided to take him literally. Reaching back, I eased it all down, slowly, revealing my bare bum. They were really staring now, wide-eyed, two with their mouths open. I knew they'd want to see my tits, so I pulled my top and bra up, letting them swing free under my chest. Bare from armpits to thighs, with everything important showing, I got back in position, laying my head on my hands.

I felt composed, serene even, and thoroughly in control. They got up, gingerly, closing in on me. Despite it all being on offer they seemed reluctant to touch, but after a good deal of peering at my crevices and some pretty vulgar comments, one went and fetched a kitchen spoon. He came back in smacking it against his hand, grinning boyishly, and I allowed my eyebrows to rise, just a little.

They beat me with the spoon, quite hard, taking turns to lay it across my bottom. Spoons hurt, but I stayed cool, never once yelping, but letting the lovely hot, sexy feeling rise in my bum. They were getting excited, surreptitiously squeezing their crotches as they waited for their turns. The beating was getting harder, and they let me know, commenting on the redness of my bottom. They said other things too, using dirty language, saying that I had 'a nice cunt' and 'we can see your arsehole'. It was getting to me, and with my whole bum warm and glowing I was about ready for sex.

I forget who suggested tying me up, but the idea was seized on enthusiastically. I told them that they were welcome, knowing that they were trying to get me flustered and determined to stay cool. That really wound them up, and three went for things to tie me up with while the fourth continued to work my bottom over with the spoon. He took a good feel too, squeezing my boobs and stroking my smacked flesh. When I didn't object I got a finger up my pussy.

The others came back with an assortment of ties, ski-boot laces and some sort of jump harness. I was stripped first, my clothes hauled off at either end to leave me naked on the table. Next came the harness, a system of broad nylon straps that pushed my breasts apart, pulled up over my buttocks and fastened around my waist. It was

26

tight, and the V-shaped crotch-strap covered my pussy but held my bum-cheeks open, leaving the hole showing. One dirty little bastard suggested that I needed gagging, and that it should be done with my own panties. They were stuffed in my mouth and tied in place with bootlaces. My arms followed, strapped up tight behind my back and fixed to the harness. Only then did I realise that one of them actually knew what he was doing.

Ties were secured to my thighs and my knees were pulled up to my chest. Bootlaces fixed the ties to the harness and I was left helpless with my bottom stuck right out and the cheeks flared wide. My ankles were pulled apart and tied to the waistband of the harness, putting the final touch to my exposure. The position had pulled the crotch-strap forwards a little, letting the cool air to my vagina and pulling the nylon up into the crease of my vulva. They were laughing, commenting on how rude and silly I looked and applauding the guy who'd done the work. I did my best to stay cool, but it was getting difficult, and I felt the first flush of real apprehension when someone suggested carrying on with my beating. I wasn't in control any more, and with my mouth stuffed full of my own panties I couldn't even speak.

They carried me to the sofa and put me in a kneeling position, bum out to the room, spread and utterly available. More crude remarks were passed, commenting on my pussy as a 'fuckhole' and my straining bumhole as a 'chocolate starfish'. With that a lump of humiliation began to rise in my throat, despite my best efforts to stay cool.

There was a brief discussion about what to beat me with, each suggesting a different implement, to the sound of general laughter and further dirty comments. One wanted to use my own hairbrush, another the cane from a pot plant, the third a ski. It was the fourth who got his way, pointing out that a snow-board would cover the whole surface of my bum and give me the spanking of a lifetime.

They fetched the board. I've been paddled before, and it's one of the most painful punishments there is, not just cutting into the poor victim's bottom, but jamming her insides up with every smack. This was going to be worse, I knew it, the snow-board being twice as big and heavy as anything that had been used on me before. I looked back, pleading with my eyes, but they didn't even notice. Then it was being raised over my bare bum.

It came down and nearly knocked me through the sofa. I would have yelled, but I could only manage a sort of strangled coughing through my panty gag. My muscles had jerked in response, and they laughed at my reaction, then once more brought the board down across my bum.

They really beat me, on and on, taking turns to use the board, swilling beer and laughing as I writhed and wriggled under the punishment. I was sweating, and I could feel the wet on my skin, hazy through my pain. Twice I farted, starting fresh laughter and dirty remarks, adding a new pang of humiliation to the welter of emotions in my head. It hurt so much that I didn't know if I was turned on or not, at least until somebody pulled the straps wide of my bum to get a better target. This tugged the crotch plate even tighter into my pussy, right against my clit. There was more laughter, and I was told how funny my bum looked with two broad white lines running across the cheeks where the harness had protected my flesh.

The beating started afresh, but now with each stroke the harness jerked against my clit. I immediately knew I was going to come. My muscles started to pulse, my cheeks clenching and my bumhole opening and closing in what I knew must be an utterly obscene display. They roared with laughter at the sight, but went right on smacking, and as my vagina clenched tight I was coming, writhing, bucking and gagging on my panties, totally, utterly out of control as I reached orgasm in an unbearable agony of pain and humiliation.

It didn't stop them. Their cocks were out, their English reserve gone in a mixture of beer and sadistic lust. My panty gag was pulled free and a cock was stuck in my mouth before I could even get my breath. I sucked dizzily, grateful for the end of the spanking, hardly knowing what I was doing.

They used me, like a doll, taking advantage of my body without the slightest thought for me. Olive oil was poured between my bum-cheeks and up my vagina. I was buggered amid wisecracks about their behaviour at school. My breasts were greased and fondled, my nipples sucked and bitten. One made me take his balls in my mouth, another pushed his bottom in my face and told me to lick his anus. That really made them laugh, with his cheeks held wide so they could see my tongue lapping at his hole. It made them serious too, intent on orgasm. One went up me, in my pussy. Another went in my mouth, the one who had been up my bum. My body was soon jerking to the rhythm of their pushes, one in each end, sending me dizzy while the others urged their friends to hurry up.

Abruptly my mouth was full of thick, salty male come. I swallowed, sucking it down even as the erection in my vagina was pulled free and more semen splashed over my burning bottom-cheeks. There was no gap; a moment later I was full of cock again, only this time it was my sore, greasy anus that got invaded as well as my mouth. The boy up my bottom was rough, and once more the harness was rubbing on my clit, bringing me to a peak so, so fast. My pussy tightened, my bumhole too, squeezing his cock and making him gasp, then grunt as he emptied himself into my rectum with a string of filthy words.

I was fainting, half conscious as my mouth was fucked and the cock pulled slowly from my bottom. A hand was twisted hard in my hair, controlling my head, which was pulled abruptly back. The cock slipped from my mouth, jerked and erupted a stream of come full in my face, over one eye, into my mouth, even up my nose. With that I collapsed back, exhausted, thoroughly used and no longer caring. My whole body was burning, from the beating, from the ropes, from the cocks that had been put in my holes. All my cool was gone, leaving me a sweaty, slimy mess, smeared with come and oil, my anus gaping and dribbling semen, my bottom a mass of bruises, broken but happy . . .

* * *

Which, frankly, would serve me right for being such a cocky little so-and-so in the first place.

So there we are, five of the principal emotions a girl can feel during punishment, each with an individual flavour. They all turn me on, and not just when I think of taking the punishment myself. When I see another girl spanked the view is lovely, no mistake, and I like to stand right behind so that I can get a good look at her pussy and bottom-hole as she's beaten. I love to stand in front too and watch her face, taking in all the emotions running through her head as she is punished. Every detail of her anguish arouses me and makes me want to feel the same, although as I know how it feels myself I also feel sympathy.

I've never seen a girl genuinely punished against her will, and I know that if I did I would do my best to intervene. Having said that, there are times when it's hard not to feel that a good spanking would be just the thing. Maybe I'm just old-fashioned, but I do think that modesty is a virtue – not physical modesty, but modesty about who you are and what you've done. Every time I see the sort of boastful, self-obsessed women we're supposed to view as role models nowadays, I can't help but think how they'd benefit from a few minutes over somebody's lap with their pants pulled down. Mark you, there are plenty of men who are just as bad, but then I don't get a kick out of seeing men spanked.

If it did happen, then I don't suppose her principal emotion would be any of the things I feel, but pure, furious outrage that anybody would dare to do it to her ...

She was what is called an 'It Girl', a brainless media darling with the luck to have passable looks and be born into the right family. She had brought a load of her friends into the restaurant to celebrate a new contract, having been paid some huge sum for a book or film or something. I knew this because she was making no secret of it, but boasting openly about how talented she was and how much of a success she was going to be.

Gian got her table, and for some reason she took against him from the start, taking every opportunity to put him down and make witty little comments to her friends. They were already rather drunk, and her acid humour drew sycophantic laughter from the others, encouraging her. As a waiter he was an easy target, not being able to answer back, although if he had done I would certainly have stood up for him.

He brought them mineral water in a carafe, which gave her the perfect chance to make him look stupid, saying that he should have brought the bottle and that if she had wanted a carafe she would have ordered it. With his poor English he got tongue-tied very quickly, and I came over with the wine list in an attempt to defuse the situation. Unfortunately all I managed to do was turn her wit onto me. She took the list and began to look at it, making occasional ill-informed comments about the wines. After a while she asked what was probably a rehearsed question and not really designed to get information at all, but just to show how clever she was. I gave her the answer in full, very politely, but she was ready for that and immediately christened me 'the snob', drawing fresh hilarity from her friends.

She ordered champagne, pink Dom Pérignon, along with a string of instructions about how it should be served. I was seething as I went down to the cellar. Unpleasant customers are common enough, but they're mainly drunken men making remarks about my figure. She was worse.

When I got back to the table I found her ticking Gian off for being slow with the starters. I could see he was getting riled, so I swapped him with Karl, hoping that Karl's heavily muscled frame and smouldering goods looks might turn her mind to other things. If anything it made her worse, but I was sidetracked after that by a group of elderly men who seemed determined to empty our cellar. Despite asking some demanding questions, they were refreshingly polite, and I spent much of the rest of the evening talking to them, leaving Marco to deal with the wine at Miss It Girl's table.

31

It was a long evening, and I was exhausted by the time tables at last began to empty. The old gentlemen had been insisting I taste various things, so I was a little tipsy too, and looking forward to winding down with my own supper and a glass or two once we were closed. The It Girl and her friends were still there, now very drunk indeed. She had made up nicknames for all the staff and was using them openly, until at last it got too much for Karl and he asked her to behave.

His rebuke was mild enough, but if she was good at dishing it out, then she was not good at taking it. She immediately launched into a tirade, calling him everything from a 'pompous male pig' to a 'needle-dick', while the others egged her on. To Karl's credit he just walked away, into the kitchens, but that wasn't good enough for her and she followed, shouting that she hadn't finished with him yet. I quickly apologised to the group I was seeing out and followed as the double doors slammed behind her.

By the time I got to the kitchen she was in full spate, actually threatening Karl physically, for all that he was a foot taller than her. He was trying to placate her, and the others were standing behind, Gian cold and angry, Marco red-faced with passion. For some reason she seemed to have taken Karl's mild rebuke as an attempt at male dominance, which really got to her. Almost with the same breath she was telling him that he ought to show respect for what she saw as her celebrity status and telling him he'd benefit from a kick in the balls.

I stepped in, hoping that as another woman I'd be able to calm things down, only to be met with a burst of invective. Karl took my part, telling her not to be rude, and the next instant she'd slapped him. There was a pause, absolute silence as he stood there with the red handprint rising on his face, and for a moment I really thought he was going to hit her back.

It wasn't Karl who lost his temper, but Marco. Before she could react he had grabbed her about the waist and thrown her back onto the big chopping block, still slimy with meat juice. As she yelled in outrage he said something fast in Italian and Gian grabbed one arm, Karl quickly taking the other. I was shocked, and demanded to know what they were doing. Marco just turned, grinning, and told me that they were going to teach her some manners; they were going to spank her bottom.

If she'd been angry before, it was nothing to the state she got into when she learned what was going to happen to her. Actually he was probably joking, just wanting to scare her, and if she'd burst into tears they'd have let her go, but that wasn't her style. Instead she screamed and cursed, demanding to be released immediately and promising violence if she wasn't. It was a mistake, because she wasn't in a position to demand anything.

They held her down on the block easily, showing up her boasts about her strength for what they were. Not that she gave in. She continued to kick and struggle and swear, calling them every name she could think of. I could only stand and stare, knowing that I should stop it, but unable to make myself. Instead I slipped the bolt on the double door into place.

Marco stated that she ought to be given her spanking bare, quite calmly, then reached up under her skirt and pulled off her panties. Her struggles got worse, a real tantrum, then stopped abruptly as the little scrap of black silk was forced into her open mouth. They tied her gag off with a napkin, and after that she could only mumble, although I could still see the fury in her eyes.

I imagined they'd bend her over the chopping block, but Marco had other ideas. He took her by the ankles and rolled her up, legs high to get at her cheeks, a position that left every detail of her neatly shaved pussy and little brown bumhole showing. It was great, so out of step with her 'aren't I perfect, aren't I wonderful' attitude, and I could feel her outrage as it all came on show. I can't deny it – after the way she had behaved, seeing her bare was so good, and watching her spanked was going to be even better.

Marco did it with his belt, which I fetched for him from his jeans. It was thick, a length of heavy black leather, and just feeling the weight of it had my excitement rising. Marco took it and showed it to her, which finally got a reaction other than pure outrage. I laughed at the sight, then again as the belt smacked down across her helpless cheeks and her body jerked in reaction. He gave her thirty hard ones, slow, measured smacks across her bottom and thighs, each one leaving a thick red welt across her immaculate flesh.

I'm afraid I masturbated as they did it, standing behind one of the big vats so that the boys wouldn't see. My hand was up my skirt, my fingers down my panties, working surreptitiously at my clitty as I watched her beaten. It was lovely, so satisfying, especially the view of her pouting pussy-lips and the way her vulva swelled and moistened as she was punished. Almost as good, and even dirtier, was the way her bumhole pulsed, the tiny brown hole opening and closing, almost as if it was winking at me. I came with my eyes glued to her rude rear view, sighing in ecstasy at the thought of how exposed she was and how she must have been feeling.

Nobody took any notice of me and the beating went on. By the end she had stopped struggling and was mewling into her panties, still kicking with each blow, but pretty subdued. When Marco finally stopped I actually thought they were going to rape her, and I would have stepped in at that, only it wasn't their intention. They let go of her and she got up, never making a sound, even when she had got her fancy knickers out of her mouth. She left with her head bowed, ignoring her friends' questions.

I locked the door behind them, pulled down the blinds and turned to the boys, certain that I ought to rebuke them but not quite sure what to say. What I found was the three of them, grinning, hands folded behind their backs, each immaculate in his uniform, except for their flies, each of which had an erect cock and a pair of balls sticking out towards me . . .

Which would be just nice for me, while of course, being a fantasy, the snotty It Girl would go home and masturbate over what had happened to her and in future think twice before putting other people down. In reality all hell would break loose, but maybe, just maybe, the spanking would have made her a better person anyway.

Spanking, as my readers can hardly fail to notice, is my favourite thing. Well, perhaps along with being a pony-girl, a piggy too, and other sexy things that concentrate on my bottom, but anyway, the joy of spanking never seems to cloy for me.

I really believe in it too. I'm sure the world would be a better place if girls got their bare bottoms smacked once a week or so, voluntarily of course. Men, too – let's not be sexist. Good, regular spankings stop me getting over-confident and self-obsessed, things that I hate in other people, as well as turning me on. Another thing I hate is the sort of women's magazine that tries to tell me how to live my life. That's the central theme in Tie and Tease, *where I first meet Beth, Elizabeth Diez-Joyce. She takes her life from the pages of* Metropolitan, *and not surprisingly I try and corrupt her. The fact that she is a small, pretty blonde with lovely olive skin is quite beside the point. At the end of the book she gives in and canes me, and this story looks at her continuing exploration of her sexuality . . .*

Pussy Pie – Elizabeth Diez-Joyce

I knew the twins would punish me if they found an excuse. In fact, I was fairly sure they'd punish me anyway, excuse or no excuse. Ever since we'd met they'd been after me, really openly too, both Melody and Harmony. I was a bit scared at first, because Penny had told me the sort of things they liked to do to other girls and I wasn't at all sure if I could take it. Penny did, and she even let Morris have her, but I'm not as dirty as her.

It was tempting, and I made myself come over the thought of them more than once. I would lie naked on the bed, imagining myself helpless in their strong, dark arms, being touched and teased, maybe spanked, being made to do rude things that I'd never have dared suggest of my own initiative. In the end I gave in. Melody rang to say that she and her sister were going up to some place in Gloucestershire, alone, and would I like to meet up for lunch as they came back towards London.

I said yes. After all, Morris wasn't going to be there, so it would be just girls, and I couldn't deny that the prospect thrilled me. Anyway, it would have been weak to say no when I knew it was what I really wanted. I did feel nervous, and pretty amazed at myself. A few short months before, I'd thought it was all so wrong. Not going with other girls, which is a really empowered thing to do, but doing kinky stuff, like bottom-spanking and tying up. Now I was going to get it, I was sure of it.

They arrived before lunch. I'd seen them in their clubbing gear before, tight sexy outfits of black leather that left most of their firm, muscular bodies showing, like a pair of Amazons. Now they were in summer dresses, light, ankle-length ones with belts at the waist, Melody in red, Harmony in blue. They looked so innocent, as if they'd just come out of church, and it seemed completely out of keeping with their reputation. I told them so and Harmony laughed. Melody smiled, showing her teeth, and suddenly, just for an instant, the dress seemed no more appropriate than if it had been on a wild animal.

I'd been imagining that we would go out for lunch, then back to my flat where they could seduce me into whatever exotic sexual games took their fancy. They had decided otherwise, stating that as it was such a beautiful day we should take a picnic up onto the downs. I agreed, but my disappointment must have shown, because Harmony laughed and promised it wouldn't be a dull day.

That thrilled me, the idea of get down and dirty with them in the grass, outdoors, where there was always a chance somebody might see. Perhaps I'd be made to lick them, on my knees in the nude while they lifted their dresses, showing just enough to let me get at their pussies, no more. They could even make me go up under their dresses, pulling their panties aside and licking, showing it all off while they revealed nothing.

We bought our food as we walked through Streatley and into Goring. They chose French bread and pâté, cherry tomatoes, Brie cheese, a big apricot pie and two bottles of wine. At the end of the road we started up the hill, on a footpath, then across private land. They just laughed when I pointed out that we might get caught trespassing.

They began to tease me as we walked, casually discussing the things we'd talked about on the phone, how I wanted to know what it felt like to be punished, how I wanted the thrill of being naked while they stayed dressed. I could feel myself getting excited, and then Harmony came up with the most wonderful idea.

'I think you should serve us, Beth,' she said. 'All afternoon.'

'Perfect,' Melody agreed, 'and so appropriate. Think of all the black girls who've had to do really menial jobs down the years, not to mention slaves. It's time we got a bit of our own back.'

'I've never had a black girl as a servant! I've never had a servant at all!'

'Look on it as racial guilt. You all have to atone.'

'But . . .'

'Butts get smacked, Beth,' Melody interrupted. 'That's what Mistress Diana used to tell the slaves who answered back when we worked in LA.'

'It doesn't work so well over here,' Harmony added, 'but my hand will if you're not careful. Now how about it, are you going to be our maid?'

'In the nude,' Melody added.

I swallowed hard. It was what I wanted, more or less exactly. That didn't make it easy to actually accept it. I could see the kick in being a white maid to two black mistresses as well, although I wasn't sure if it was really ethical. Not that it mattered much what I thought, because they were already getting into role.

'Carry this, Elizabeth,' Melody addressed me, passing the big picnic rug and her bag of shopping.

'Yes, Mel,' I answered, keen to play if still a bit unsure.

Her reaction was instantaneous. She swung on her heel, her hand lashing out and catching my cheek. It wasn't hard. I'm sure she could have knocked me down with a slap if she'd needed to. It didn't need to be hard, it was the gesture that counted, and suddenly I understood just how strong sexual role-play could be.

'That's Mrs Rathwell to you, you insolent little baggage,' she snapped, 'or ma'am, perhaps.'

'Yes, ma'am, sorry, ma'am,' I managed.

My cheek was stinging and I felt small and confused, wondering if I could really take it. I knew I could break role, but I was scared that if I did they wouldn't want to play with me. It went against everything I'd been taught, everything I'd believed in, but I forced myself to swallow my pride and accepted the things Harmony had been carrying, trying frantically to remember her surname and getting it just in time.

'Thank you, Miss Dauray,' I said as I took her shoulder bag and the rest of the food.

For a moment she smiled, then turned away, as haughty as her sister, linking arms with their backs to me so that I was forced to walk two paces behind. We had come out on top of the downs, to an area of short grass and scrub, looking out over the Thames Valley, a really beautiful scene that somehow made it all the easier to believe.

Melody picked the spot, a patch of soft, short grass in the shade of a beech, sheltered from prying eyes but really much too open for me to feel safe in the nude. Somehow I suspected they didn't want me to.

'Lay out the rug,' Melody ordered.

I complied, quickly placing the rug on the ground, then laying out the picnic things. They watched me work with a wonderfully lazy detachment, as if it was something they would simply never, ever be called on to do.

'It seems you have some trouble understanding the difference in our status, Elizabeth,' Harmony remarked. 'It is very real, I assure you, and in order to impress this upon you, you will serve naked today.'

'Not naked, please, Miss Dauray. Make her not do it, Mrs Rathwell, please.'

'Naked,' Melody said, 'and one more word out of place and you will be whipped.'

'Yes, Mrs Rathwell.'

I looked around, wondering if I really dared. I also wondered if Melody would carry out her threat and whip me if I answered her back again. She was trying to look cold and haughty, but I could see that animal look in her eyes and I knew the answer would be yes. I'd probably get it with some twigs, held down with my bottom bare for a firm, salutary thrashing, an idea that thrilled me but scared me too. I hesitated, wondering if I should just give in to my feelings and let them have me, only for my fear to get the better of me.

With my hands fumbling for the buttons of my blouse, I began to undress. As each one came open I felt more and more exposed, and I was sure somebody would come,

40

catching me stripping. The twins sat sipping wine, ignoring me save for an occasional glance to make sure I was doing as I had been told.

My blouse came open, making my cleavage seem really blatant, then off, leaving my breasts feeling huge and exposed even though they were hidden by an ample bra. I put my hands behind my back, to the clip, my fingers shaking as I snipped it open. The catch came open and fell away, leaving my breasts feeling really heavy in their cups and so rude. I knew I was being dirty, and it wasn't easy, but I dropped the bra, and they were bare, two big pink titties, nude in the cool air, nude outdoors.

Harmony gave me a knowing smile, which I did my best to return. I felt so vulnerable with my breasts out, but I knew it was only half way. My bottom already felt fat and obvious in my trousers, and my privates were tingling, making me wonder how it was going to feel when I was showing everything. I undid my trouser button and tugged down the zip, then pushed them down with a timid, guilty glance behind me. They came off my hips, down my thighs and to the ground, leaving me with my panties showing. I'd put sexy ones on, peach-coloured satin with a lacy panel over my bottom. It had felt good at the time, knowing they showed my bottom off nicely and wondering if it would make the twins want to smack it. Now they just seemed rude, and my bum felt enormous, a great wobbly thing with the crease showing through ridiculously tight panties.

I still wanted to keep them on. It's one thing being caught in your panties, another to be caught nude. There's a big difference between topless and nude; topless is daring and sexy, nude is dirty and vulnerable. They were coming off, I knew it, just from the look in Melody's eyes. I pushed them down quickly, getting it over with as fast as I could. They fell to the ground and my bum was showing, my privates too, all bare. Only then did I realise that I should have taken my shoes and socks off first. I was in trainers, and it was hard to get at the laces, making me adopt a whole series of silly, rude postures before I managed to get

41

them off. Harmony watched me, giggling at my plight, then laughing aloud as I tripped and had to go down on all fours to save myself, sticking my big bum out, right towards her.

'Oh, Beth, you are comical,' she laughed. 'Now do hurry up.'

My face was red as I stepped out of my clothes. I was nude, not just showing my bits, but stark naked, in the open, my titties and bum bare to anyone who came by. Without the girls there I would never have dared, and as it was my heart was hammering as I stepped over to the rug and dropped a little curtsey to show that I was ready.

Melody clicked her fingers and pointed at the ground, and I realised that I was to do it kneeling. I went down, onto my knees, acutely aware that the position left my bottom sticking out and the back of my privates and my bottom-hole showing. It made my titties more prominent too, swinging them forwards under my chest so that they felt big and heavy. They felt sensitive too, and my nipples were hard.

They held out their glasses and I hurried to serve, turning to Melody and then her sister, each time thinking of what I was showing the other from behind. As I poured Harmony's wine something touched my bottom – Melody's toes. I gasped, but I didn't dare move, and managed to pour as the ball of her big toe traced a line down between my bum-cheeks. She prodded the hole and I tightened it instinctively, blushing to have my anus touched, then gasping again as her toe wiggled in the entrance to my hole.

'You are wet, Elizabeth,' she informed me, and gave my bottom a little kick. 'Are you a virgin?'

'No, of course not,' I stammered. 'No, Mrs Rathwell, I'm not.'

'Not in your cunt, silly girl,' she chided. 'Up your bottom.'

'Yes!' I squeaked, disgusted but with a fresh twinge of arousal.

Melody gave a little snort, maybe amusement, maybe contempt. I've always been shy about my bottom, and I know some dirty men like to put their cocks up girls' back passages. Nobody had done it to me, never. Other than putting a finger up in the bath to clean myself, and of course wiping, I never even touched my anus. To them it was something to be played with, and I was sure both of them would have taken cocks up theirs, and liked it. Now I was naked and it was showing, and from the way I had reacted I was sure they knew I was shy about it.

They didn't molest me any more, but made me serve, with my feelings growing stronger and stronger all the time. I handed out their wine and food, all the while so conscious of my nudity that I couldn't stop shaking. Both hardly seemed to notice me, addressing me only to give orders or to tell me to hurry. It went on for ages, and it was torture, expecting all the time, and never getting it.

If they ignored me, then they didn't ignore each other. I knew they were intimate, even for twins, and that they joined in together when they played with people, but I hadn't realised how far it went, nor how casual they were about what was really incest. Melody was sitting with her legs up, leaving the white crotch of her panties showing, taut over her fleshy sex-lips. She didn't care that she was showing it, and when Harmony joked that there was a damp patch on her sister's gusset, Melody simply reached down and pulled it aside, exposing the naked swell of her privates as if it was no big deal at all.

That had me shocked, because the view was plainly intended for her sister, but Harmony simply stuck her tongue out and wiggled it. Melody nodded, and the next thing I knew Harmony had gone down on her knees and buried her face in her own sister's sex. I could see her licking, rubbing her nose on Melody's clitoris and licking the hole, then going higher. Melody sighed and leaned back, pushing out her sex into her sister's face. I was awestruck, watching one twin lick the other, so casually, so playfully, totally indifferent to the taboo they were breaking or to the fact that I was watching.

Melody came in her sister's face, crying out her name and clutching at her hair, then giggling as they both sat back. I was ignored, completely, but I could feel the wet between my thighs and knew that however shocking what they had done might be, it was also a turn-on. Melody made herself decent and held out her glass for more wine, and that was that; they went back to the picnic as if nothing had happened.

I was still scared, but I wanted it more than ever. They let me have some wine, making me lick it up from a plastic plate on the ground, which got to me even more. It wasn't enough, though, simply being their maid, not nearly. Slowly my need for something to happen outgrew my fear, until I could stand it no more. I wanted my punishment, and I realised that to get it I was going to have to be naughty.

Most of the food was gone, and I was hungry, not having been allowed to eat anything at all. It was obviously a really insolent thing for a maid to do, eating in front of her mistresses. So, with the full knowledge that it would lead to me getting punished, I picked up the apricot pie and took a big bite. Melody turned to me immediately, her full lips pursing in an angry frown.

'What are you doing, Elizabeth?' she demanded.

'Eating, Mrs Rathwell,' I answered. 'I'm hungry.'

I expected a sharp order, an instruction to get into some thoroughly degrading position, maybe to have my hair pulled to make me get across her knee. She did nothing, but shook her head and turned to her sister.

'One simply can't get the staff these days,' she observed, casually. 'You're useless, Elizabeth. You're not fit to empty my privy.'

Harmony laughed; Melody turned away, reaching for her wine glass. She wasn't going to do it. I'd worked myself up, got over my fear, offered her the chance to punish me, which was so precious to me, and she wasn't going to do it!

I was swinging my arm around even as her fingers touched the stem of her wine glass. She saw an instant before it happened, but it was too late. The apricot pie went right in her face, exploding and spraying bits of crumbly pastry and filling into her hair and over her dress.

44

I pulled it back, about half the pie coming away in my hand, as Harmony burst out laughing. Melody had frozen, her face filthy with crumbs and sticky apricot jam. Her mouth was open, her eyes shut; a blob of jam hung from her nose.

As her fingers went slowly to her face, I got that fearful, excited feeling that comes when you've done something really naughty and you know you're going to get in trouble, right that moment. I hadn't felt that way since I was a little girl, and it was so good, so fresh, so free. Harmony was on her side, her legs towards me, laughing so hard that she was shaking and clutching her sides. Her dress was a little up, showing her legs, and before I really knew what I was doing I had whipped it up, pulled open the back of her panties and pushed the pie down them. Her knicker-elastic snapped back against her skin, and I gave her bum a firm slap even as she yelped in shock.

She rolled, sitting right in it, and I saw the expression of surprise on her face turn to disgust as the pie squashed up between her buttocks and around her privates. I put my hand to my mouth, hardly believing what I had done as her disgust changed slowly to shocked outrage.

'You have had it, Elizabeth,' she announced, shaking her head as she climbed around onto all fours.

I backed away, shuffling on my legs as Melody flicked a piece of jam away and opened one burning eye. The next instant she had moved, Harmony too, and I went down, rolling on my back as they grabbed me, my legs flying high in the air. Melody got my hair, Harmony my ankles, twisting and forcing me to turn. I went, squealing in delight but also shock and pain as I was rolled onto my front. Melody got me around the waist, and I was giggling and kicking as she forced me up into a kneeling position. I knew what was coming and was begging her not to do it, but wanting exactly the opposite.

The smacks never came. Melody held me tight while I looked back between my legs. I could see my dangling breasts and my bare pussy, and knew what a display I was making. I needed spanking, and I had been sure I was

45

going to get it, but Harmony was collecting what was left of the food. She gathered it up, tomatoes and pâté and cheese, scooped into both hands and squeezed into a filthy, soggy mess as her sister held me helpless. Melody was so strong, and I knew it was useless to struggle. All I could do was give a little despairing groan as the double handful of mess was slapped between my bottom-cheeks, right up the crease and all over my privates. I could feel it, cold and wet and slimy, in my pubes, even up my hole, and it was my turn to screw my face up in disgust.

Harmony laughed and wiped her filthy hands on the clean white flesh of my bottom-cheeks, smearing them with food. I was looking back, and I saw her scrape up the last of the cheese and pâté. She edged forwards, and I felt her weight on my back as she mounted me, curled her hands under my chest and took a breast in each hand, smearing them with muck, wobbling them in her hands and then smearing the mess down my tummy, also on her sister's arm.

'Her face,' Melody urged. 'Do her face.'

'All in good time,' Harmony answered. 'I've been wanting my hands on these fat little tits for months.'

'Me, too,' Melody said, 'so splosh her first, then we can both have a feel.'

Harmony laughed and her weight shifted forwards, just giving me time to shut my eyes before her hands found my face. She smeared it well in, rubbing the mess into my cheeks and over my eyes, then forcing a handful into my mouth by pinching my nose until I had to gasp for air. That left me gagging and spitting bits of cheese rind and meat jelly, which only made them laugh.

With me thoroughly soiled, Harmony dismounted and Melody let go, allowing me to roll over in the grass and wipe the mess from my eyes until I dared to open them. It was impossible not to grin, as I was well pleased with myself. I might have been splattered, but Melody's face was still covered in pastry crumbs and bits of apricot jam, while a good half the pie was down Harmony's knickers.

'If that was a punishment I want more,' I laughed, licking the mess of jam and crumbs from my fingers. 'I thought I was going to get spanked!'

'Punishment?' Melody answered. 'No, no, Beth, that wasn't the punishment. The punishment is that you're going to eat the picnic, starting with the pie.'

'Eat it? But . . .'

'Eat it, Beth, darling,' Harmony copied. 'Eat it all up.'

With that she turned over, onto all fours, looking back with a grin at me. Her beautiful bottom was lifted high and she reached back, pulling her dress up over tight white panties, clean and fresh except where the pie that was down them showed. It looked really filthy, hanging heavily in her panty crotch and bulging the material out between her muscular cheeks. In places it had stained through, a rich, deep yellow, in a line down between her cheeks to her privates, where a drop of sticky yellow jam had squeezed through.

'Lick it all up, Beth, until she's clean, there's a good girl,' Melody said. 'I'll hold your head to make sure there's no nonsense.'

Melody twisted her fist into my hair, gently but firmly as Harmony reached back to take hold of her panties. Most of the pie stayed in them as she peeled them down, making a gooey puddle of jam and crumbs in the pouch. There was a good deal still between her cheeks, smeared on the glossy brown skin of her privates and higher, in her crease. I could see the dark knot of her anus, wrinkled and smeared with jam.

That was what my eyes were fixed to as Melody pulled me in by the hair. Not Harmony's full, dark, pussy, nor her big, firm buttocks, but the tight hole of her anus. I could lick pussy, I could kiss another's girl's bottom. A bumhole was different, ruder by far, and dirty, not something a girl should be touching at all. To kiss Harmony's anus was dirtier than anything I had imagined in my fantasies, and now I was expected to do it, and not just to kiss it, but to lick it clean.

Melody's grip was firm, not painful, but stern enough to let me know there was no going back. Harmony watched, moistening her lips at the prospect of my tongue on her bottom. I puckered up, ready to kiss the glossy brown skin in front of me as Melody tugged my hair. I did it, kissing Harmony's bottom, one cheek at a time, gentle pecks, nothing really, only they were on another's woman's bare bottom, something so intimate.

'That's right, kiss ass,' Melody said. 'Kiss it like the good little slut you are.'

I did it again, kissing the full cheeks, pecking at the crumbs and jam, then starting to lick as my passion rose. I could smell her, her skin and the scent of her sex, mixed with the rich tang of apricot jam. Soon I was fully willing, lapping away, leaving Harmony's buttocks clean but wet with my saliva, all but the filthy mess in her crease. Melody kept hold of my hair, directing my head to make sure I did a thorough job of her sister's bottom. Harmony was groaning by the time her cheeks were clean, and pushing her bottom up to spread them wide.

'Now her hole,' Melody ordered and my head was jerked back and held, inches away from Harmony's open bottom. 'Then when it's clean you can lick cunt.'

I could see her bumhole, a little open, the centre a star of damp, bright pink flesh surrounding by little bumps of glistening black. A girl's bumhole, and I was about to have to kiss it. I shook my head, unable to make myself, only to have Melody jam my head in between her sister's buttocks. All I managed was a muffled gasp and then my face was in it, held hard between the big cheeks, smeared with pie as well as the mess which had already been rubbed in. My nose was in her cleft, my eyes just high enough to see the full, dark curves of her buttocks, with her shoulders and hair visible too. I was almost smothered, and my lips . . . my lips were pressed right against her anus.

'Kiss it!' Melody ordered.

Harmony was panting, really eager, and pushing it back in my face. I could taste her, and smell her, and then I was doing it, puckering up my lips, pouting, and kissing her bumhole, right on the ring. I was telling myself I'd been made to do it, that I was a decent girl, that I'd never kiss an anus by choice, but I was doing it, kissing again, then licking, as with a sob of mixed ecstasy and revulsion I poked out my tongue and began to clean my friend's anus.

I did it all, slurping up very last crumb, every smear of jam, until Harmony's bottom was spick and span, glistening with saliva. There was an earthy, acrid taste in my mouth, but I felt so aroused, so much in need of more, and as Melody at last let go of my hair I didn't pull away, but let my head slip down. My tongue found Harmony's sex and I began to lick, listening to her sighs of pleasure as I dug the pie out of her vagina, then turned my attention to her clitoris.

Behind me I heard Melody give a little chuckle, an amused sound, as if she had known how dirty I could be all along. I didn't care, all I wanted was to lick and lick, to worship the firm, muscular, yet so female bottom that was in my face, to clean her anus for her, to make her come.

I felt Melody's hand touch my hair, and then Harmony's panties had been pulled up, trapping my head and smearing my hair with the filthy remains of the pie. I kept licking, the feel of having my head trapped against a woman's bottom in her panties just adding to my lovely, sexy arousal. Melody found my breasts, feeling them, then slid a hand down over my bottom, tickling the hole and slipping into my vagina. She began to masturbate me, alternately fingering my hole and rubbing her knuckles on my clitoris as I licked her sister.

Harmony's panting became frantic. She cried out, calling my name, then her sister's. She came right in my face, bucking her bottom so that my trapped head was jerked back and forth but my mouth stayed in contact with her sex. It went on for ages, with my tongue on her clit, until at last the muscles of her underside stopped contracting against my face. I didn't pull back, because I was coming myself, and I wanted my head trapped in her panties as it happened, and my tongue in her too, only not in the rich, thick cream of her vagina, but up the tight hole of her anus, with my mouth full of the bitter taste of her bottom.

49

It was so dirty, so utterly dirty. I came like that, my head held tight in her filthy white panties, my tongue well up her bottom-hole, licking and slobbering at the dirty little ring I hadn't dared to kiss, which it had shocked me to see. I was lost, my tongue right up her, pushed in as far as it would go as her sister brought me off from the rear, bouncing my breasts, slapping them, fingering my hole, sliding her thumb higher, touching my own bumhole and piercing the virgin ring as I hit the most glorious, beautiful orgasm of my life.

It was too much. Once I'd got my head out of Harmony's panties, all I could do was lie on the ground, panting, my head spinning with emotions as I struggled to come to terms with what I'd done. I'd licked a girl's bottom clean, of my own accord; there was no use pretending. I was full of guilt, but at the back of my mind a little rebellious voice was telling me that no harm was done, nobody was hurt, that it wasn't wrong, and that before too long I'd be doing it again.

More fun than searching for Mr Right, surely?

Many women have a lot of guilt and self-doubt to get over before they can really enjoy their sex lives. Beth was corrupted, coaxed into being dirty before she discovered how nice it was. Others get there of their own accord. Trisha Ellis appeared in A Taste of Amber *as a racing pony-girl, tall, lithe, intelligent, liberated and balancing a respectable job as a barrister against a secret and exotic sex life.*

In this story she is much younger, aware of her sexuality, but still learning to come to terms with it . . .

The Music Room – Trisha Ellis

It was really too hot to move, one of those summer afternoons when you know you ought to be out doing something but just can't be bothered. I'd thrown on a pair of panties and an old T-shirt, just for the sake of decency, but that was all. I certainly wasn't getting dressed up just because old Grunewitz was in the house. Besides, it had been great to see the old fool's eyes bulge when I'd let him in. He'd been staring at my tits so hard that his little round glasses had steamed up. I had earned a dirty look from Gwen, and I suppose they do stick out a bit, and my nipples show rather without a bra on, but that's just nature.

Hiring Grunewitz was typical of my parents. They were sure Gwen and I had some great hidden talent, and we had had to suffer an endless line of music tutors, art tutors, sports coaches, of whom Grunewitz was just the latest. Daddy's big in the City, and Mummy's always been the arty type. Actually, I think she was a stripper or something when they met, but of course it's never mentioned. So their pretensions get taken out on us.

Anyway, he'd had a good stare, then turned his attention to the back of my panties as I walked away. They were cream silk ones, small and quite loose, so most of my cheeks showed and a little bit of the crease at the top. I wiggled on purpose, just to steam him up, and I swear I could feel his eyes on my bum. Gwen had told me to go and get dressed, but I'd ignored her, as always. Grunewitz had been getting pretty hot under the collar, and suggested starting the lesson right away, calling her Guinevere, as he always did.

Now she was practising scales, over and over, the piano tinkling away downstairs, endlessly repetitive except for Gwen's mistakes, of which there were plenty. She was no good, and never would be, any more than I would ever be any good at the viola, which was what Mummy was currently trying to force down my throat.

I was just wondering if I had the energy to go and sunbathe topless on the lawn outside the music room window when the piano stopped. Grunewitz's voice sounded, deep but too faint for me to catch the words. Gwen answered and then the irritating tinkling of the piano began once again. It was too much. I had to get out, even if it was just to the pool. I could skinnydip, and with any luck I'd give Grunewitz a coronary.

The music stopped again as I went downstairs, and I caught a funny little sound, like a sob or a moan of despair. I imagined it as Grunewitz's reaction to Gwen's piano playing and couldn't help smiling. It came again as I passed their door, and I heard Gwen say sorry and Grunewitz's frustrated grunt. The music started again, then stopped as Gwen muddled it up, only this time there was a sort of smacking sound and a little cry, very definitely female. Grunewitz was a stuffy old sod, but I couldn't imagine him hitting Gwen for making a mistake. Still, that was what it had sounded like, someone's face being smacked, not hard, but enough to be felt.

I couldn't help but look. I mean, I had to, didn't I? The keyhole was big, easily big enough to peep through, and I crept up to the door, knelt down and put my eye to it. I don't really know what I expected to see, but certainly nothing like what was going on. Gwen was sitting on the piano stool, as neat and prim as ever in her little white summer frock, except for the fact that it was turned up and tucked in underneath itself. That wasn't all. She had her panties down, right down, around her ankles, leaving her little round bottom stuck out over the back of the stool, quite bare.

53

That was bad enough. I'd figured Grunewitz for a dirty old man, but he had my sister sitting at the piano with her bare bottom showing, and it was obviously some sort of punishment for her incompetence. I say obviously, because her bottom wasn't just bare. She had it pushed well out, and on the crest of each cheek was a little patch of pink, flushed skin from where the dirty old bastard had smacked her.

My mouth was wide open in surprise and shock. This was my sister, my big sister, and she'd been made to take her panties down and show her bum so that she could be smacked, smacked because she couldn't do her piano lessons properly. I could feel her emotion for her; the awful humiliation as she had lifted her dress, then more, really burning as she took down her panties and stuck her bum out over the edge of the stool, all bare and ready for his lecherous attention. I wouldn't have done it. I'd have smacked his face and kicked him in the balls, but then Gwen was always the sweet one, the polite, obedient one.

I should have opened the door. I should have given him a piece of my mind. I should have told him I was going to tell Daddy. I should have, but I didn't. Instead I just stayed there, staring transfixed at my sister's naked bottom. It was a pretty rude view too. She was full onto me, with it stuck out far enough to let me get a glimpse of the little brown hole down between her cheeks and a puff of her pussy hair. I was sure she'd know her bumhole was showing, and that Grunewitz would see it when he leaned down to smack her, which must have been awful. It was impossible not to think of myself in the same position, bare bum stuck out, my own bottom-hole showing and the smell of my pussy in the air. I just hoped Gwen had wiped herself properly.

Grunewitz stepped into my view and I moved quickly back, thinking he had heard something. He hadn't, but the sudden feeling of guilt and shame for peeping was awful. For one horrible instant it was as if I was the one doing something wrong. It was as if I was being bad, peeping at Gwen's nakedness and humiliation, and in that instant the thought that if I was caught I too would be spanked flashed through my mind. It was no more than a second, but it left me blushing and angry, not so much at Grunewitz but at myself. After all, I was in my house, and he was effectively abusing my sister. I shouldn't be guilty, I should be indignant.

I was too, in a way. I mean, there he was, fifty if he was a day, balding, greasy, with a horrible moustache and a nasty little pot belly, and he was making Gwen show her bare bottom, and smacking it! If he'd been attractive it wouldn't have been so bad, and I'd have understood why she went along with it. As it was it was awful, a dirty old man like him thinking he had the right to see a pretty nineteen-year-old bare, never mind to smack her bottom!

Not that my outrage stopped me watching. Gwen's always been so bossy to me and, I had to admit, I really rather liked the idea of watching her get a spanking. Big sisters are so superior, and I doubt that there is a little sister alive who wouldn't at least smile at the thought of her elder having to take her panties down for punishment. I did, and I wasn't even going to try and pretend otherwise. In fact, I was even hoping it might go a bit further.

I could feel myself trembling as Grunewitz moved out of the way, and I knew that my feelings were more than just ordinary excitement. My nipples were stiff for one thing, and my tits felt really big and heavy under my T-shirt, the way they always do when I'm turned on. The music started again, and once more Gwen got it wrong. Grunewitz walked forwards, reached down and smacked his fingertips down on her bum. She yelped, the same odd little sound she had made before. I felt sympathy, I really did, but at the same time a little nervous twinge went right through me.

It made me feel more guilty than ever, but I wanted him to do it again. In fact, I wanted him to spank her properly, across his knee with her legs kicking and her panties flying around on one ankle, all the while squealing and pleading for him to stop. It was a cruel thought, and I knew it, but I couldn't help it, no more than I could help the damp patch that I could feel spreading out on the crotch of my panties. I was getting horny, over my own sister's pain and humiliation, but I didn't want it to stop.

Once again she tried her piece, and once again she failed and got her little smack. It was so unfair, because it must have been impossible to concentrate with her bare bum showing, never mind knowing that every little error would bring his fingers down on her behind. Her bottom had really begun to pink up, and as I watched he told her to stick it out more. She obeyed with a little, broken sob, pushing her bum out into a yet ruder position, her cheeks now wide enough to give me a clear view of her wrinkled little bumhole and also the back of her pussy-lips. Again I imagined myself in her place, and without thinking I was sticking my own bum out and feeling grateful for the skimpy silk panties that covered my own modesty.

Grunewitz passed in front of my view again as poor Gwen tried her piece. She failed and he barked an instruction, the anger plain in his voice. Her answer was another broken sob, and she began to move, climbing onto the stool, kneeling and once more sticking out her bottom. Now it all showed, everything, and to him as well as me. Her feet were stuck out, her neat black shoes towards me, her dropped panties hanging pathetically from around her ankles. Her thighs were pressed tight together, but that didn't hide anything, not with her bottom stuck out. It was an awful position, so vulgar, so embarrassing, with her bottom-cheeks apart and her little brown bumhole showing. Her pussy was visible too, every detail, the lips pouted out in a nest of crinkly hair, the inner lips and her clitty on view and a tell-tale bead of moisture over the actual hole.

How Grunewitz resisted pulling out his dirty little cock and pushing it up her from behind was beyond me. He had to be hard. I mean, what man wouldn't be with a girl like Gwen in such a pose? I was hoping he wouldn't, for her sake, but I did want her spanked, so badly. It was going to happen too, and not just a few little pats. He told her, quite calmly, then put his arm around her waist, holding her in position. She did nothing, but I could hear her breathing, and then it began.

He cupped her bottom, feeling each cheek like the dirty old man he was. Gwen shivered and I found a lump rising in my throat as his fingers slipped between her crease, loitering on her pussy lips, then her anus. He had touched her bumhole, a dirty old man like that, with his filthy fingers lingering on my big sister's bottom-hole. I was shivering, really hard. For all my outrage I wanted to touch myself, and as he lifted his hand and brought it down firmly across Gwen's poor, poor bottom I had to shut my eyes to stop myself from doing it. I heard the smack of palm on bottom flesh and Gwen's yelp of pain and surprise. My eyes came open and I pressed my face to the door. I began to watch it, to watch my own sister spanked.

Gwen's bum was bouncing to the smacks, wobbling and parting, showing off her anus and pussy, as dirty as could be. She didn't seem to care; certainly she was too far gone to try and hide it. I look the same spanked, just the same, my long red hair in a pony-tail, bouncing to the smacks, tits swinging, rounded bum wobbling, plenty of pussy hair and rude, pouty little lips between chubby buttocks, all on show. I'd had it, from a boy, some dirty little pervert who took me into the loos while I was up at uni for interview. He'd made me watch in the mirror and I'd looked just like Gwen, rude and dirty, bent over, bum stuck out, thoroughly undignified, just right to be spanked, just right to be beaten by some dirty, gloating man. Only it was worse now, worse for Gwen, because at least my boy had been young and good-looking. Grunewitz was a dirty, filthy old bastard.

He was getting harder too, really smacking his hand down on her poor, unprotected behind. In answer she was kicking her feet and doing a silly little shuffling dance on the stool, wiggling her bottom and lifting one knee, then the other. She was squealing too, really squealing, like a stuck pig, in time to his slaps. It looked ridiculous and it looked rude, so rude. Spanking's like that, really dirty and undignified for the poor girl who's getting it, but hard to resist, hard to resist because it leaves our pussies soaking and our bums throbbing and warm and lovely. Gwen's was bright red, her pussy an open pink hole into her body, readied for cock as she was beaten, and all the while my shock and outrage were building and I was praying over and over that it would never be me and at the same time just wishing it was.

I'd have looked the same, just the same, bum high and bare, puffy little pussy and dirty little bottom-hole on show, my cheeks wobbling about in the air, squealing and kicking and writhing and bleating . . .

Suddenly it was just too much for me. My panties were down in an instant, then my top was up. My tits swung out, big and heavy and bare, into my hands as I thrust out my bare bottom. I began to feel myself, squeezing my breasts because I knew exactly where my hands were going to go if I stopped.

Gwen was sobbing. I could hear her, snivelling and moaning over her spanking and what he was about to do. I felt bad, I really did, but I was too turned on, too much in need. I couldn't hold it, I never can. My hands went back and took hold of my bottom. My cheeks came open and in went my fingers. My crease was slimy and damp with sweat, my bumhole a ring of bumpy flesh in a nest of hair. I touched it, stroking the little hole and thinking how nice it felt even as I filled with self-disgust. Poor Gwen was being spanked by some dirty old man, and what was I doing? Was I trying to stop it? Was I filled with anger and righteous indignation? No, I was glued to it and I was feeling my bum and I was stroking my dirty little bottom-hole and I couldn't stop myself.

Gwen's bottom was red, a round little ball of hot girl-flesh with her pussy and bumhole stretched taut in between. He was still spanking, slapping one cheek after another and grinning as he did it. It was not the look of an angry artist dishing out punishment to an incompetent pupil – anything but. It was the look of a dirty, filthy old bastard who's tricked a pretty young girl into dropping her panties for a spanking.

As my finger sank into the wet cavity of my bumhole I put my other hand to my pussy. I was wet, sodden in fact, with juice running into my lowered panties and my thighs wet and slippery with it. I began to stroke, and as I did so I began to move my body, making my breasts swing so that I could feel their weight as I masturbated. I'm big-chested, and normally it's a nuisance, but when I'm masturbating it's wonderful. They feel so big, so heavy, like two fat melons hanging from my chest, and I just love to feel them move as I rub myself.

I was going to come soon too, even though I'd just started. My gaze was fixed on Gwen's bottom, Gwen's wide, naked bottom. Her skin was red with beating and slick with sweat, her vagina gaping with involuntary arousal, her bumhole winking lewdly at me. Grunewitz was going to fuck her – he had to, I didn't see how he could resist – just as soon as he had made a thorough job of her punishment and ensured that she was too far gone to care.

Sure enough, his cock came out, pulled one-handed from his fly while he smacked poor Gwen's bum with the other. It was big, dark and wrinkled, with a heavy hood from which the red tip had began to peep. I don't think I've ever seen such an ugly cock, but as he began to tug at it I was thinking of how it would feel in my hand, in my mouth, up my pussy . . .

I nearly came at that. My finger was well up my bum, in the tight little tube I love to explore, just because it makes me feel so, so dirty. My pussy was empty but I wanted her filled, filled with Grunewitz's big, ugly, dirty cock, right in me with my bare, smacked bum stuck out behind. That was what stopped me. I hadn't been smacked, although I should have been. It was my sister who had been smacked, and my sister who was kneeling on the piano stool with her nude bottom all red and sore.

Grunewitz was a bastard, a real bastard. He wasn't content with just humiliating and spanking Gwen, not even with taking a quick one up her from behind. He wanted it slow, and he wanted her to feel it as she was fucked. First he pulled her dress up, high over her tits to leave them hanging in her bra. They came out; her bra was tugged up and they fell loose, big and heavy, like mine but larger still, really quite fat actually, for all her tiny waist.

He had a good feel, stroking his dirty great cock all the while and moving between her tits and her bum, touching her pussy, fingering her, touching her anus, even popping a finger up her back passage, just like mine was inside me. Even that wasn't enough. The filthy bastard put his fingers to her mouth and made her suck them, not just the one that had gone up her pussy but the other too, the one he had put in her bottom-hole. Gwen took it, she actually sucked his dirty finger, and as she did so he took her by the hair and pulled her head around. I knew what he was going to do

And I knew it would be too much for me. Sure enough, her mouth came open and in it went, his fat, dirty cock into her pretty mouth, to be sucked and licked as he held her tight by her ponytail and pawed her spanked bottom with his other hand.

I came, and as I came I pulled my finger free of my bumhole and put it in my mouth, sucking and tasting the same taste as I knew my sister would have in her mouth. I felt ashamed, so very ashamed, but I couldn't stop myself and I was sucking and gulping down air and rubbing frantically at my clitty as I came and came and came.

That should have been it, but in the music room Gwen was still sucking Grunewitz's cock and it was impossible not to watch. When I got my eye back to the keyhole he was hard, his prick sticking out of his fly and into her mouth. I'm no prude; I'll suck a boy's cock if he asks, sometimes even if he doesn't. This was different, her face so pretty and sweet, his cock so huge and ugly. That she had it in her mouth just seem so totally, utterly obscene, yet it was nothing to what he intended.

I had pulled up my panties and put my tits back, but I was still feeling horny as I watched Gwen suck. He took his time, using her mouth until I thought he meant to come down her throat, only to pull free. His prick flicked up as it left her mouth. It was huge, or at least it seemed huge, and really ugly, dark in places, pink in others, gnarled and fleshy, with a bulbous red tip, all glossy with my sister's saliva. There was so much wet that for a moment I thought he had come in her mouth, but as he gave her a gentle slap in her face I realised her ordeal was not over. She turned, lifted her bum in a way that made it quite clear she knew what to do. That meant it wasn't the first time, that she got made to strip with every lesson, that she got spanked and fondled, fingered and made to suck cock, probably every time.

She looked round, watching with an unreadable expression as he went behind her. His body blocked my view, but I could see her face and I saw her expression change as he pushed that great ugly prick into her body. He began to fuck her, holding her hips and pushing himself into her body with obscene little jerks, each of which made her gasp and sent a shudder through the soft flesh of her thighs and middle. Her tits began to swing with the motion.

I started to feel my own once more, and as I put my eye back to the keyhole I saw that he had done the same, bending down to fondle Gwen's breasts as he fucked her. He was mumbling as well, tell her how lovely her tits were and how beautiful she was, how much he liked to spank her and how much he liked the feel of his cock in her tight little cunt. He used the word 'cunt', a word Gwen and I never used, and at that my feelings overcame me again. My panties came down, then off, and I was masturbating naked at the door, my bottom stuck out, my breasts in my hands as I watched my sister used by a dirty old man.

I didn't know how he'd done it, or why she had put up so little resistance. He hadn't forced her – I'd seen it with my own eyes – but he had made her do things far dirtier than anything she'd done with a boyfriend. Maybe he'd blackmailed her in some way. Maybe he'd even paid her, which was somehow worse. Whatever he'd done, he now had his cock in her hole and was fucking her, slowly and easily, enjoying her naked body, her reddened bottom and heavy, swinging breasts.

He pulled it out in the end, all greasy with her juice, only to push back again, rubbing the filthy thing in the crease of her bottom. I thought he was going to bugger her, to ram his great fat cock into her tiny hole and fill her rectum

61

with spunk. He'd have done it to me; I'd have asked him to. I knew it, and as my hand went back and once more found my slimy, dirty little hole I knew exactly what I'd have done in her place. I'd have let him strip me, and spank me and feel me up. I'd have let him pull out my tits and take down my panties. I'd have let him make me suck his cock. I'd have let him finger my bumhole and I'd have sucked his finger clean. I'd have let him fuck me and rub his cock in my crease. Only then I'd have pulled my bum-cheeks wide and begged for it up my hole, deep up my tight, dirty hole, all the way in until I could feel the weight of his penis bulging out my box, filling me where no cock was ever supposed to go, buggering me and spunking in my hole.

I was going to come again, I was so close. Grunewitz was moving, pulling to the side, once more showing me Gwen's bum, all red and sweaty with her own juices smeared between her cheeks. His cock was filthy, slimy with sweat and pussy-juice and worse, and it was going back in her mouth. She took it and began to suck and I was pushing my finger further up my bumhole, deep in, feeling the hot, slimy flesh inside, wriggling around to make me gasp and shiver as I rubbed my clitty. He had taken his balls out and was masturbating in her mouth, cupping his balls then jerking at his shaft, and all the while watching Gwen with her cheeks sucked in as she mouthed and kissed and nibbled at his fat, red knob.

I was slimy behind, a real mess, and my clitty was burning under my finger. Gwen had lost control and her fingers had gone back to her own mushy, sopping sex. I began to bugger myself, jamming my finger in over and over up the sticky, slimy hole of my anus. Gwen's fingers went up her vagina, deep in, then stretching the hole to make it gape, black and wet, running with juice. My own hand went back to my pussy, my clumped fingers sliding easily into the wet cavity. Grunewitz began to jerk harder and his teeth set in a manic grin. Gwen began to snatch at her sex, rubbing from anus to clitoris, smearing her own slime over her pussy. I was coming, my anus tightening on my finger, starting to pulse. Grunewitz erupted, jerking his cock from Gwen's mouth and doing it full in her face. I cried out as his semen splashed over her, closing her eyes and soiling her nose, going into her open mouth and smearing her cheeks and chin. My finger went deep, touching something, and I was biting my lip to stop myself screaming. Gwen came too, kicking her feet and slapping at her sex, smacking the meat of her pussy as she likes to do, as I've watched her before, coming and coming, spanked and stripped, fingered and fucked, with a faceful of Grunewitz's come and the taste of her own pussy in her mouth, the taste of cock, the taste of her own bumhole . . .

My fingers were back in my mouth and I was sighing and moaning, trying not to be too loud and really too far gone to care. I was nude, I was filthy and I'd just had the best orgasm of my life, and if Grunewitz caught me, well, he could do as he liked; so could Gwen. They could beat me and bugger me. They could make me go nude all day with a carrot stuck up my bottom. They could tie me and fuck me and spank me and I'd do anything, even to Gwen, even in front of him, to let the filthy old bastard have a good show before he spunked all over us as we writhed and wriggled together on the floor, tongues in mouths, fingers up holes . . .

I came again, a third time, just a little one, but the dirtiest of all, over my own sister. After that it took me a bit before I got my senses back enough to realise that grovelling nude on the floor in a puddle of my own juices wasn't really the way I wanted to be caught. I didn't know why Gwen had surrendered to such degradation, but I didn't want it to include me, not really. I pulled my knickers on and mopped up with my top, then ran quickly into the laundry for another.

I felt pretty bad. At best I'd watched my sister tricked or bribed into really dirty sex with an old pervert. At worst I'd watched her blackmailed, even raped, although she'd never actually tried to stop it. Either way I'd come over it, with my finger up my bum, which I know is dirty, but which I can never resist when I get carried away.

I was sure they would have heard me and expected them to come out, but they didn't, and at last curiosity overcame me and I sneaked slowly back to my place at the keyhole. Gwen was dressed, Grunewitz likewise, and they were sitting side by side in the window bay, right at the edge of that part of the room I could see. Grunewitz was smiling, as well he might have been, but so was Gwen, a happy, satisfied smile which showed quite clearly that whatever she had done, it had been exactly what she wanted.

Not that getting what you want is always easy, especially if it's something kinky. Many people find it hard enough asking someone else out, never mind for a favourite sexual position. Asking for someone to indulge a fetish is harder still, unless you know people who admit to liking it.

That is the theme of the next story, which explores the efforts of Paulette, a pretty black girl who we met briefly in Tie and Tease, *to get her bottom smacked after being turned onto the idea by acting as make-up artist on a rude photo-shoot. She succeeds, after a fashion . . .*

Getting that Spanking – Paulette Tate

It was all getting too much for me, this whole spanking business. I had to try it, but there was no way I was having it get out at work. Private life was worse, and I could just see how I was going to get teased if it got around that I liked my bottom smacked. Besides, I knew some of the boys; they'd think that spanking meant taking a belt to my back and legs as well as my bum. I wanted it the English way, the way Amber Oakley and Penny Birch had described it, across someone's lap with my pants rolled down over my bare bottom.

Unfortunately they were too well in with Amy McRae for me to ask them. In fact, I wasn't sure if Amy wasn't getting a bit of the same herself. Anyway, I wanted it from someone older, someone who would be very patient with me and not necessarily want sex afterwards. It almost had to be a woman, and I'd actually evolved this image of a steel-haired, British Empire type who would like nothing better than to get what she thought of as an impudent young girl across her lap.

I tried to get it out of my head, but it wouldn't go. Again and again I got this image of a bare female bottom stuck out, pants down, being spanked, preferably my own. Even after I'd been given a parking ticket my thoughts were of how the warden would look bent over the bonnet of my car with her uniform skirt up, her pants around her ankles and her fat white bottom decorated with red handprints as I gave her what she so thoroughly deserved. I even imagined the onlookers cheering me on, which was probably quite realistic.

So I had to have it, and in the end I pinched Amber Oakley's number out of Amy's phone pad and asked her advice. That took some doing, but she was very sweet and understanding, and not pushy at all. First she made sure I genuinely wanted it, and when I'd convinced her she said she'd do her best. She didn't know anyone who fitted my description offhand, but she would let me know.

It took her a week to get back to me, but when she did she seemed to have the solution. My spanker was to be a lady called Jean, an ex of her godfather. Jean was a Scot, which appealed, as it made me think of Miss Jean Brodie. Amber wasn't sure how old she was, but she'd been in her early twenties in the late Sixties, so presumably over fifty. She had agreed to spank me, and just hearing that sent a shiver down the whole length of my spine. It was so intimate. I knew that somewhere in England there was a woman who now expected me to go across her lap and have my bottom smacked. Not only that but my virgin spanking had been discussed over the telephone by several people.

Amber had called on my mobile while I was at work, so it had been a bit difficult getting the details down. I'd managed though, scribbling it one-handed onto a post-it and then hastily folding it away. The address was a place called Mill Cottage, in Sussex, which sounded very English, the ideal place for naughty girls to be spanked. I was to go there at the weekend, arriving at tea time.

The thought of meeting a perfect stranger and asking her to spank me was pretty shocking, but I wanted it badly enough to go through with it. Not that it was easy, and even deciding what to wear was a major trauma. My bum looks best in jeans, or so I'm always told by the boys, and that's coming from black guys, who appreciate girls' bums. It didn't seem right, though, especially the cut-down ones I sometimes wore when I wanted to show a bit of cheek.

For an English country setting jeans were too vulgar, too ordinary. A frock seemed more suitable, something long and light so that it could be lifted easily, or maybe a smart suit with a tight woollen skirt so that I could really feel it as it was pulled up. On the other hand it might be nicer to have her unbutton my trousers and pull them down, so loose cotton trousers might be the thing, or even cords.

That seemed to be the question: up or down, which was the bigger turn-on. Being bared was a big part of it, and I wanted to get it right, for myself. Also for Jean – not that I had any idea what she liked, but I wanted to be appreciated. In the end I decided that as my pants were bound to be pulled down, I would wear a dress so that I could get both sensations. It was more English, too, and in the end I chose a white cotton summer dress with white pants underneath. I wore suspenders and stockings too, with a little waspie to enhance my waist and make my hips and bum flare when I was in position. It felt good, and fully dressed I was well ready for it.

I thought about it all the way down. Dress up, pants down, and spanked, until my bum was warm and glowing. What happened then depended on how I felt, and what I was allowed to do, but if my confidence held I knew I'd finish off with an orgasm. Jean would know full well that I was turned on; after all, that was what it was all about. She might be embarrassed by it, though, and send me up to a bedroom to masturbate, or even tell me to do it sitting on the toilet. That was a nice thought, and I could imagine myself sitting there with my sore bottom, feeling sexy and punished at the same time as I brought myself off under a finger.

By the time I got there I was in a fine state. The place was in a maze of lanes to the south of East Grinstead, really pretty countryside, with little fields and high hedges, even a ford. It didn't look as if it had changed in years, not since spanking a wayward girl was considered a perfectly reasonable thing to do. In such a setting it was easy to imagine farmers' daughters getting put across the knee in the yard, having their dresses turned up and their big drawers pulled down for a spanking, given in front of the farmhands without the slightest thought for their modesty. Better still, it could be a landowner's daughter, a beautiful, carefree girl, over the governess's knee with her clothes disarranged to get at her bare bottom, a white summer dress and white pants, just like my own.

Mill Cottage was perfect, a converted water mill on a little stream in a wooden valley, right on the edge of the Ashdown Forest. I'd got a bit lost, and only found it because I saw the sign, but it was everything I'd imagined in my fantasies. Part of that had been getting my spanking on the lawn, in the open air, and the lawn of Mill Cottage was visible from the lane. That meant I might get seen, which added a new thrill to my mounting excitement. I felt that was how it should be – not done in front of an audience on purpose, but done where it happens to be convenient. After all, if I'd been naughty I should be spanked, and it shouldn't matter if I was seen or not.

I knew Amber had done her best to arrange it for me, but I'd had no idea she had gone to such lengths. As I parked the car I saw Jean, a slim, elegant woman who looked nearer sixty than fifty, maybe more, with her abundant white hair caught back in a bun. She wore a long dress, belted at the waist, in dove grey. Her face was intellectual, somehow stern as she looked up at me. She smiled, warm yet ever so slightly condescending, the smile of a spanker to the girl she is about to punish. Suddenly it wasn't going to be so hard.

'You must be the new girl,' she greeted me.

'Yes, Claudette,' I answered.

'Well, you're a little early, my dear,' she went on, 'but as you're here perhaps you would be kind and clear away the tea.'

I understood immediately. She wanted to create an inequality, making me feel subservient so that I got the full thrill out of my spanking. It was roleplay, the way Amber and Penny had described it, and I was more than happy to go along. I took the tray into the kitchen, which was immaculately tidy, and washed up the tea things, my excitement getting higher and higher all the time. She was still outside, sitting primly in a white cast-iron chair, reading a book, as if the fact that I was about to be punished was the least important thing in the world. When I finished I came outside, folding my hands in my lap as I waited for her to speak.

'Thank you, my dear,' she said. 'Now a little weeding if you would, just along the borders. There's a trug and a trowel in the shed.'

'Yes, miss,' I answered.

It seemed the right thing to say, and she gave me her condescending little smile again. I went for the gardening things and she began to read again, apparently taking no notice of me at all. It was obvious where it was going though. I didn't know the first thing about gardening, and I was bound to make mistakes. I would be criticised, mildly, then more sternly, then spanked.

I was really trembling as I worked. Occasionally she would glance over to me, and sure enough, after a little while she pointed out a couple of bits I'd missed, telling me off really quite sharply. That put me in a right state, and a few minutes later, when her book suddenly shut with a snap behind me, I knew the time had come.

'Really, girl, don't you recognise any plants at all?' she chided. 'Those are young snapdragons; I'd just had them bedded out. Oh, look, you've pulled up nearly half of them!'

She bent down, her face set in the most wonderfully cross expression as she quickly worked the little plants back into the soil. Her movements were delicate, very precise, fussy, and I could just imagine those same hands being applied to my bottom. They were about to be.

'Well, you obviously aren't to be trusted weeding,' she said, shaking her head as she stood up. 'You've quite ruined the bed. What shall we do with you?'

She was going to make me ask for it, and I knew I had to. I was blushing a bit, and fidgeting with my fingers, because it was so like a real telling off, but I managed to choke the words out.

'I . . . I think you'd better spank me,' I managed.

It was clumsy, badly played, nothing like as good as her, but I'd said it, out loud.

'Spank you?' she answered sharply, looking right at me through narrowed eyes as if she doubted what I'd said.

She wasn't going to make it easy, and I realised that for her it might be my embarrassment and shame that was as important as smacking my bare bottom. It was the least I could do to play along.

'Spank me,' I repeated, 'on . . . on my bare bottom.'

'You think I should smack your bottom? Is that what normally happens to you, if you make mistakes at home?'

'Yes,' I mumbled.

It was a detail of her own, a little piece of fantasy, and again, I was keen to play.

'I'm . . . I'm spanked quite regularly,' I went on. 'Over Mother's lap, sometimes over my big sister's.'

'For a little thing like pulling up the wrong plants?'

'Yes.'

'Good heavens! I had no idea modern families were so strict.'

'Very strict. Sister spanked me last week for borrowing her high heels without asking.'

'Gracious, and you feel I should do it to you as well?'

'Yes.'

'Well, I must say, I'm astonished. I really haven't thought about that sort of thing for years, not since I was a girl. I mean, yes, I sometimes feel you girls could be a little better-mannered, and a little more careful, perhaps, but to spank you?'

'Please; it would make me feel better.'

'Better?'

'To be punished. It would, I mean it.'

'Well, I don't know . . . Oh, very well, come on then. You had better get across my knee.'

She had changed so suddenly. One moment doubtful, concerned, the next testy and stern. A few quick steps took her to her chair and I followed, trying to look hangdog but so wonderfully excited. The chair was visible from the lane,

71

and my bottom was going to be sticking out towards it, in full view of anyone who came past.

I went down, laying myself across her lap, the position I'd imagined so many times. My toes were touching the ground, my hands, too, leaving my head hanging down by her skirt and my bottom the highest part of my body. I'd asked for it gentle, at least at first, but as her hand came down across the seat of my dress I realised she wasn't even going to bare me.

She did it quickly, a dozen firm swats, each making my bottom wobble a bit but not really hurting at all. It was nice, though. I felt genuinely chastised, and as she stopped I realised that she was giving me the chance to get up. I stayed put, wanting more but reluctant to break role by asking for it.

'Are you punished now?' she asked.

I stayed still, saying nothing. She sighed, and I felt her hands take hold of my dress.

'Well, perhaps if I do it across your drawers,' she said.

She sounded uncertain, a little put out even, but my dress was coming up and that was what mattered. I shut my eyes and concentrated, feeling the cotton ride up my legs, tickling my thighs, then higher and the tuck of my bottom and a little bit of my pants were showing. Higher still it went, up onto my back and it was out, my bum, stuck high over a woman's lap, clad in nothing but an inadequate pair of pants. They'd pulled a little up my crease while I was weeding, and most of my cheeks were showing, meaning I was going to get it on the bare skin.

Jean began to spank, a bit harder this time, and very methodically. The smacks came full across my seat, stinging a little, but more ritual than pain. It was warming me, and turning me on, but most of it was in my head. I was across a woman's lap, for real, being spanked across the seat of my pants, and it was everything I had imagined it would be. There was the feeling of helplessness, of being taken care of, of being given attention. I heard a car pass and knew I'd been seen and that someone knew that I had been spanked, me!

It stopped after maybe thirty smacks. I was breathing hard, feeling punished and excited, but neither as punished nor as excited as I might have been. Again she was giving me the chance to get up, but I wanted more and I wanted my pants taken down.

'Surely you now feel chastened,' she said. 'I don't want to hurt you, my dear.'

'No,' I answered, 'you're not. More, please, do it bare.'

I could hear my own voice, hoarse with need, breaking role, but I couldn't help myself. Her hesitancy sounded genuine, but I knew it was a pretence, just there to make me beg. If she kept it up I was going to.

'I do feel that would be a little indecent,' she went on. 'I mean to say, I am in favour of discipline, and I won't pretend I haven't wished, once or twice, with some of the other girls, but on your bare bottom?'

'That's how I'm done at home,' I managed, trying to roleplay. 'Always on the bare, always with my pants down, no matter who's looking.'

'Yes, but . . .'

'Please, please, pull them down, spank me, punish me.'

She didn't reply, but a moment later I felt her thumbs in the waistband of my pants. They came down, not slow, not fast, just taken down as if merely to get them out of the way because it had to be done. I felt it though, every inch as my bottom came bare, seeming very obvious behind me, also very big compared with her trim figure. She settled them around the tops of my thighs, leaving my whole bottom gloriously, utterly bare, just as a girl's bottom should be for a spanking.

There was a pause, and then she started, harder now, as if I had really started to make her angry. The slaps stung, making me gasp and I started to kick my feet a little to try and dull the pain. It didn't work, but it did seem to encourage her, and the smacks came harder and faster, still full across my cheeks. It was firm, solid discipline, a punishment. Another car passed and I knew my bare bum had been seen, jumping and jiggling over her lap with my pants down and my dress high.

I was really coming on heat, my nipples hard and my pussy feeling warm and puffy. Each slap seemed to go to my sex, increasing my need while what was being done to me ran over and over in my head, *spanked bare, spanked bare, spanked bare* . . .

When she stopped I was ready, my bottom glowing and my pussy wet with juice. If she'd given an order I'd have obeyed, but she said nothing. I rolled off her lap, sitting down hard on the grass, smack on my hot bottom. She looked down at me, her face full of compassion and, I think, wonder. I wanted to show my appreciation, to let her see how well she had handled me, what she had done to me right in front of her.

I rolled back, face on to her, and gripped my pants, pulling. They came down my legs, to my ankles and I cocked my knees wide. My pussy was spread, my pants stretched tight between my ankles, and I began to masturbate. She just stared, her gaze riveted to my open sex. My finger was on my clit, rubbing, taking me quickly high. I was mumbling my gratitude, thanking her brokenly for my pleasure.

As I started to come I went back, rolling up so that she could see the cheeks she had smacked so well, and the dark flush on my skin. I knew the position showed everything, my sex, the full width of my bum, even the little chocolate brown hole down between my cheeks. That was how I wanted it, completely open, showing everything, holding nothing back. She gave a little gasp, her hand going to her mouth. I pulled my dress high, over my breasts, my bra too leaving me nude from my neck to my ankles. My fingers went back to my pussy, sticky and wet with my juice, my clitoris a hard bump at the centre. I was coming, thanking her, crying out, screaming and then slumping exhausted to the lawn, spanked and frigged, spent and happy.

'Thank you,' I managed as I pulled myself up onto one elbow. 'That was lovely, perfect. Still, I suppose you've been doing it for years.'

'Well, not . . .'

My phone rang, in my bag, and I scrambled across on all fours, giggling at the sight I was making with my pants still around my ankles and my dress up to my neck. I got the phone out and answered, shrugging to Jean as I did so. It was Amber.

'Hi, Paulette, where are you?'

'With Jean, of course.'

'No, you're not; she just rang me. Be fair. I understand if you've got cold feet, but you might have called.'

'No, seriously, I'm here, at Mill Cottage. Jean's sitting right next to me. She just gave me the most wonderful spanking.'

'Eh? She can't have ... Hang on, did you say Mill Cottage?'

'Yes.'

'It's not Mill Cottage, silly, it's *Hill* Cottage. Poor Jean's been waiting there for two hours. You'd better hurry. Hang on, did you say you've just been spanked?'

I didn't answer. I couldn't. I closed the phone, and as it clicked shut I felt the blood start to rise to my cheeks.

Oh, well, a smacked bottom is a smacked bottom, or so I always tell myself as I'm turned over the knee of some particularly dirty old man.

You would think that any woman with the courage to ask would be able to get what she wants sexually. This is not always true; I've been turned down for spankings by men keen enough to get me into bed. Being kinky tends to get you labelled, too, much like any too overt display of sexuality, and certainly being involved with the sex trade.

Personally I would judge being a stripper as less degrading than being a shop assistant or a secretary. That is the theme of the next story, which follows the attempts of Chloe, one of the rough girls from Brat, *to make herself respectable . . .*

Making an Impression – Chloe Chapman

It looked like I'd fallen on my feet first time. I'd only been at Winter and Doyle a week and I'd been bumped up to stand in for Mr Hatton-Brown's PA while she was on maternity leave. Not only that, but he seemed to think that there was every chance she wouldn't come back at all and, if so, it would be me who got the job. Sure, I knew his choice had a lot more to do with my looks than my ability as a secretary, but that's just the way the cards come out. I was even ready to do a bit of cock-sucking if I had to; why get stuck up?

The only hassle was that he wanted me to change my look. At college I'd got into a bit of a gothy thing, with spiky green hair and black make-up. Black everything, really, except for my hair and nails, which I liked green. Green's my favourite colour, but not for a whole look – just the highlights. I'd got some great body jewellery, too, those neat little ones from Wildcat, with spiked balls at one end and round gems at the other, green gems.

I knew it was a bit much for temping, even in London, so I'd toned it down. Out went the kinky boots and mini-dresses; in came sensible shoes, trousers and tight tops. I kept my hair and put sleepers in my nipples so that they didn't show too much. That made me look pretty respectable, or at least I thought so. So did my sister, Sally.

She'd wanted me to join her stripping and get a really neat double act together. I'd been tempted, but it seemed

77

such a waste of my time at college. Besides, I'm not as strong as her, and the way people like to look down on girls who strip or do lap-dancing gets to me.

Sally might have thought I looked pretty straight, but it wasn't good enough for Mr Hatton-Brown. He wanted me like something out of the Fifties, only modern, if you see what I mean. Skirt suits for starters, and crisp white blouses and heels. I was supposed to lose weight as well, and do my make-up a certain way; my hair too.

It was all very well for him, but I just didn't have the money for all that, even if I was willing to give it a try. I did my best, losing the green nail varnish and toning down my make-up, but while I didn't mind looking like the other girls in the office, I didn't want to look a total straight. The next day I got the lecture. He called me in from the outer office where I worked. I knew what was coming.

'What did I say yesterday?' he began.

'To try and look smarter,' I answered.

'No, Chloe, not to try and look smarter, to look smarter. Not try, Chloe, do. Understand?'

'Yes, Mr Hatton-Brown, but –'

'No buts, Chloe. If you look bad, I look bad. Understand?'

'But –'

'Be quiet and listen, Chloe. How you look reflects on me. If you look a fright, it makes me look bad. I need respect in this job, not just from the people below me, but from clients too, and the directors. What are they going to think if they see a secretary who looks like she's just stepped out of some dumb sci-fi movie?'

'Well –'

'I'll tell you what they're going to think. They're going to think her boss is weak. They're going to think she's got no respect for her boss. And if she's got no respect for her boss, then why should they, right?'

'I think –'

'No, Chloe, you don't think. I think. You do your work and you look the way I want you to look. You're a pretty girl, Chloe. OK, so there's a bit of puppy fat on you, but

78

that'll come off. You should join a gym. That may take a little time, I understand. The rest I want now: no buts, now.'

'I just can't afford it, Mr Hatton-Brown.'

He didn't answer, but reached into his suit and pulled out a notecase. It was full of fifties, more money than I earned in a month, and he peeled some off, not even bothering to count, and threw them down on the table. I didn't know what to say, but I took them quickly enough.

It took me a week to get it right, but at last he was satisfied. I wasn't. Looking in the mirror in the morning, the young woman who looked back just didn't seem to be me any more. It was as if he'd taken over my personality, making me his woman instead of my own. Even my attempts to get a splash of green into the outfit had failed. Mr Hatton-Brown preferred blue.

I went to see Sally at lunchtime, feeling pretty rotten and in need of some comfort. She was stripping at a bar in Soho, just a few minutes' walk from the office. It might have been in another world. Sure, most of the businessmen who were watching could have walked into Winter and Doyle and no questions asked. That was the end of it. The bar was all mirrors, red and gold furnishings, the works. Sally was on when I came in, wearing a little glittery number like Columbia at the start of *Rocky Horror*. She had glitter boots too, with stack heels.

She likes to take it slow, and tease, but I knew she'd end up naked, because she'd told me it was part of the deal. Sure enough, she went all the way, ending up with some fancy dance poses that left everything showing, and I mean everything. Even I thought it was cute, and I'm her sister, while most of the men were really staring. Nobody took much notice of me, except to give me funny looks as if to wonder what such a prude was doing in a strip bar.

Sally and I had a good chat afterwards, in the little room the girls used to change. She was really supportive, but it didn't make me feel any better. In fact it made me feel worse. I was brooding all the way back to the office, feeling miserable – hungry, too, because I'd missed lunch. Sally

79

had been eating a great big burger, with chips and relish, but then she'd have danced it off in a few hours.

That was bad enough, but it was only part of it. Sure, she got fed up sometimes, but more with the way people treated her for being a stripper than anything. Going bare didn't matter to her. She could go on stage and show everything, nipples, everything, even her pussy and bumhole with some of her dirtier moves. It's supposed to be about the most degrading job there is, but it was me who was feeling small and exploited, not her. My job might be respectable, but I didn't feel half as confident as her. People make a big fuss about nudity, and I don't really understand it. I mean, what's wrong with going bare? What's wrong with my body that I should be ashamed to let people see it?

Anyway, people might get to see Sally's body, but it was her choice. She was her own person, and I felt like an ornament for Mr Hatton-Brown to show off. All that was bad enough, but she was earning more than me too, a lot more.

Given the way he treated me, I expected him to start demanding favours. I'd been going to accept. In fact, the idea of getting down behind his desk with the door locked and sucking his cock for him had been fun, a bit cheeky, a bit naughty. Now I wouldn't have done it for the world, but I was still hoping he'd ask, just so that I could refuse. If he then found some reason to sack me, then that was just too bad; there were limits.

It was only after nearly a month that I realised he was gay, and had no physical interest in me whatsoever. That really pissed me off, not so much because I wasn't going to get the pleasure of turning him down, but because it meant he hadn't picked me for my looks. Probably he'd picked me because he thought I was a pathetic little girlie who'd do as she was told.

I'd lost my weight by then, two inches off my hips and bust, one off my waist. Everyone was complimenting me on it, saying how good I looked, but I didn't feel good, and I didn't feel as sexy. Men like big boobs and cheeky bottoms, at least all the ones I've been with do. If having them talk to my chest can be a pain at times, at least they don't see me as some sort of robot.

Mr Hatton-Brown seemed impressed, as least as much as he ever was. While I'd been there I'd got to know some of the other staff better, and they said that he was basically a control freak. What mattered to him was that I was something he had chosen, not myself. To me it seemed more like I was becoming his slave.

The next week was the industry awards, an excuse to meet up in a big hotel and get drunk. Mr Hatton-Brown asked me to attend, and when I came in the next morning he gave me a list of what I was to wear, an exact list. Basically it was a little black dress, fancy undies, stockings and high heels. Over that he chose my make-up, my hair-do, even my perfume, so that I felt more like a mannequin than ever. He even made me wear a red ribbon in my hair.

On the day, we drove up to the venue in one of the company Mercedes, a big black thing with a chauffeur driving. The place was a converted country house, really huge, with an enormous hall at ground level and the biggest staircase I'd ever seen leading upstairs. For a while I was alone, only to be taken aside by Mr Hatton-Brown.

'Right, Chloe,' he began, 'as you know, this is still work, so no getting drunk or flirting with the hotel staff.'

'Yes, Mr Hatton-Brown.'

'On the other hand, there are a lot of important people here, very important people. I want you to make an impression. Now, if anyone from another company approaches you, particularly any of our big clients, you can have a little leeway. Just be discreet, understand?'

I nodded. I could see what he was getting at. Commanding as ever, he wanted to be sure I flirted with the right people, maybe went further. Nor did he want me giving snotty comebacks to clients who thought they might be onto a good thing. Well, it was better than being bossed around the office, and I can play the tease as well as anybody. On the other hand, I wasn't going to bed with some beery old git.

It didn't take long. The first guy approached right after the big introductory speech, in the bar. He was called Charles, fifty-odd, and grey-haired, but very neat and very self-confident. I let him buy a bottle of champagne to share and played the flirt. He was nice, in his way, not pushy or anything, but he just seemed to assume that we'd be going up to his room for sex in due course. I could have kicked when the time came, but I didn't. After all, I hadn't actually had anything since I'd started work at Winter and Doyle.

Sex was so-so. He was the oldest man I'd been with, so I reckoned that maybe old-fashioned men were all like that. Mainly he told me what to do, you know, suck my cock, get on all fours, wiggle your bum, that sort of thing. He didn't try to snog at all, or to give me a frig or a lick. I was quite turned on by the end, but he just thanked me and put his cock away, not even bothering to wait until I'd got dressed and tidied myself up.

The second guy I picked myself. When I got back downstairs I seemed to be pretty popular, with several men around me all the time. They were all eager, and I could tell each one was pretty pissed off about the others being there. I could see it staying the same all evening, so I picked the best-looking and whispered in his ear. The others took it quite well. One even joked that it was his turn next as I led my choice away by the hand.

He was called Mark, a big black guy who was an assistant department head for one of our client firms. I was expecting a lot of fun, at the least a big cock I could suck and lick, hopefully while he returned the favour. What I got was told to dance, stripping for him while he lay on the bed and sipped champagne. He liked my bum and I gave him plenty, wiggling and bending down like Sally, really showing off, until I was stark naked and sweaty. By then he had about ten inches of thick brown cock sticking out of his fly. I wanted it badly, and when he told me to bend over the dressing table and stick my bum out, I was right there.

It was a great position. I could see myself in the mirror, my face all flushed and excited, my boobs squashed out on the table and him behind, his cock sticking up like a flagpole. He took off his trousers as I watched back over my shoulder, never once taking his eyes off my bum. I'd set my legs apart and I knew I looked a sight, with my glistening bottom wide open to show off my pussy, which felt ripe and ready for cock.

He buggered me. I didn't expect it at all, and if I'm no virgin up my bum, then it's just as well, because he didn't even bother to get me ready properly. All he did was rub his knob in my pussy until it was all wet and slimy, then put it to my bumhole. He'd been right on my clit, leaving me moaning, so by the time I realised it was too late. I felt him push and my hole was so wet with sweat and the juice on his cock that it went in a little.

I called him a bastard, but he had me by the hips and was pushing, forcing it past my hole. He was far too strong for me and I was pretty randy, so I let him, relaxing my hole. In he went, right up my bum, jamming it in inch by inch. I kept calling him a bastard, over and over, in between grunts and gasps as he forced his way up. I knew it was all in when I felt his balls push against my pussy. My bumhole stung, and felt really stretched, like when I'm on the loo and trying to get a really big one out. I could feel it inside me too, not touching, but like a weight, like a great heavy log in my box.

He took me by the tits and began to push, calling me a 'sassy white bitch' and more as he buggered me. I have to say it was good. It had hurt going up, but once it was in I just felt breathless. My nipples were right between his fingers too, and if he was a bit rough, then I couldn't deny I was getting off on it. Before long I was being as dirty as he was, begging for it deeper and harder and watching myself given it up the bum in the mirror.

I could see him behind me, his dark skin against my pale, humping away to make my big bottom squash and jiggle with the pushes. His balls were slapping on my pussy too, bumping my clit, and I think I would have come if he hadn't got there first. It would have been so good, so dirty, reaching climax with his cock up my bottom. I love that,

the way my hole squeezes on the man's cock, just like my
pussy, only it's not my pussy, it's my dirty little bottom-
ring.

Instead he called me a dirty little whore one last time
and jammed his cock so hard up my bum that I screamed.
I never felt it, but I just knew that he'd done his thing up
my bottom. There was a stab of disappointment, but it felt
so good and so dirty that I wanted to frig off while it was
still in me. He didn't give me the chance, but pulled out,
which hurt more than when he'd put it up.

My pussy never did get seen to. As soon as he was out
I lay back on the bed, my legs wide open, showing
everything in the hope of getting a lick. He just walked into
the bathroom and washed his cock at the sink. I did get
told I had the best bum of any white girl he'd been up, and
I'm sure he meant it as a compliment, but that was it. He
went without waiting for me, just like Charles. I was left
on the bed, sweaty and sore behind, also more frustrated
than ever. I could have frigged off – I nearly did – but I
knew that there were plenty more men waiting for me, and
one of them had to be a bit more attentive.

I had a quick shower and sorted myself out, teasing my
pussy while I did it but never letting it go too far. Cock
was what I needed, and a skilful tongue to get me to my
climax. Back downstairs almost the first person I met was
the guy who'd said it was his turn next, Derek. He made
the joke again, then suggested straight out that we go up
to his room. I hesitated, because he was a good forty and
a bit of a slob, with a bristly moustache and a beer gut. On
the other hand I've found that the best-looking guys are
often users, while the less attractive are used to having to
try harder. He squeezed my bum anyway, and was steering
me towards the stairs, so I went.

I thought he was a bit drippy at first, but his manner
changed as soon as he got me into his bedroom. The first
thing he did was to ask me how old I was. I told him I was
twenty and he gave a sort of grunt, then said I looked more
like sixteen. He meant it as a compliment, I suppose, so I
smiled. Actually, I wasn't too pleased. He then told me to

turn round and stick my bum out, which was the sort of thing I'd been expecting. I did it, putting my hands on my knees and pulling my back in to make it as round as possible. He went a bit goggle-eyed at that, and got down behind me.

Some men are like that; they really worship a girl's body, as if they'd got their hands on some rare and wonderful treasure. Maybe it was like that for him; after all, I don't suppose he got much. I was looking back, and his eyes were absolutely popping out of his head, staring right at my bum. I'd thought he would strip it and get down to it, but he took ages. First my dress came up, held by the hem and inched up, bit by bit, over my thighs, then my bum, until it was rucked up into the small of my back. That left my bum in the lacy knickers, which were pretty tight and see-through at the back so my crease showed. He liked that, because he began to stroke it, mumbling about what a lovely bum I had and saying I was more of a peach than an apple, which made me giggle.

It took ages before he pulled down my knickers. He had a really good feel, squeezing my cheeks and kissing the lacy bit at the back. My legs were getting sore, but at least he was paying me some attention, and it seemed likely that any man who wanted to kiss my bum wouldn't mind licking my fanny. I knew my knickers would come down in the end – they always do – and I was quite grateful when I felt his fingers in my waistband and he began to pull.

He did it really slowly, kissing every inch of my bum as it was exposed and flicking his tongue in my crease. It was nice, but I couldn't handle his face, so I'd turned forwards and shut my eyes. When my knickers were far enough down he took hold of my cheeks and pulled them apart. I knew he was looking at my bumhole and I was wondering if I was going to get buggered again and feeling a bit resentful about it when I felt his moustache tickling in between my cheeks. He kissed my hole, right on it, and I knew that I was going to get my lick. After all, if a man's prepared to kiss a girl's arsehole, then he wasn't going to be fussy about a bit of pussy-licking.

85

Kissing my bumhole must have been the climax of his fun, because as soon as he pulled back he stood up, just tugging my knickers down a little further, to the tops of my thighs. He was still staring at my bum, and I suppose I did look cute, with it stuck out and framed in suspenders and my lowered knickers. The way he was looking, you'd have thought he was going to eat it.

He told me to bend over the bed, so I did, with my bum stuck out so I'd be nice and easy for entry. I could see that his cock was stiff under his trousers, but instead of pulling it out he began to look around the room. He kept looking at me and licking his lips, and I wondered what he was doing, until he noticed the cheese plant on the balcony and pulled out a three-foot bamboo from the pot. I was going to get a whacking.

If I hadn't been so turned on, and so drunk, I'd have told him to fuck off. Instead I just bit my lip and held still, wondering what it was going to feel like. My friend Lydia says it's a turn-on. I'd seen her whacked and she loved it. Derek was flexing the bamboo and grinning, with a really demented look on his face. I held still, knowing I could scream the hotel down if I had to and really rather enjoying the idea of getting the stick across my bum. He came round behind me, tapped it on the plumpest part of my cheeks, lifted it and gave me one.

God, it hurt. It was like I'd sat on a red-hot stove, stinging right across my bum and making me yelp and fall on the bed. I jumped up, squeaking like crazy and rubbing my bum, then calling him a bastard and a pig. He just told me to stop being a baby and get back over the bed. I did it, I don't know why, but over I went with my bum stuck out. I could see it in the dressing table mirror, looking fat and pale, with one bright red line across the middle.

It had really knocked the breath out of me, and I was panting and wincing in anticipation of the next one, dancing on my toes too, as if I was dying for a pee. He told me to keep still and called me a baby again, which got me and I tried my best to keep my bum still. The cut came down and I yelled out and fell over again, clutching at my burning cheeks, before getting slowly back into position. He said I was a good girl and brought another one down, even harder.

I managed not to fall over this time, but still jumped up, gasping and bouncing up and down on my toes until the awful stinging pain began to go away. My bum was getting warm, like Lydia said a whacked bum did, and I found myself actually quite wanting the next one. I got back in position, looking over my shoulder. There were now three red stripes decorating my poor bum, red on white, showing how I'd been whacked. That was really strong. A man was beating me and it was going to be obvious for ages; my bum marked to show what had been done to me.

He waited until I'd faced the front again and gave me my fourth. It was lower, right where my bum tucks down, and it stung like anything. I held still, though, just kicking a bit with the first of the pain. The fifth was harder, and laid right across the others, leaving a couple of places where the stinging didn't go away. I looked back and saw the deeper red marks, thinking of how bruised I'd be and how I'd be able to feel it and remember I'd been whacked for ages.

The sixth was even harder, and I fell on the bed again, sobbing a bit and clutching the cover because it hurt so much, but thrilled too. I'd have tried to take it if he'd wanted to go on, but somehow I knew he wouldn't. Someone had given Sally a dirty video once, called *Schoolgirls get Six,* and I was sure that was what he wanted me to be. Anyway, I might have been sobbing on the bed, but I'd never been so ready in my life. When I got my head together enough to look back I found that Derek was half-undressed and had his cock out. It was fat and pale and he was holding it in his hand, stroking it and looking down on my body.

As he came closer I slid back a bit, letting my legs trail over the edge of the bed so that he could get at me. I had my thighs cocked open as far as my knickers would let them go, and I was ready, but instead of putting it in me he began to wank over my beaten bottom. I told him I was

87

on the Pill and that he could have me. He took no notice,
but just pulled harder, his eyes glued to the mess he'd made
of my bottom.

I stuck it up, hoping to get his cock in me, only to have
him come, spraying spunk all over my bum and back. It
was on my lovely dress, I was sure, and I could feel it down
between my cheeks, warm and wet, right on my bumhole.
Some was on the cane marks too, which stung. It felt lovely
and disgusting at the same time, and I really wanted my
pussy seeing to. I asked for a lick, but he just wiped his
cock on my knickers and stepped back.

My pussy felt so, so ready, and I asked again, begging,
only to be turned down with a mumbled remark that I was
a slut. He'd got really embarrassed, and dressed in a hurry,
then left, leaving me randy and frustrated on the bed. I felt
so used, but this time I really couldn't do without my
climax.

I let my hands go back, feeling my smacked bottom and
rubbing the slimy semen into my cheeks. It was on my
dress, my knickers too, and I felt so soiled. I'd been fucked,
buggered, whacked and spunked on. My pussy and
bumhole were slimy with come; my bottom was burning in
pain, the cheeks criss-crossed with red lines. I normally get
embarrassed about the size of my bum, but now it felt
wonderful, so big and girlish, really sensitive too. I smeared
the spunk all over my bottom, then let my fingers go back
between my cheeks. My bumhole felt sore and itchy, like it
always does after having one up it. I put a finger in,
thinking of Mark's cock.

That was how I came, face down on the bed, one hand
under my tummy to get at my pussy, my beaten, slimy
bottom stuck up, all bare and open, one finger in my
bumhole, feeling the buggered hole and the ring of stinging
flesh. I cried out when I came, my ecstasy mixed with
resentment at the way I'd been used, but still very, very
happy for the experience.

It was actually all right when I'd come down. I cleaned
up as best I could, managing to get the spunk off my dress
but abandoning my knickers as just too soiled. The idea of

88

being knickerless for the rest of the evening made me giggle. I even began to wonder if I might not go to bed with another man, preferably one who'd treat me with a bit of respect and maybe actually sleep with me.

That was the mood I was in when I saw the card on the floor. It was by the door, and must have fallen out of Derek's pocket while he hurried to get dressed. I picked it up, recognising our own company logo. It was one of Mr Hatton-Brown's, and on the back was a brief note in his hand writing "Chloe, black dress, red ribbon. Will do as she's told."

I just stood there, gaping as it sank in. Mr Hatton-Brown had sold me. Not for money, maybe, but he'd sold me just the same. It even explained the way the men had behaved, getting their jollies as if I was a tart who would do want they wanted, no more. Not only that, but it explained why they'd been so rude to me too, getting me to do really dirty things because they thought I'd been ordered to take it, not because they wanted me to enjoy it. I had enjoyed it, but I was wishing I hadn't.

At first I didn't know what to do, other than raid Derek's mini-bar. There was champagne in it and I drank the bottle, feeling angry, miserable and ashamed until the alcohol began to get to me and my anger drowned out everything else. There were tears in my eyes, but I choked them back, determined to find the courage to go and show Mr Hatton-Brown up in front of the entire conference. I had to tell him, to call him a pimp in front of all his rotten friends, and I'd go just as soon as I'd eased the tension in my bladder.

Only I didn't. Instead I went out onto the landing, staggering a bit, but not so drunk I didn't know where I was going. At the top of the stairs I stopped, swaying, looking down on the throng below. Mr Hatton-Brown was there, talking to the bastard Charles who'd fucked me first. Mark was nearby, at the bar, Derek near the door.

I got their attention by throwing the champagne bottle down the steps. It shattered on the marble with a major bang. Everyone turned round and the room went quiet. I sat down, hard on my bum, spreading my knees. My pussy was showing, to all of them, wet and pink and glistening, the hole they all thought they could put their dirty cocks up when they pleased. Mr Hatton-Bastard-Brown was already hurrying towards me and I called him a whoremonger, which was the best word I could think of.

He reached the stairs and I let it go, a great, golden fountain of pee. It arched out from my pussy, right down the stairs, splashing among the broken glass, catching him. I laughed at that and really squeezed, sending a spray right in his face as he tried to get at me. He slipped in the glass and went over, back down the stairs in a mess of pee and broken glass. I was laughing, I'd never laughed so much, and as my pee ran down the marble steps in a little yellow waterfall and several hundred faces stared at me in utter horror, I decided that Sally was going to get her double act.

Good for her. Girls grow bolder, and each generation seem determined to shock the last. Sometimes they do, but it is wrong to assume that people who don't do openly outrageous things are necessarily dull and quiet. Some women mellow with age; others just become more discreet.

Kate, my cousin, is well built, with a full figure and a tumble of brown curls. She appears in several of my books, but mainly in **Bad Penny,** *was a pretty outrageous teenager, but married, twice, settled down and had children. Despite all that, underneath, she's still the same girl who made me suck her brand new husband's cock . . .*

Builder's Bum – Kate Bassington-Smyth

I did hesitate as I walked past the bank, but only for a moment. After all, Ginny Scott had done it, so why not me? All the way back from Henley I was wondering what was going to happen. With Jeremy in Hamburg and Pippa and Jemima at school, the house would be empty. I just hoped they'd be sensible about it.

They'd done a good job, painting the exterior woodwork as well as the walls, also a fair number of odd jobs I'd managed to find for them. All three were still there when I pulled into the garage, clearing up. Greg was, anyway, bending down to check the lids on the paint pots with a good three inches of his huge, muscular buttocks showing over the top of his trousers. Jason was leaning against the ornamental Japanese cherry, drinking tea, his skinny frame making Greg seem even bigger. Mr Sullivan was also drinking tea, but walking along the front of the house, looking over the gleaming new paintwork.

I had already decided that it was best to get on with it rather than put it off, so I put the car away and came back outside. Mr Sullivan greeted me with a wave, holding out a piece of paper.

'All done, Mrs B-S,' he announced. 'That's the lot.'

I took the paper, pretending to scan down the list of materials and charges. The total was just over thirteen hundred pounds, which seemed reasonable.

'Fine,' I said, handing it back to him.

There was a pause.

'Er, Mr B-S said you'd settle up when we'd finished,' he said.

'I can't pay it,' I answered. 'I haven't got the money.'

'Look, love, we had an arrangement,' he went on. 'We can't wait till your old man gets back, you know.'

'I'm sorry, but I can't pay it,' I told him.

'Look, we've done the work. We want our money.'

'I don't have it.'

'What, a rich bird like you? You must have.'

'I don't. My husband only gives me housekeeping, and with the children away I don't need much at all. Anyway, my husband will want to look at your work to make sure you've done a proper job.'

'We've done a top job. See for yourself.'

'I don't know anything about these things. You'll have to wait, I'm afraid, and that's all there is to it.'

'Look, your husband said you'd pay on completion.'

'I haven't any money, I tell you. Be reasonable; you were with Mrs Scott.'

'You know Mrs Scott?'

'Yes.'

There was a pause, each of us looking at the other. I could see him thinking, wondering if I really meant it. His mouth curved up at one end, just a fraction, but I knew I had got what I wanted.

'You want it like Mrs Scott?' he asked.

'Yes.'

'Just like Mrs Scott?'

'Exactly.'

'I'll have a word with the boys.'

He walked off, leaving me trembling with excitement. I had done it, and now I was going to have to have sex with them, all three of them – rough, hard men, very different men from Jeremy. OK, so I could just have asked them, but it wouldn't have felt the same. That way they'd have been considerate and tried to please me. This way they'd just use me for their fun.

I knew they'd accept. They'd done it to Ginny Scott, so they'd do it to me. She hadn't given me the details, just admitted that she'd given them sex in return for a job. At the time she'd been drunk and giggly, but I'd been sure she was telling the truth and now I knew she had.

Both Greg and Jason were nodding, then turning me lust-filled glances as Mr Sullivan started back across the lawn. I wondered what they'd do. Perhaps I'd be sent up to my bedroom and they'd come up one after the other, using me on my own bed, three men, three sweaty, crude builders. They might make me strip for them, or serve in my pinny and skimpy underwear. Maybe the others liked to watch and I'd get it on the lawn, made to perform while they waited their turns.

'All right,' Mr Sullivan addressed me, 'we'll do it. Like Mrs Scott, yeah?'

'Just like Mrs Scott.'

'Right. Get some fancy gear on then and we'll call it half an hour. How about down the end of the garden? No chance of being seen, that way.'

'Fine. Give me an hour.'

I walked into the house, trembling harder than ever. So it was going to be in the garden, which meant the others watching – maybe all three together. They wanted me in nice clothes, too, and I tried to imagine the sort of things builders might enjoy as I went up to the bedroom.

My first thought was to put on cut-down jeans and a little top, leaving plenty showing. I imagined it would be the sort of thing they'd like their wives to wear. It wasn't right, though, because I was sure that part of their fun would come from having a rich woman to play with. Expensive clothes would be better – silk underwear and a tight dress, sexy but chic.

I showered quickly, dried and put a little powder and make-up on, then laid my clothes out, knickers, bra and suspenders in heavy pale blue silk, a set Jeremy had brought me back from Milan. For a dress I chose a knee-length Chi Avina which probably cost more than they would expect to make in a month, between them. Silk stockings completed my look, which I was sure would impress.

Not surprisingly I was feeling nervous as I stepped out into the garden. Only one house overlooks our property, and that not very much, but I found myself glancing at the hedge several times until I was sure I was out of sight. There's a little patch of lawn with a few old plum trees which Jeremy likes to call the orchard, and that was where I wanted it to happen, down in the warm, long grass.

I couldn't see any of them, which seemed a bit odd, as I'd imagined they'd be really eager. Still, I was a little early. Jeremy had slung a hammock between two of the trees, a big one made of soft, thick rope. I climbed in and made myself comfortable, with one foot trailing over the edge so that I was showing a little leg. Closing my eyes, I waited, expecting Mr Sullivan's Irish accent or Greg's coarse Cockney at any moment. They'd be first, I was sure of it, Jason being much the youngest. He'd come last, once I was wet and slippery . . .

It came as a total shock. One moment I was dozing happily, thinking of how wet and open my pussy would be. The next I'd been grabbed, something tough and sticky had been forced down over my mouth and the sides of the hammock had been pulled up around me. I was helpless in seconds, my mouth taped and my arms and legs trapped in the mesh of the hammock, never giving me a chance to call out. The first thing I saw was Greg, looking at me, his fat, unshaven face split into a broad grin. Jason was visible too, winding a thick roll of masking tape around my body. Beyond him Mr Sullivan was working on one of the hammock fastenings with a Stanley knife. I only realised as the rope parted, and I came down with a bump.

I didn't know whether to be scared or excited. Not that it mattered what I felt, because I was wrapped up in the hammock like a cocoon, with just my head sticking out of the top. They were obviously going to have their fun with me, and that was what I'd wanted, so I lay still while the other hammock rope was cut, trying to fight down my sense of panic. What I wasn't sure was how they intended to have any fun with me when my mouth was taped and I was wrapped up too tight for my dress to be lifted.

I soon found out.

Greg rolled me over, face down in the grass. I looked back, wondering what they were going to do. They were looking down at me, at my bottom. The hammock was wrapped tight around me, and I could feel my flesh bulging through each hole of the mesh. Suddenly my bottom felt huge, really fat and round. Mr Sullivan had stood back, and Jason had the knife. Greg cocked a leg over my body and squatted down, lowering his great buttocks onto my back. He didn't put all his weight on me but it still squeezed the breath out of me. I felt pressure on my legs and realised that Jason had sat down too. He had the knife, and I felt a trace of fear as his hand touched my bottom.

I felt it all. They had a quick grope and Jason started to cut the hammock open, my bottom swelling out through the hole as each rope snapped in turn. He cut away enough to leave it sticking out of a big gap, and I thought he'd try and pull my dress up to get at me. Instead he took a pinch of it, right over my crease and I realised that he was going to cut my beautiful designer gown open. I wanted to wriggle, to kick, anything to stop him. I could only make muffled squeaks through my gag. He took no notice, and I felt my beautiful dress split as he cut a hole and pulled it wide. My bottom came out, bare but for my panties, protruding through the hole in the hammock in a mess of ruined silk. Sticking out like that it felt fatter than ever, with the panties stretched taut across the cheeks. My position was so embarrassing that for a moment it took my mind off my ruined clothes, until I felt him take a pinch of my panties and knew that they were coming off too. He didn't have to cut them, he only had to pull them down, but he didn't, he slit the seat. I felt the silk rip and the cool air on my bottom, bare and open, my bumhole showing because of the way it was sticking out. Greg took hold of my cheeks and hauled them apart, his thick, sweaty fingers right down in my crease. Jason's hand went down between my thighs, pulling my flesh to get a look at my pussy.

'Hairy, ain't she?' he commented. 'Nice cunt, Mrs B-S, but you ought to shave.'

'I like 'em hairy,' Greg put in. 'Look, she's powdered it for us and all.'

'She's well wet,' Jason added and I felt a finger at the mouth of my pussy.

It went up, Jason giving a childish snigger as he fingered me. I was wet, and it went in easily, deep in me, where he started to wiggle it around. The casual, appallingly intimate remarks had really got to me, making me excited and humiliated all at once. His finger was in me, touching my pussy in such a rude, intrusive way, using me just as he pleased. A second finger went in me and he began to fuck me with them.

'Nice arsehole, looks tight,' Greg drawled.

'Nice arse, full stop,' Jason added. 'I like a big arse, just so long as it's firm and the waist is nice and tight.'

'I'm going to fuck it,' Greg added, making my muscles twinge.

'Here, look, Greg, it's winking at you!' Jason laughed. 'Hey, boss, her arsehole's winking at us!'

'They don't call 'em brown eyes for nothing,' Mr Sullivan quipped. 'Now, come on, she'll want her tits out before you start any of that stuff.'

'Yeah, right, I want a feel of them and all,' Jason agreed.

Jason's fingers pulled from my vagina. I was rolled back, putting my bare bum in the grass. It was my breasts that felt huge now, squashed under the hammock mesh and bulging out of the holes in the same way my bottom had done. Jason stood over me, looking at my breasts instead of my face, just like he always did, only now he had them to play with. I watched, resigned to the ruin of my dress, as he extended the blade of the Stanley knife.

'Don't worry, Mrs B-S, we ain't going to cut you,' he assured me, 'just get your tits out.'

He sat on my stomach, the others watching as he took hold of my breasts and pulled them through the mesh, leaving them sticking up, really swollen, as if they were bound. Each made a ball of blue velvet, with my nipples

97

poking up to make little mounds at the top. He had a feel, squeezing and groping, his face set in a happy leer. I shut my eyes as he picked the knife up. I felt a nipple pinched, tweaked, then let go as he took hold of my dress. There was a tug at the velvet and I felt the pressure go, my flesh pushing out as the hole opened. I was whimpering, not daring to look as he repeated the process with my other breast. His fingers found the holes, one by one, ripping my pretty dress wide to let my breasts burst free, held in only by lacy bra cups.

'Nice,' he drawled. 'You don't know how often I've wanted to get these out, Mrs B-S.'

'Good and big, real bouncers,' Greg added, squeezing his crotch.

'Let's have 'em all the way out, then,' Jason went on.

I had hoped he'd spare my bra, but that went too, cut and torn, both cups, leaving my breasts sticking out of the mesh in circles of ruined silk and velvet. Because of the way they were pushed up they were swollen and dark with blood, the nipples achingly hard. My breathing had got really deep and I was trembling inside, wondering if I could handle what was being done to me. I've always preferred big, rough men, and so many times I'd fantasised about being thoroughly used, sometimes being tied up too. Now it was real, and my stomach was turning itself in knots as Jason's coarse hands explored my breasts, squeezing them.

'Slap 'em; they like that,' Greg's voice sounded from above me.

Jason responded with a hard slap to one breast, then the other, making me squeak behind my gag. He laughed and did it again, firm, stinging smacks that made them wobble and bounce, like two fat jellies on my chest. I had opened my eyes, and I watched as he did it, laughing as my flesh moved. My nipples were so hard, my flesh red, and getting redder. It hurt, quickly leaving me moaning and whimpering in my throat, one moment trying to writhe away, the next pushing them up for more. They felt huge, bloated and hot; rude, too, stuck out the way they were.

'In the face – remember her face,' Mr Sullivan said.

Instantly Jason's hands went to my cheeks, smacking fast, one after the other, leaving my face warm and tingling. Then it was my breasts again, slapped and fondled, slapped again, as above me Greg put his hands to his trousers. His great belly flopped out as he undid the button, then his cock and balls as he shoved them down and took his underpants with them. He had huge balls, really hairy, and a fat, stubby cock with a heavy foreskin. I couldn't take my eyes off it as he scooped it all into his hand and began to feel himself, leering down at my body.

Jason stopped and moved lower. I winced as two hammock ropes were cut. Greg's eyes moved down as my dress was slit and ripped apart. Jason's hands delved in between my thighs, pressing on my pussy, catching my torn panties and ripping upwards, tearing the silk away from my pussy. Greg licked his lips and began to pull at his cock.

'Fucking time, Mrs B-S,' Jason told me happily.

Without warning he grabbed my legs, pulling them up so that my bum pushed out through the hole in the hammock. I squeaked as the ropes pulled tight on my breasts. He held me up by my ankles, his eyes feasting on my bare sex as he fiddled with his fly. It came out, a pale, skinny cock, long and erect in his hand. He moved up to me, his cock nudged my pussy and then he was in me, holding me by the legs and moving his prick in my body, watching as it went in and out of my hole.

It was just what I'd wanted, being taken and fucked, used the way they wanted, only I hadn't imagined they'd tie me and humiliate me first. Greg was getting hard, and as he knelt at my head I knew he was going to make me suck his cock. He nudged it at my face, his great hairy belly really close. His fingers came down, tearing the tape off my mouth with one harsh movement. I cried out, only to have my mouth stuffed full of penis. He tasted of sweat and man, of cock and dirt as I began to suck him. Shuffling close, he pressed his belly to my face, his hairs tickling me as he plunged his cock deeper into my throat.

I was being had at both ends, used on the grass, fucked in my pussy and in my mouth. Crude words, I know, but that was how I wanted it, rough and hard, dirty and done without the slightest thought for my modesty. I felt Jason jerk and my pussy was full of semen. As he pulled out I could feel the wet, then on my sex as he emptied himself over my pubes and my thighs. He wiped his cock on a torn edge of my dress and moved back, dropping my legs. I rolled a little, giving all my attention to Greg's cock and wondering what Mr Sullivan had in mind for me.

Greg pulled back and I knew it was going in my pussy. Sure enough, he grabbed my legs and swung me round, prodding at my hole. Rolling me on my face, he squatted on my thighs, pushing his cock down into my crease. It touched my bumhole, which was wet with my own juice and Jason's come. As he pushed I remembered his threat to bugger me, only for his cock to dip lower and slide up my vagina.

He was crushing me, his weight pressing me into the grass as he fucked me with little, short jerks. It had me gasping, then moaning at the feel of my full vagina and the grass pressing to my sex. Jason came to my head, feeding me with a cock slimy with semen and juice. He started to harden as I sucked him clean, my head jerking on his cock to the rhythm of Greg's pushes. Jason took my hair, twisting it in his fist to make me suck deeper.

'Always the dirtiest, these posh tarts, ain't they?' he said merrily. 'Watch, I'm going to make her lick my arse.'

He pushed himself forwards, sticking out his cock and balls, his legs splayed wide. I kissed his balls as he pushed them in my face, then underneath them. If they hadn't had me helpless I wouldn't have done it; I couldn't have made myself. As it was I had my head pulled hard between his legs, my lips pushed to his balls until I took them in, then to his anus. I kissed it, hardly knowing what I was doing, then started to lick and Greg laughed to see me being so filthy. His balls were lying in my face as I cleaned him, his cock half-stiff, flopped over one cheek. He was rubbing, moving in my face, pressing his anus against my lips.

'Dirty fucking bitch!' he drawled. 'Who'd have thought she'd lick my arse, eh Greg? Not to look at her you wouldn't, eh? Why don't you fuck her up hers?'

Greg said nothing, just grunted and pushed right up me. For a moment I thought he'd come, only for him to pull out and nudge his cock down between my bum-cheeks. My bottom-hole was slimy and I knew it would go in, whether I wanted it or not. I didn't want it to hurt, so I let my ring relax, feeling the most wonderful, the most dirty sensation as the fat head of his erection began to fill my anus.

'I'm doing it, it's going up,' Greg breathed. 'Fuck, she's tight.'

He grunted, pushing, and my ring gave in, the head of his cock jamming suddenly into my rectum. I gasped and Jason laughed, then Greg pushed again and up it went, the whole, fat length of his penis, forced up my bottom until his balls met my empty pussy.

'Yeah, right up the brown eye!' Jason called as Greg lifted his belly to show off my penetrated anus. 'Fuck it good, Greg. Come on, suck my balls, bitch.'

I took his scrotum in my mouth obediently, sucking and panting with the effort of buggery. Greg's belly was slapping on my buttocks as he had me, his cock straining out my poor bottom-hole, pulling it back and forth. It hurt a bit, and my rectum felt bloated, while the feelings of being used were stronger than ever. If my hands had been loose I'd have masturbated, stroking my clit while my bottom and mouth were used for men's pleasure.

They wouldn't make me come, I knew it. These were builders, and had probably never licked a woman in their life. They probably thought I came with their cocks in me, and with Greg's cock up my bottom and Jason's balls in my mouth I was as close as I would get without my clitoris touched. I was grunting and mewing anyway, and I'm sure they thought they'd done it. My turn would come later, at last, lying on my bed in the nude and thinking of how I'd been caught and tied, my body used, my mouth filled with semen, my anus violated.

Greg came, and I bit on Jason's balls as the fat man's full weight was jammed down on my bottom. Jason gasped, Greg grunted, pushing again to knock the breath out of my body, and I knew that there was come up my bottom, adding an extra dirty touch to my feelings. Jason stood up, then Greg pulled out of my bottom with a sticky sound to leave me panting on the ground. I could feel the wet on my buttocks from the sweat of Greg's belly and between my thighs from my own. My bottom-hole was oozing semen, sore and I was sure, very red. I could taste Jason in my mouth and smell both of them, also my own excitement.

'Make me come,' I begged, hoping that they might know enough to do it.

'Nah, that's the boss's job,' Jason answered.

'We've had ours; now we watch you get yours, just like we did for Mrs Scott,' Greg added.

Jason bent down and picked up the masking tape. I let him do it, sealing my mouth as it was obviously part of the game. I'd had no idea that Ginny Scott was so kinky, not even that she liked being tied up, never mind the sort of abuse they'd given me. I was glad though, because I'd wanted it rough and I'd got it, even up my bottom, which I never dare ask for but always makes me feel so beautifully dirty.

I lay on the ground, waiting, tied and ready for my orgasm. Jason and Greg made themselves comfortable, sitting with their cocks and balls hanging out, Jason chewing a straw, Greg absently watching his semen dribble down over my bottom. A voice sounded from the house and I turned to see Mr Sullivan walking towards us, a heavy bag in each hand. Greg got up.

'Not here, boys; her husband might notice,' Mr Sullivan said. 'Put her on the midden, she'll like that, and we can rake it over when we're done.'

'What you got?' Jason asked.

'This and that,' Mr Sullivan answered. 'Mainly what's left of the paint.'

I knew what he was going to do. I could see the outlines of the paint pots through the bags, big tins of white gloss and blue masonry paint. It was going on my body, soiling me and making an utter ruin of my already torn dress. My bum would get it too, and my boobs, even my pubic hair, a dirty, sticky mess that would take hours to clean up. I'd have said no if I'd been able, despite a little voice in my head telling me it was just what I needed. I was going on the midden, too, among the grass clippings and leaves, the old tea-bags and bits of vegetable.

Greg lifted me easily, just hooking a hand into the hammock mesh. I was carried and dumped on the midden, face down so that I came up with bits of grass stuck to the semen on my face. They rolled me, putting my bottom in it. I could feel the hot, rotting grass on my skin. Something was in the sticky mess between my bottom-cheeks, maybe a bit of old carrot. The smell of cut grass mixed with the smell of decay, rich and strong, then with paint as Mr Sullivan levered a screwdriver under the lid of a pot.

Jason and Greg stood back, grinning as they watched. I could see my bare belly, the skin white and smooth with my pubes showing over the gentle bulge. Mr Sullivan stepped close, poising the pot right over my pussy, letting me watch, letting what was going to be done to me sink in. Then he tipped and out it came, a thick trickle of paint, then clots, for all the world like a cow doing a pat, splashing on my belly and pooling in the V of my thighs. It felt cold and wet, heavy too, as thick clots splattered on my bare belly, then on the ruins of my dress as he moved up, on my breasts, one then the other, soiling my whole front. Some splashed on my neck, my face too, but I couldn't shut my eyes, I needed to watch too badly.

My bottom came next. I was taken by the feet and rolled over again, face down in the midden with my bum stuck up. I could feel where the grass had stuck to Greg's sweat and semen and I felt the paint squelch between my thighs and into my pussy as they parted. I tried to look back, over my shoulder, just in time to see Mr Sullivan start to pour, emptying a great thick stream of blue over my poor, bare bum. I felt it hit, splattering my ruined panties and dress, running down between my cheeks, cool against my abused anus, sticky as my cheeks clenched and unclenched in my emotion.

103

I was pushing my bum up, I couldn't help it, behaving like the dirtiest little tart in front of three builders. The paint went on my legs, on my back, splashing in my hair. I squirmed away, praying he wouldn't ruin it but knowing he would and wanting him to. He did, pouring out the last of the tin into my curls, down my neck and over the top of my head, utterly ruining my hair. I was going to have to wash it in turps, that or be shaved bald, and I was calling them bastards through my gag even as I stuck up my bum in the hope of getting my pussy attended to.

I got it, but not the way I wanted. Greg made the suggestion, picking a squashy, overripe plum from beneath the trees. It went up my pussy, bursting at the mouth, the rotten pulp squeezing out around the hole. Jason laughed and took another, from the tree. That went up my bottom, forced past the stinging, slimy hole and into my rectum. Another went in my pussy, a fourth – so rotten the stone had popped out – in my mouth, the tape quickly replaced. Greg squeezed my chin up and the plum burst, filling my mouth with the sweet taste of decay.

They were laughing, commenting on the filthy mess of my soiled body and the way I was acting. I was called a slut and a whore, and all I could do in response was stick my bum up to show them my filthy sex, with paint clogging my pubes and filling my pussy. The plum came out, squeezing out as my muscles tightened, slimy with paint to lie between my thighs. Jason moved, walking to near my head, grinning. I watched, breathless as he scooped up a big double handful from the midden, a mess of egg shells, old tealeaves, rotting plums, bits of decaying grass. It went in my face, rubbed in, mixing with the grass and semen. My face was pushed in, rubbed in the rotting grass until I was kicking and struggling for breath, pulled up and pushed in again. I came up gasping and blowing bits of grass from my nose.

Jason pulled my head around and I saw Mr Sullivan. He was holding the big garden syringe, the nozzle in a bucket. Greg had a tub of grease, thick yellow industrial grease, his finger coming out with a thick blob as Mr Sullivan filled

104

the syringe. I knew where it was going, and with a sob I pushed up my bottom. I wished I'd known Ginny Scott was so dirty, and I could just picture her, her plump curves stripped like mine, her body tied, her clothes ruined, her golden hair and milk-white skin filthy with paint. Then a syringe up her bottom for an enema, in public.

I lifted my bottom further, pushing it right up, my cheeks peeling apart with a revolting sticky sound. My eyes were screwed up in disgusted expectation as Greg's finger pushed down between my spread cheeks. He touched, teasing my anus wide, a thick, callused finger sliding up my bottom, nudging the plum aside, wiggling about in the chamber. It came out and I farted, making Jason laugh. The nozzle touched, my bumhole gave and it was in me, up my bottom, cold water flooding my rectum, swelling out my belly. My muscles were tightening, my anus pulsing on the nozzle, my pussy squeezing closed to bubble paint out down my vulva, only to open and fill again. I couldn't stop swallowing, my throat working over and over as my bottom filled.

My eyes came open, wide as the pressure inside me began to sting. I felt a tug at my side, looked down to see Jason with the knife, cutting at the mess over my right arm. I knew what they were doing, freeing my arm to let me masturbate, to frig off and come over my own soiling, over my utter degradation as I squirmed in filth on the midden.

I was going to do it too, my arm wriggling free as the ropes snapped until at last I could reach back. My hand found my slimy bottom, pulling the cheeks wide. I felt the hard brass tube in my anus, touching where it joined. Out it came and I let go at once, water and semen and muck spraying out around my fingers as I jabbed and patted at my bumhole. The plum burst out, several feet in an arch of filthy water, drawing fresh laughter from the boys. Fluid was dribbling into my pussy as I found the hole, then squelching out around my fingers as I entered myself, deep in, squeezing paint and semen and dirty water over myself. Twisting back I found my clit, my thumb going into my pussy.

Hot fluid hit me as I started to rub, Greg, fat cock in his hand, laughing as he urinated over my filthy body, over my breasts and in my face. Jason joined him, his spray aimed between my legs, over my pussy, splashing on my hand as I masturbated. They were pissing on me, urinating over my helpless body, laughing as they soiled me, and I was going to come over it at any moment. Mr Sullivan was hard, jerking a big pink cock over my body, and as I started to come, so did he, his semen arching out to splash on my sodden buttocks and in my crease.

I screamed into my gag, the tape pulling at my lips. Greg's urine was splashing on my breasts, Jason's into my pussy-hole and up my open bottom. My clitoris was burning, agony, too sensitive to touch, but as I pulled back Mr Sullivan's hand slapped down between my legs, pushing mine aside to frig me mercilessly into another peak, then another as my vision went red, blurred, then black as my battered senses finally gave in.

Cold water brought me round, the hose playing on my body, washing the mess away. Jason was using the knife, cutting me free, both the hammock and my clothes, leaving me naked on the midden. I had to stand to be washed, in the midden so nothing would show. Stark naked as they took turns to hose down my body. They behaved like they owned me, laughing and commenting casually on my body and the way they'd had me. I didn't answer back, just grateful that they'd used water-soluble paint for the sake of my hair.

It had been far, far beyond what I'd expected, but the orgasm had been wonderful, one of the best of my whole life. I was sore, but happy, also thankful, and as I bent over to let them hose down my bottom and sex I was wondering if Ginny Scott would appreciate a few pots of my home-made plum jam.

Who would think it of a respectable middle-class housewife? Well, me for a start. Charlotte, the slim blonde fitness instructor from Brat is also outwardly respectable, fitting into contemporary culture while keeping her dirty habits to herself. In her case she tries to be honest with her boyfriend and, as the next story shows, this can work in unexpected ways . . .

Chastity – Charlotte Petersham

Gus never really understood my need for masochism. Oh,
he was quite happy to go along with it, and he never
preached, not like some men. In fact he loved having a girl
who liked dirty sex, and if that meant indulging my kinky
fantasies from time to time, then it was fine by him. What
I mean is that he didn't understand my need for sexual acts
that hurt or made me feel submissive. To him a thrill was
a thrill, and it was beyond him that something could be
painful, or humiliating, and sexually exciting at the same
time.

For one thing he had been to public school, and he'd
been caned. He had hated it, and couldn't understand how
I could enjoy it. That didn't stop him whacking me, and he
admitted he got a kick out of having me touching my toes
with my feet set well apart and my bare bottom stuck up
high for his attention, my favourite position. He claimed
not to enjoy my pain, but he certainly enjoyed the pleasure
that came with it, because after my caning sessions he was
always rock-hard. According to him that was because any
man would be rock-hard with me bending bare bottomed
in front of them, but I wasn't so sure, or at least I didn't
want to believe that.

It was the same with anal sex. He loved putting it up my
bum, and he said it was because he liked my tight little
bottom, and that my bumhole felt good on his cock.
Personally I wondered what other tight little bottoms he
had enjoyed, but he wasn't admitting anything. Anyway,

he certainly didn't regard buggery as abnormal, and I was happy to go along with that.

What he didn't like was my tendency towards exhibitionism, especially wanting rude things done to me in front of other people. Other men were out, and the only other girl I knew who could handle that sort of thing was Natasha. Gus did not like Natasha, who he thought was a spoiled brat and far too full of herself. He did cane me in front of her, once, but got cross when she wouldn't do anything with him, which spoiled it.

After that, I was pretty sure what he was going to say when Tasha invited me to come to France with her and Percy Ottershaw. They were both wine writers, which was how they'd met, and the idea was to drive to Paris first, getting a bit of shopping in, then to tour the Champagne region and Chablis, then back to Calais. Percy was her sugar daddy, although not many knew that. Unfortunately Gus did, which was my fault because I'd got a kick from telling him what Percy liked to do with Tasha. Percy was also the one who had introduced me to the pleasures of being caned, but that Gus didn't know.

Gus was actually invited, too, although as it was in the middle of the week it was out of the question, and I think Tasha knew that. I really wanted to go, but Gus just laughed when I suggested it, calling Tasha a slut and Percy a dirty old man. I told him not to be silly and that I was hardly going to let a fat old buffer like Percy do anything to me anyway. He just raised his eyebrows and asked if 'doing anything' included letting Percy watch while Tasha punished me.

I tried to act outraged, but it was no good. He might not have known about Percy, but during one of my naughtier moments I'd admitted to liking the idea of being caned in front of his uncle, who was a very tall, stern man; also high enough up in one of the big banks to give him an added frisson of power. He just laughed at my tantrum and said I was as big a slut as Tasha and not to be trusted.

We had a bit of a row after that, and I seriously considered going anyway, but I did care for him and I knew I wouldn't. Besides, I didn't really have a leg to stand on, because he was really good to me, and faithful, while I was the dirty one. He was right, too; Tasha had every intention of getting into my knickers on the trip. She hadn't even bothered to pretend otherwise.

Gus was sulking, and wouldn't speak to me, just lying on the couch reading a book about medieval England. I suppose I was sulking too, a bit, but I was still hoping to talk him round. It stayed like that for a long time, with me thinking of how to get round him, and what promises I could make and what treat I could give him. I imagined he was thinking along similar lines, only to get a surprise as he suddenly turned to me.

'OK, you can go,' he said, quite calmly, 'but you're to wear a chastity belt.'

'A chastity belt?'

'Yup, like this.'

He passed me the book, held open at an illustration. It was a woman, very stylised, in full medieval dress, but with a cut-away at the level of her hips to show her chastity belt. The expression on her face was one of bland acceptance. Not mine.

'You bastard!' I answered, on impulse really.

He laughed.

'It's you,' he told me, 'it really is. You're always telling me you get a kick out of feeling you're under my power. With a thing like that on you would be.'

I said nothing, trying to think of a snappy answer. Unfortunately, he was right. Being under someone else's power was part of the thrill for me. With Gus I always had to tell him what to do in advance, but I like to be told to bend down and strip my bottom. No, I like to be ordered to do it.

When I didn't answer, he chuckled. I threw the book at him and I would have hit him if he hadn't caught it, but the idea was embedded in my mind. Accepting was just a matter of getting over my own pride. Gus was still chuckling to himself, and he obviously thought it was a funny idea, not a sexy one. In fact I think he expected me to turn him down, which would have put my trip that little bit further out of reach. There was a drawback to that. If I accepted he had to let me go, and to get me the belt. I waited a while, sitting with a deliberately sulky pout on my face, long enough to make him think he'd won.

'Oh, all right,' I said eventually, then paused. 'Put me in your horrid belt.'

He turned, genuinely surprised. I gave him a smile and a shrug.

'You'd wear it, really, like this?' he demanded.

I nodded.

'For nearly a week?'

Again I nodded.

'You'd get off on it, wouldn't you? You're a pervert, Charlie. A lovely pervert, but a pervert.'

For the third time I nodded. I couldn't very well disagree. I was going to enjoy it, and I suppose I am a bit perverse, by some standards. I was also going to France.

Gus was right, it would make me feel controlled, and if he saw putting me in control as humorous, then I could handle that. Of course you can't pick up chastity belts at Marks and Spencers, or even Harrods, I don't think. We needed a specialist.

After a failed shopping expedition to Soho, I found some quite nice ones, in a woman's sex shop in the city which Natasha had taken me to before. They were a neat, slim-line design, like tanga briefs, only in thin anodised aluminium with rubber padding inside. The lock was placed so it would fit over my pubic mound, very flat, and operated by the tiniest of keys. There was even a carefully shaped slot so that I could go to the loo, both ways, but there was no way to fuck me while I was wearing it. Not unless I found a man with a cock as thin as a pencil, anyway. They also provided enough protection to my bum to stop me being caned effectively. While they would have been a bit suspicious-looking under trousers or a tight skirt, under a loose skirt nobody would be any the wiser. I quite liked the idea of walking around in a chastity belt and nobody knowing, and after trying them on I'd just about come to terms with the whole idea.

Unfortunately Gus wouldn't let me buy them. He said he had a better idea. A friend of his, Anthony, had quit the city and bought a forge in rural Dorset. He was working as a blacksmith, or rather pretending to, Gus said, because he'd made enough money not to have to bother. They'd been to school together, and were pretty close, although I'd never met him. The idea was that he would be able to run me up a proper medieval chastity belt in the forge, and Gus said it was that or nothing.

I tried to bargain, even finding some nice designs on the Net that wouldn't have shown so much. There was even a chain-mail one that I liked, but which he said would be too easy to pull aside. He was adamant – medieval or nothing. I ended up giving in, just as long as it was properly padded for the sake of my skin and allowed me to use the loo. Gus agreed, and that was that.

I was pretty embarrassed, because I knew it would mean having it fitted, going half-naked and wearing it in front of a complete stranger. Gus pointed out that I was always going on about being disciplined in front of another man, and I had to admit he was right. It was exciting, but it was still humiliating, one of those things Gus could never understand. He said he might even whack me if I was a good girl, which really got me on heat and we ended up having sex on the couch after I'd been spanked with a spoon.

Anthony agreed without hesitation. In fact he thought it was funny, just like Gus, and they had a hearty laugh together on the phone over the thought of putting me in it. Having decided my fate, they arranged that we should drive down to Dorset at the weekend, which we did, arriving at the village near Chard where Anthony lived at lunch time on the Saturday.

He knew already, of course, so there was no dissembling, and he was regarding me with a sexual interest from the start. He was good-looking too, taller than Gus, and darker, if not so broad-shouldered. Suddenly, taking my clothes off for him didn't seem so embarrassing.

Gus was different in front of Tony. When he was with me he could be quite sweet, but he was normally very reserved, always with a barrier up. With Tony there was no barrier. He was much more relaxed, sharing in-jokes and stories about their school. That for me was better, and I quickly started to relax.

We lunched in the village pub and then went to Tony's forge. This was the real thing, a long, low building of red brick. The original forge had gone out of business before the war, and Tony had bought the building and restored it. Most of his work was actually making fancy iron work for other newcomers, and as I looked around I could see that he knew what he was doing.

Tony shut the big wooden doors behind us with a bang that made me jump, then swallow as he picked up a tape measure. It was time for me to undress. I was blushing as I did it. In the pub everything had been so normal, the three of us talking as equals. Now I had to go bare from the waist down so that I could be fitted with a chastity belt, in front of two men.

My submissive feelings rose quickly as I peeled off my jeans and shoes. I hesitated at my knickers, looking up at Gus to see if he wanted me to go all the way. He nodded and I pulled them down, unable to raise my eyes to them as they watched me expose myself.

With me bare Tony went to work, measuring me and selecting metal, choosing his tools and so on, all the while humming to himself and treating my body with no more regard than if I'd been a horse. It took ages to make, and I had to sit there, naked from the waist down, for most of the day. I had an old pinny, but it was still obvious I was bare, and I kept thinking somebody was going to come in without troubling to knock. Nobody did, but it kept me on edge.

Finally it was finished, and frankly it was scary. For a start it was huge, a massive thing of beaten black iron, high-waisted and shaped to the curve of my hips and bum. It was hinged at the back and closed at the front, with interlocking iron teeth like one of those ghastly man-traps. Under my crotch the teeth opened a little, enough to let me go to the loo, but not for a cock to get in. A clasp at the front allowed a heavy padlock to be fitted, which would hang down over my pussy.

It really was medieval. Even the padlock was a great black thing that looked about a hundred years old, with a huge key. As for the gap at the crotch, it would work, but I would have to wash my bottom after every time I went to the loo. Just knowing that was humiliating enough, but actually putting it on was so strong. I could feel the tears starting in my eyes, which always happens to me when I'm put in bondage, but I choked them back, unwilling to show so much emotion in front of Tony, and really Gus too.

They were happy, both with the look of the thing and the fit, although Tony had to make a couple of changes before it was really snug. It looked clumsy, but it followed the curve of my lower back and even my belly. Getting it on and off was tricky, and I was glad I'm supple, but as Gus pointed out, it wasn't as if it would be coming up and down like a pair of knickers.

Being men, they were as fascinated by the physics of the thing as the sexual implications. For me it was mostly in my head, however real the awful thing was. They got pretty steamed up, though, and Gus told me to show Tony my caning position, touching toes, and still with nothing on below my waist. I did it, although my face must have been crimson. It was all coming out as they talked, and Tony was looking at me with a mixture of disbelief and lust. I stood up, feeling really unsure of myself. So many times I'd imagined the scene, with a man looking on as I got into my pose. Now it was for real and I could feel my pulse racing and the hot blood in my cheeks and neck. Gus was smiling, with a knowing sparkle in his eyes and a bit of a bulge in his crotch. Tony's lust was more obvious, written plainly on his face, and as I stepped into the middle of the room he quickly adjusted his cock in his trousers. I've seen men do that before, when they begin to get hard and it makes their cock uncomfortable. Both of them were getting stiff, and it was the thought of me showing off that was doing it, maybe even the thought of me getting a whacking.

It is a rude position, showing everything, and I mean everything. Somehow it always feels right, better than being bent over something, or rolled up on my back, perhaps because it forces me to keep control of my body. They made me stay like that for ages, just looking at me. I was excited, and would have loved six of the best followed by being made to kneel and suck them off in turn.

Sadly it didn't happen, and I was left to cuddle up to Gus on the sofa while Tony went to fit the padding to the chastity belt. We knew it would take a while, and Gus started to kiss me and stroke my breasts, ending up in a frantic knee-trembler with me bent over the sofa. He did it over my bum and wiped up with tissues, then gave me a lick.

I think Tony guessed, because he was grinning when he came back. He had padded the belt with leather, brown and heavy but soft too, like thick chamois. The belt now had that rich leathery smell, and he had managed a sort of frill around the edges to give it what he considered a more girlie look.

For some reason getting into the finished product was even more humiliating than fitting it. It was really heavy, and although I had to admit it was comfortable enough, I knew that I'd never be able to forget that I was wearing it, not for a moment. It made me sit in a really prim posture too, straight-backed with my bottom stuck out a little. The boys liked that, and Gus fitted the padlock, clicking it shut with a wicked grin on his face. A shiver ran through me at that sound, and I knew I was genuinely trapped, unable to fuck without his say-so, not through my own choice, but because of the belt.

The next step was to see how I should travel while wearing it. I'd brought several outfits down to see what it looked like with them. Jeans were out of the question, making it quite obvious what I was wearing. The hinges at the back even showed. Even with loose trousers it looked really obvious. Not that anyone was going to think I was wearing a chastity belt. After all, why should they? What they were going to think was that I was incontinent and was wearing a nappy, which was even more humiliating. It was like that because of the way the padding bulged out at the sides. When I pointed out how it looked to Gus and Tony they laughed themselves sick.

Skirts were better, but even then they had to be loose. In the summer I'd have been in real trouble, but as it was a pleated wool skirt hid the thing to all but careful inspection. Even then it was going to be both awkward and embarrassing, but then it was supposed to be.

So that was it, and Gus made me wear it on the drive back to London, sitting bolt upright in the passenger seat. Back at the flat he took it off long enough to fuck me on the bed, then locked me in it for the night, tossing the key in his hand and chuckling to himself as he left. He hadn't made me come, deliberately, and I wanted to, but with the belt on it was impossible. I just couldn't get at my clitty, no matter how hard I tried and what strange positions I got into. I could touch, just, with my little finger pushed in through the iron teeth, but only in poses so awkward that I knew I'd never get there.

It was worse when I needed the loo. The belt made it hard to sit down properly, and I ended up squatting over the bowl with my feet on the seat. That was bad enough, but I made a terrible mess and had to have a bath and a shower before I was properly clean. All the while my feelings of control and sexual humiliation were growing stronger, and my need to come worse and worse. I even tried to rub myself off on the belt, but I just couldn't get the friction.

In the end I went to bed, feeling incredibly frustrated, only to find that it was only comfortable on my back, because of the padlock. In the end I managed to sleep, only to dream of being in a medieval dungeon, spread out on a rack while hooded men tried to break my lock with a hammer and chisel. Gus let me out in the morning, and I was pathetically grateful. How I was going to get through five days with it on I just didn't know, and the prospect was as terrifying as it was exciting.

The day came and I let him lock me into the awful thing before Percy came to collect Tasha and me. I told

116

Tasha and she made me show it to her, Percy too, going pink as I lifted my long dress up to my neck. She pretended to be outraged, asking how Gus dared to think he could restrict my sexual freedom. Underneath I could tell she was a little aroused, amused too, but would rather it had been her who had the key. Percy just gave a dirty little chuckle.

For the next five days my whole life revolved around being in the chastity belt. Not only could I never forget that I had it on, but being in it dictated what I could wear, how I could sleep, how I could sit, even the details of my personal hygiene. Percy remarked that it was a bit like travelling with a baby.

Natasha took it as a challenge, swearing she would have me out of it before we got back to England, or at the very least make me come while I was in it. She tried to pick the lock, in the loos on the ferry, but failed. We had always intended to share a bed, not that Gus knew, and on the first night she tried to make me come by massaging me, kissing and licking my body all over and finishing on my breasts. It didn't make me come, but it got me so high that I was writhing on the bed, getting into position after position in the hope that she would be able to get at my sex. She tried to poke her tongue through the teeth over my pussy, and managed to lick my sex lips, anus and perineum a little, but not my clitty, which made it worse than ever. Tony had done his job well, and I ended up sweaty and frustrated. Natasha sat on my face and made me lick her to her own orgasm.

Paris was great, and while shopping I came as close to forgetting that I was in a chastity belt as ever. That evening we drove out as far as the country where they make Brie cheese and chose a hotel in a village near Meaux. We'd been talking about what to do with me a lot as we drove, with an intimacy that had got me going again, Tasha too. After dinner we let Percy watch as we played in our room, cuddling and showing off for him until he could hold back no more and took out his skinny little cock. Tasha sucked it while I posed, on my knees so that he could see the pink

117

flesh of my pussy through the jaws of the belt, just feet in front of his face, but totally unobtainable.

The next day was Champagne, and we arrived in Epernay for lunch and spent the afternoon tasting. We were drunk by the end, and I was more aroused than ever. Our intimacy was really building up, and that evening Percy watched us in the shower. Tasha said she would pee for him, which he always liked, and she had climbed up on the bidet and spread her thighs when she suddenly stopped.

I wondered what she was doing as she told me to get into the shower and lie down, and then I realised. Going down on my back, I spread my legs, rolling them up high to push out my crotch with the belt bulging up over my pussy, the padlock lying upwards to get it out of the way. Tasha squatted down, holding my ankles and pushing her pussy up against the teeth of the belt. I heard her sigh, and suddenly hot pee was gushing out over my pussy. Some splashed on the teeth, spraying our bellies and breasts. Most went in, right on my sex, filling my open vagina and trickling down between my bum-cheeks. It was great, so rude and sexy, and for a moment she even managed to get the jet onto my clitty, bringing me up towards orgasm, only to die to a trickle just when I thought I was going to come.

The frustration was terrible, worse than ever. I was left lying on the shower floor, wet with Tasha's pee, legs spread with Percy looking on and playing with his cock. I'd been close, really close, and I was sure I could do it. What I needed was more than I could bring myself to say, but I nodded to Percy and he nodded back.

He let his cock go down, leaving the bathroom until it had gone limp. That always seems to make men want to pee and, sure enough, he managed it. He stood over me, cock out of his fly, and pissed on my body just as if he had been using a urinal. He did his best, aiming it at my pussy, and catching my clit. It didn't work, though; his pee didn't have the force of Tasha's, and it was less of a turn-on having him doing it to me. All I got was peed on.

I showered down while Tasha sucked Percy back to erection. She was as high on sex as I'd ever seen her and insisted on sitting on his lap with his cock inside her so that I could lick everything from his balls to her clitty. She had a great orgasm, moaning deeply and playing with her breasts as my tongue lapped at her sex, which left my head in a spin. Percy's cock was in her, right in front of my face, and I'd already licked his balls, so as it slipped out I took it in my mouth, sucking Tasha's cream off it while she laughed to see me behave so rudely. He came in my mouth, and I swallowed dutifully, much to Tasha's delight.

The next morning was spent driving up the Marne Valley, from village to village, tasting. Percy seemed to know everybody, and aside from our purchases we collected plenty of free samples. I tried to spit, but by lunchtime I was tipsy again and thinking of what the evening would bring. Gus really had me under his thumb. True, what I'd done with Percy would have made him furious, but the fact remained: I couldn't fuck and I couldn't come.

We chose to picnic, buying bread and goat's cheese and driving up into the woods above the vineyards. At a secluded spot we ate and drank, then lay in the dappled sunlight, drowsy and replete. Tasha had her head in Percy's lap and he was stroking her hair. Both were being far more intimate than they ever were in London, where she never admits to what they get up to. Now it was different, there was only me to know, and I wasn't at all surprised when after a while she unbuttoned his fly and got his cock out.

She began by nuzzling her face against it, then kissing and finally taking it all in her mouth. He sighed and moved his legs, and as he did so his foot caught a bottle of champagne. It went over, the stopper flying out with a gush of bubbles. Tasha cursed and came off Percy's cock, reaching for the bottle and picking it up. She made to put the stopper back in, but stopped suddenly, turning to me with her face set in a grin of pure mischief.

'I can do it, Charlotte,' she announced. 'Come on, dress off.'

'What, here?'

'Here's perfect, nobody will come. Come on, darling, I'm going to make you come.'

'But the belt.'

'Never mind the belt, just strip off and roll up, like you did in the shower.'

I obeyed, quickly shrugging off my dress and bra. Knickers were pointless over my belt, so that left me in nothing but a pair of shoes. I rolled up, presenting my bottom and the mouth of the chastity belt to them, knowing my pussy showed pink beneath.

'Better get you turned on properly first,' Tasha said and crawled quickly over to me.

She just stuck her bottom straight in my face. Skirt thrown up, knickers tugged down and a leg cocked over my head. I started to lap at her as soon as she had settled her bottom. My nose was against her bumhole, my tongue on her pussy as I began to lick. She was right, it did turn me on, quickly, especially when she began to play with my breasts. I knew Percy was watching, and I could hear the slapping noise as he played with his cock, getting off on watching his girlfriend queen me.

Tasha got off before she came, scrambling round between my legs. I held them wide and high, with my hands under my knees as she took a bottle of champagne from the chiller. Percy was hard, tugging at his cock as he watched Tasha remove the foil and wire cage. She popped the cork away, and as the bubbly spurted from the bottle she put it to my pussy, right against the teeth of the chastity belt.

I gasped as a gush of champagne exploded against my sex. It was cold, and hard, harder than her pee, but it was also fizzy. My mouth went wide as my vagina filled with champagne; the spray was right on my clitty, tingling on the sensitive flesh, making me gasp with pleasure. Again she did it, shaking the bottle, then applying it to my pussy, then again, until I had begun to moan and sigh, sure that with just a little more effort she could make me come.

There was a wet pool under my bottom, my cheeks and the rear of the belt splashing in it as I bucked in ecstasy.

Percy came forwards, taking a second bottle, and moments later a fresh spray of fizzy wine burst on my pussy. They took it in turns, one shaking, one spraying as my moans turned to gasps, to little whimpering cries. It was all round my clitty, prickling me, bubbling down over my sex. My vagina was over-flowing, my anus twitching, cold and wet. It was so good, and all the better for the rudeness of my exposure and being in the open air. Then it was good enough, and with one final drawn-out groan I came.

I was clutching the belt as I did it, my fingers locked on the hard iron. My pleasure went on and on, beautiful and slow, my clitty pulsing in the stream of fluid. My tummy was wet, and my breasts; so were Tasha and Percy, but they seemed not to care, keeping up the spraying until at last I slumped back and said that I had had enough.

After that it was sex with everything. We were triumphant, and Tasha made a point of having me do all the things of which Gus would disapprove. Several times I sucked Percy's cock, even after it had been up Tasha's bottom one particularly debauched evening. I posed too, flaunting myself for their entertainment, and got peed on more than once. I watched Tasha punished, beaten with a hazel switch, and took it myself, both of them using bundles of twigs to get at the area of my bottom that showed around the edges of the belt. I even spent an evening as their dog, crawling around on the floor and being fed come from Tasha's hand. Every time, though, when I was high enough, they would make me come, spurting champagne up me and over me until I reached my orgasm.

At last it was over, and we returned to England. It had been quite an experience, and I was sorry that it was over. Not too sorry, though. Enforced chastity had made for some inventive fun, but it wasn't really practical to be belted all the time. So they dropped me at Gus's flat and I climbed the stairs with a knowing smile, thinking of Champagne. He was there, and greeted me with a satisfied nod, then caught the key to my chastity belt as I threw it to him.

Which just goes to show, girls don't have to be made to do dirty things, they're quite capable of doing them of their own accord. In fact, anyone with the urge towards sexual punishment, watersports or any of the other minor taboos will probably get what they need eventually, whatever their background.

Naomi appears in In for a Penny *as one of the regulars in Morris Rathwell's all-girl wrestling contests, a tall, black-haired girl who can hold her own against all but the best. Wrestling is what turns her on, and her story shows how she learned to take pleasure in it . . .*

Flirt – Naomi Yates

It was such a thrill, a real thrill, the sort that leaves me with wet knickers and an itchy feeling in my fanny. The boys didn't even think it was a big deal, but it was for me. Billy Ryan had punched Evan Donnell a couple of times and thrown him on the ground, that was all, just to put him in his place.

I suppose I was a bit innocent, what with the convent and life on the farm. Belfast was different, and if it made me nervous then it made me excited too. After watching Billy I wanted him for my boyfriend, but I didn't want to be easy. I wanted to make him fight for me.

Innocent I may be, but I know how to flirt. Because I was new, I wasn't really in with the popular girls, and that made it a lot easier. They were like the hens in the barnyard, with Patti Lachlane at the top. What she said went and, as far as she was concerned, Billy was hers. Not that he cared. He would go with whoever took his fancy, and he would never let her pin him down. If he had, he'd have lost a lot of face.

That was how it was, the girls in one group and the boys in another, only really mixing at dances and stuff, and for the occasional date. Billy was the king, but he needed to show it, and that meant not letting anyone boss him around, not the other boys and not the girls either, whatever Patti might say.

He was game for me, maybe because he knew I didn't care what Patti thought, maybe because of the skirts I wore. I'd taken the hems up, really high, so high that I got a serious lecture from Mum. Not that she could do anything, not at my age, and not with me bringing in nearly half the money to the house. I'd bought some fancy knickers too, real silk, and cut high to leave most of my bum showing. With three brothers I know what a flash of a girl's knickers can do to a boy. Their favourite thing used to be to pretend to be fixing the Landrover in the road outside the farm, lying on their backs so that when the girls came out of St Mary's they could look up their skirts.

Billy was no different. He loved to look, watching my legs as I went past, never really obvious, and always cool, but watching just the same. I gave him his first flash when he was with a group of mates, hanging around outside Renshaw's, where they'd been drinking. I went past, smiling back when his friends whistled, but looking right at Billy. I hadn't planned it, but there was a five pence on the pavement and it was too good a chance to waste. For all they knew it was a pound, so I just bent, not at the knees, but from my waist. I'd checked in the mirror, and I knew it would show my knickers and a bit of bare bum, just enough to get them going. Boy, did they whistle, and I heard one or two very rude remarks as well. I was blushing as I walked on, for real, but I was wet too.

I did it on my bed; I couldn't help it. Whatever the sisters say, I like to touch myself and I don't see it does any harm. First I gave myself a little show, bending in front of the mirror, just the way I had for Billy. It made my bum show, just a little bit of cheek, with the silky panty-seat covering the really rude bits. I wished it had been more, maybe my whole bum, if the wind had lifted my skirt. That would have got him going, all right. The knickers were cut so high he'd have seen nearly everything, everything except the place he wanted to put his cock. I climbed on the bed thinking about Billy and how he could have had me.

Some of the others would have been interested, too. He'd have got rid of them, just using his strong, hard voice. One or two might have fancied their chances, but a couple of quick punches would have put them in their place. I'd have seen, and I'd have felt, my fanny start to tingle and my nips go hard. He'd have followed me, his mates coming behind, wanting to see the fun. I'd have walked, but not towards the city, not where I'd be safe.

I'd let him catch me somewhere quiet, maybe down by the university, where not many people go out of term. They'd have cornered me and Billy would have come forwards, trapping me against a wall with his arms. He'd have kissed me and I'd have let him. He'd have felt my tits and put his hands up my skirt and his mates would have whistled and called out rude suggestions. The others would have been really horny, and he'd have made me give them a little show, holding my skirt up at the back to show my bum. I'd have let them see my tits too, pulling my top and bra up. They'd have loved it. Some would even have got their cocks out, but Billy wouldn't have let them do me, I'd have been his.

Billy would have made me go down on him like that. I'd be kneeling, my top pulled up, my skirt lifted, tits and bum on show, just the way boys like them. Billy would have got out his cock and I'd have sucked it, right there, in front of them all, hard in my mouth. My fingers would be down my knickers, just like they really were, rubbing at my fanny and feeling the tight little bump down between my lips. They'd all be watching, saying how dirty I was, how rude I was, and what a great guy Billy was, and then he'd come in my mouth, and he'd make me swallow and I'd come too, and they'd all know . . .

I did come, just the best climax, and if I'd have to confess it and get a penance, then it was worth it, worth it many times over.

Billy asked me out the next day. I went, to a film and a pub well out of our area, where he knew none of his friends would be. When we said good night we snogged, and I let him feel my tits and put a finger in me. Nothing more, though, and I used my mum as an excuse for not inviting him in. He said he wanted me and I said maybe. He called me a tease and I told him not to be pushy. If Billy Ryan wanted me, then he was going to have to put out a bit more than a movie ticket and a few drinks. I did tell him that I wasn't a virgin.

He wanted me after that, playing it cool in front of his mates, but dead keen whenever he got me alone. I let him know I might, but never allowed him more than a grope. It was turning me on, and the more eager he got, the more I teased. I hadn't really thought about Patti, expecting her to ignore me the way she ignored most of the women he went after, as if they didn't exist. Anyway, the main reason she bossed the other girls was because of her family and because she was a hard bitch. I didn't think she'd actually try and pick on me.

I got it wrong. She and three mates came up to me one day while I was sunbathing down near the river. Patti stood over me and told me straight out. She called me a tart and told me to keep away from Billy. That wasn't all. They were going to slap me about and throw me in the river, just to make sure I learned my lesson. I ran, but Jeanna caught me so I threw her in a bank of nettles. Patti was close and grabbed my arm, yelling for her friends to help. Fat Siobhan was miles behind and little Mary didn't dare, so I rolled on the ground with Patti. She bit and scratched and tried to punch, but I got my weight on her and held her down. It was muddy and I put her face in it, but big Siobhan was coming so I ran and this time they couldn't catch me.

All the way back I was angry, and I was wishing I'd had a chance to do more to her. It would have been good to push her in the river, or in the nettles, like Jeanna. Better still, I could have sat on her back and stuffed nettles down her tights, loads of them, in her knickers too, and held her down like that. Alone I could have done it, if she'd ever had the guts to take me on alone. I knew she wouldn't, because for all her hard ways she only comes up to my neck, and I hadn't spent most of my life on a farm for nothing.

I went on thinking about it when I got home, imagining how much I could have humiliated her. My heart was still pumping fast, and even though I'd really won, I wasn't

126

satisfied. It was only while I was lying on my bed in just my towel that I realised I wanted to play with myself again. I tried to do it over Billy, but the feeling wouldn't come. Underneath I knew what I wanted, and after a bit of stroking my fanny and tits I managed to get over my feelings of guilt.

If Patti and I had been alone, and if it had been just a bit more private, then I could really have gone to town. For a start I'd have had her knickers off, right off, not just down, so her bare bum and legs showed to all the world. No, she'd have been better stripped, stripped stark naked and made to run home in the nude. I'd not have let her off the nettles either, nor the mud. I'd have tickled her fanny and whipped her tits and belly. I'd have left her red and smarting, with all those little spots that nettles make, on her bum and in the crease, right on her dirty little hole, to make her burn and itch and wriggle. I'd have done her face with mud and made her eat a mouthful, right out of my hand, swallow it too, like boys make us swallow come.

I'd taken off my towel and my hands were on my fanny, one to hold the lips apart, the other to rub my bump. I could see Patti in my head, her skin reddened and filthy, her hair in a mess and her mouth full of mud. There'd be mud in her fanny too, a great handful pushed up her hole, well up, right in her, clogging her hair and filling the hole. I'd soil her breasts and I'd soil her hair, and when I was done I'd stand right over her and show her my hole, with my knickers aside so she knew what was coming. She'd look up at me and I'd let it all go, my piss in her face and all over her body. It would go in her hair and I'd make her open her mouth and pee down her throat . . .

This time I cried out when I came, and afterwards the guilt was really bad. Not too bad, though, not bad enough to stop me doing it again. I hadn't had a fight before, not since hair-pulling and scratching when I was a little girl. It came as a shock to get so excited, and to have been so dirty. I mean, pissing on her!

It had felt so good, though, and it made me want to have Billy fight over me more than ever. I knew how he'd feel now, when he'd won, and how good it would make me feel. I wasn't going to let him unless he did but, once he had, he could do as he liked. I'd let him keep the lights on. I'd swallow for him. I'd go in doggie for him. If he really wanted to I'd even let him put it up my bum.

Billy got to know that there had been a fight over him, and boy did it make his head swell. He was boasting and saying what a big man he was, and the others just egged him on. I knew it would be soon, because he was sure I wanted him, and sure I would go all the way. Now was the time, and so I began to flirt with Evan Donnell.

Evan was tall and skinny and had red hair. None of the girls fancied him, it just wasn't on, but now I'd beaten Patti, nobody was even going to try and tell me what to do. I think he must have been a virgin. He was certainly desperate, because he was always coming on to girls, but no one would have him.

First I just teased, wiggling a little when I walked past him and smiling when we met. I hoped Billy would get jealous and give Evan a pasting just to show off, but he took no notice and I had to go further. One day I asked Evan to help with the zip on my dress, and there was a big lump in my throat as his long, bony fingers touched my neck. Another I went up some steps right by where he was reading. Well, pretending to read, because I'm sure he was really just trying to look up girls' skirts. He certainly saw up mine, right up, because I called to him and did a little wiggle to make sure, then called him a dirty sod for looking.

I went to Billy then, and said that Evan had been looking up my skirt. He just laughed and said it was what I expected if I went around showing off my legs to everyone. That made me cross, but I bit it down and said I'd be nice to him if he sorted Evan out for me. He asked what I'd do, straight out, and I had to offer to give him a suck.

He made me do it in a men's toilet in the park, down on my knees while he sat on the seat. I knew my shoes showed under the door, and with my heels everyone would know it was a girl. A man saw and laughed because he guessed, but Billy didn't care. He held me by the hair and wanked in my mouth. He came in my throat and made me swallow his stuff, then wiped his cock in my face and said he'd teach Evan a proper lesson, that evening.

All the rest of the day I was so wet and so excited that I couldn't sit down. I came in the Ladies after I'd sucked Billy, sitting with my knickers down and knees wide apart, thinking of Billy's cock and what he would do to me after he'd beaten up Evan. It wasn't enough and I went home for more, waiting until Mum had gone shopping before I took off my clothes and lay on my bed, stark naked. It was how I would be, down on the grass by the river. Billy would strip me, pull off my clothes, maybe tear them. He'd make me go nude, right down to the buff, out in the open. He'd make Evan watch, letting him see what he could never have, never ever.

I'd be so willing, so rude. I'd suck Billy's cock and lick Billy's balls. I'd play with my tits and rub at my fanny. Evan would see, all of it bare, my tits and my bum, my fanny and hole, all of it there, all of it Billy's, and so, so far out of reach. When Billy was hard I'd get on my back, my legs open wide to let him inside, deep in my fanny to make me moan and make me sigh, to make me gasp and make me cry. Evan would watch, feeling beaten and shamed, not daring to move, not daring to breathe.

Billy would show me to Evan, on my back and on my knees, sucking his cock when it had been in me, taking it from behind, showing my bottom, as rude as can be. My cheeks would be open and my hole open wide, my fanny so eager and wet. He'd pull open my bottom and show off the hole, watching as I filled with his cock. He'd know I was dirty, know I wouldn't stop him, and up it would go, in my dirty bottom, right to the hilt, his balls on my fanny, so dirty, so rude, showing to Evan, a woman's surrender, absolute surrender.

Evan would see and Evan would know. I was Billy's, Billy's alone, giving in to things that would never, ever be his. I would come, twice at the least, crying and laughing

129

as I rubbed at my bump. Billy would come, deep in my bottom, making me cry again, in pleasure and pain. Evan would come, jerked off in his hand, his eyes on my body, his head full of want and of fear. I'd still be on heat, spread on the ground with my thighs well apart, rubbing my bud as Billy finished the show, taking his cock, thick with the taste of my body and making Evan take it in his mouth . . .

I came with a scream. My dirty thoughts had gone beyond what I had expected, far beyond. To want to be watched by Evan while Billy and I made love was bad, but thinking of Billy making Evan suck his cock clean was really, utterly filthy, and after it had been up my bottom! I'd never known I could be so dirty, but for all the guilt it was good and I was starting to wonder just how bad a girl I really was.

Billy had it all arranged. He'd told Evan to meet him by the river, a quiet place among some trees where nobody was going to come. The choice was a pasting from Billy and his mates, so Evan was sure to come, that or leave Belfast, which Billy joked was what he expected Evan to do. Walking down to the river was like floating on air. I was really excited and wanted to kiss and be held. Billy obliged, snogging and feeling my bum, taking my tits out and kissing my nips, until by the time we arrived I was ready for anything. I was knickerless too, having pulled them off so that I could tease Evan, showing him what he couldn't have, because I knew that Billy would never actually let him watch.

Evan was there, looking as lanky and spotty as ever, a real freak with his curly red hair and his big feet. He didn't look scared, but I knew he soon would be, and laughed and called him a pervert to get him going. I was squeezing my thighs as Billy got ready, so randy I wanted to wank, then and there. Billy had pulled off his top, showing his muscles and tatts. He looked like a statue, so strong and such a man.

I had to do it, I couldn't stop. As Evan squared up I opened my thighs, showing my fanny, warm and wet and ready, Billy's prize for being my knight. Billy smiled and winked, admiring what was his. Evan looked too, the dirty little sod, and Billy smacked him one for his trouble. Just seeing that punch put my heart in my mouth and my fingers between my legs. I was wanking, and I just didn't care, and as soon as Billy had dealt with his business I was going to be fucked.

Billy hit Evan who went back with the punch and my bump seemed to jerk under my finger. Evan came back, low and hard, his big bony fist catching Billy right in his middle, his knee coming up as Billy bent and then Billy hit the ground with a thud. I was coming, my thighs wide apart, my fanny on fire, my mouth as open as my eyes and Evan was coming towards me, his hand on his zip.

A moral tale, in ways, primitive too. The same is true of the next story, which comes from Henry, who appears in several books as Amber's godfather. It takes the form of an erotic fairy tale from the viewpoint of Sigismund the Black, a brash lordling of reprehensible habits . . .

Four Flavours – Henry Gresham

Sigismund, known as the Black, sat with his four favoured aspirants for marriage and the councillor Torquil. Each maiden was of the highest birth, and lovely, causing his pulse to quicken and his penis to stiffen in his britches. Sephany stood to the left, a girl close to his own height, yet as slender as a wand, with pale hair and skin, and features of exquisite delicacy with huge, pale eyes that seemed forever full of strange, sweet thoughts. Her breasts were high and proud, her hips and belly neat, her bottom a pert ball of firm flesh above long, delicate legs. Her sole garment was a gown of opalescent gossamer, through which the full beauty of her body was displayed without discomfiture.

Next was Charbonelle, curled on the rug with all the elegance of a cat, her coal-dark eyes fixed on his as if daring him to choose any other than herself. Her hair was a mass of fiery red constrained in a band of beaten gold, her skin a rich tan, glossy with oil. Pride showed in her face, and power in the taut, muscular lines of her body. Although full and feminine, her breasts, buttocks and thighs were sleek and hard. What few garments she had were burnished black leather, encasing her breasts and sex but doing nothing to hide their contours.

Bethan sat cross-legged, easy and calm. Luxuriant brown hair fell from her head to the floor, rich and thick, framing her face, which showed an expression both calm and beautiful. Her body was ripe and full, with heavy breasts, a softly swelling belly and rounded hips and bottom, the very essence of fertile womanhood. A short kirtle of green cloth was all that covered her opulent curves, her pose allowing the uninhibited display of her sex.

Last, and kneeling with her hands in her lap as if to shield her sex, was Lioqué, who alone of the four seemed timid. Her body was full, although less so than that of Bethan and hidden beneath a gown of flowing blue silk. There was both beauty and pride in her face, but without the open force of Charbonelle. The depth of het violet-blue eyes seemed enough to drown in, but fell short of the ethereal quality than came from Sephany's.

Sigismund grunted. To choose among them seemed an impossibility. With a displeased shake of his head he turned to his councillor.

'It seems, Lord,' Torquil began, 'that each maiden may seem to represent one of the four prime elements. Sephany is air, delicate and fey, dreaming unknown thoughts, an exquisite thing not given to ordinary man. Charbonelle is fire, hot and eager, charged with energy and lust, the consort of a warrior prince. Bethan, then, is the earth, rich and yielding, fertile and deep, a mother to provide heirs. Lioqué is water, shy and yielding, deep and secret, a nurse to soothe you when troubled.'

'Profound, no doubt,' Sigismund growled, 'yet entirely useless. Whom do you recommend?'

'You must allow all to come to you,' Torquil advised, 'one each night, and on the fifth day you must choose.'

'At last a worthwhile suggestion,' Sigismund boomed. 'So be it.'

Sprawled naked on his bed, Sigismund gave a critical glance to the appointments of the room. A cover of sweetmeats had been laid out, including such delicacies as larks' tongues, grigs soused in wine and honey ants, each selected in the hope of tempting the tastes of the exquisite Sephany. She had been chosen first, and he was eager to get to grips with her delicate body, his cock stirring in its

134

thick nest of hair as he thought of how her exquisite face would look with a foot length of penis thrust into her mouth. Drapes and ornaments in tones of blue, white and gold had been chosen to best accentuate her looks, with delicate and subtle styles and furniture inlaid with turquoise and mother-of-pearl.

The door swung open and closed discreetly, admitting Sephany, as beautiful as the dawn with her ash-pale hair in a loose cloud that fell to her knees. As before she wore only a diaphanous gown, revealing the pale buds of her nipples and the neat crease of her hairless sex. Her eyes seemed deeper and more mysterious than ever, and as she approached Sigismund she shrugged the gown from her shoulders and stepped from the tangle of silk, naked. He gave a growl of lust at the sight and took hold of his cock, which was already half-way to erection. As Sephany reached the bed he took her firmly by the hair and pulled her head down. She bent without resistance, climbing onto the bed even as she gaped wide to take in his cock. With her little bottom stuck high and her back pulled in to enhance her slender curves, she began to suck, easing her mouth up and down on his penis while he watched in delight. It was indeed a sight to revel in, with her delicate face making a perfect contrast with the thick, dull-pink shaft of his penis.

She sucked well, using her lips and tongue with exquisite skill and all the while holding her pose to show off her bottom to best advantage. Soon his cock was a solid column of flesh in her mouth, with the veins standing proud and dark to heighten the contrast between his raw virility and her sweet beauty. Only when he felt himself at the edge of orgasm did he pull back, taking her by the hair again and pushing her face into the bed to force her bottom into greater prominence. She made no resistance, but submitted gracefully to being entered from the rear, simply giving a soft sigh when he pushed his full length rudely into her body. Putting his great hands on her hips, he spread her tiny buttocks, revealing the junction of his cock and her sex and also the tight pink orifice of her anus.

With what he regarded as the perfect view of a woman he began to fuck her, grunting and moaning as his pleasure rose.

Sephany took him with an air of serene acceptance, sighing quietly to herself as she was ridden and occasionally adjusting her knees and elbows to make herself more comfortable. With his attention fixed on her spread bottom, Sigismund paid little attention to her response and soon came, erupting gout after gout of semen into her vagina until the white fluid was running down her quim and out over his balls. She held her place, giving only a gentle sigh of satisfaction even when he rammed his erection home to the very hilt as the last of his come drained into her.

Four more times that night they enjoyed each other, Sephany accepting Sigismund's lust without complaint. Each time he chose a different position, taking her on her back with her long legs rolled high, then from the side with her neat posterior pushed out into his lap. Next she mounted on top of him with her hair flying as she was bounced on his penis and lastly she seated herself in his lap while he fondled her quim and tiny breasts in an effort to make her come while he was inside her. She did not climax, but when he had taken his fifth orgasm inside her she went to lie on the bed and used her fingers to bring herself to ecstasy, all the while with her huge eyes wide and staring at something invisible to Sigismund.

Determined to make her react more fully to his manhood, Sigismund took a pause, refreshing himself with brandy and a selection of delicacies. Sephany ate nothing, but sat quietly on the bed with her knees hugged to her chin and her wet quim peeping out from between her thighs. Her mouth was set in a dreamy smile, which Sigismund chose to take for satisfaction. When ready he had her suck him to erection once more, then went about making full use of her beautiful body. His cock went into the shallow valley between her breasts and also the crease between her buttocks. He had her masturbate him while she sucked on the tip of his penis and he sat her on his face to lick at her quim and bottom. He ate honey ants from her vagina and shared larks' tongues in a long kiss. He took her across his knee and spanked her bottom to a glowing pink, then had her kiss his feet to thank him. All of this she accepted with an easy pleasure, and when her bottom was hot from spanking she once more brought herself to orgasm under her fingers. Sigismund put his cock to her face as she did it, and came in her mouth as she gaped in her ecstasy, but even this lewd act drew only a soft sigh from her after she had swallowed his come.

Finally they slept, with Sigismund laid out flat in exhaustion and Sephany curled up beside him.

On the next night Sigismund waited the arrival of Charbonelle. Again he had ordered refreshments laid out, rich meat and strong wine, spiced delicacies and brandy of Ai-Corahai. The furnishings of the room were now in red, black and gold, with polished woods and a rug woven with the design of a phoenix. After Sephany's mute acceptance of his lust he was looking forward to the undoubted challenge of mating with the fiery Charbonelle. He expected the encounter to be energetic, and his cock was already stiff in his hand in anticipation. As the door swung wide he realised that he was not to be disappointed.

Charbonelle stood foursquare before the bed, her feet planted firmly apart and her hands folded beneath her magnificent breasts. Plate of polished bronze covered her breasts and quim, shaped to the contours beneath with no detail omitted. Her hair was loose, an unruly mane of vivid red hanging almost to her waist. She was gloved and booted in black leather and in her hand she held a plaited whip. Her face was set in a smile that showed both cruelty and lust. As she came forward she gave a warning snarl, then sprang onto the bed, flourishing her whip.

Sigismund met her with a roar and they went down together, rolling on the bed in a tangle of limbs and scarlet silk sheets. Her nails bit into his arms and her teeth found the flesh of his shoulder as she tried to force him down. Sigismund resisted, grunting at the pain of her assault and bunching his great muscles. She was strong, and full of a demonic energy, yet his bulk and power quickly told and on the second attempt he managed to hurl her down on the bed. She gave an angry hiss as he tore the whip out of her hand and mounted her, forcing her thighs apart with one knee. He tore her quim plate away, twisting the bronze and snapping the leather, then did the same for her breasts, exposing the firm, sweat-slick mounds with the nipples rigid in erection. Jamming himself between her thighs, his cock found her vagina and slid easily into the wet hole, filling her even as her arms went around his neck and she grappled his body to her own.

As Sigismund began to fuck her Charbonelle's talons sank deep into his back and her teeth locked in his chest. She tore at him as he rode her, biting and scratching, hissing and spitting, mouthing obscenities and demanding deeper and harder penetration. With the blood singing in his head Sigismund continued to pound into her, ignoring the pain until it faded to become a hot, angry pleasure that drove him to ever more powerful efforts. Finally he came, cursing her as he filled her vagina with semen and the blood ran hot down his back. She came with him, screaming and flicking her tongue at drops of blood that had fallen on her face, her orgasm lasting long after his own had begun to subside, with her writhing her quim against the coarseness of his pubic hair in order to get friction to her clitoris.

When her thrashings had at last subsided Sigismund dismounted and crossed to the buffet. He could feel the blood running warm down his back and his body felt as if he had just won through a hard skirmish rather than enjoyed a woman. Taking up a flask of strong red wine, he put it to his mouth, only to drop it as Charbonelle leaped onto his back. She was scratching and biting, attempting to pull him down and get at his penis at the same time. Sigismund gave a roar of anger and reached back, grappling for her. He found hair and pulled, drawing a cat-like hiss from her as her nails dug deep into her skin.

Wrenching her free by the hair, he turned and grappled her body. She fought like a tigress but he managed to get

138

her onto the bed. Grunting and sweating with the effort, and taking several more bites and scratches in the process, he managed to bind her hands into the small of her back with a length of one of the sheets. Placing her in a kneeling position, he strapped each of her ankles to a bedpost, leaving her knees wide and her fine bottom high and open with quim and anus showing beneath the ruins of her leather panties and bronze plate. Her breasts were swinging loose from her chest, now seeming larger and more vulnerable as she was upside down.

Sigismund climbed from the bed and refreshed himself, downing two full flagons of wine and eating a large steak before he felt ready to resume congress with Charbonelle. Thinking that she might be hungry, he attempted to feed her a piece of meat from his hand, only to receive a nip from her sharp teeth for his pains. Tearing free the soft leather that had covered her quim, he balled it in his fist, then held her nose until she was forced to gape. Shoving the pussy-scented leather into her mouth, her tied it off with silk. She was helpless and seemed resigned to it, yet when Sigismund put a hand to her quim to test her lust she immediately began to rub herself on him.

Blowing the air out from his lungs, he began to amuse himself with her. Taking his cock in one hand to masturbate, he gave her a dozen light strokes with her own whip, leaving her upturned buttocks criss-crossed with fine red lines. He explored her breasts, bottom and quim, teasing her nipples and easing his fingers into the damp cavities of her body, stroking and slapping and tickling until she was grunting deep in her throat and writhing her body in her need. Having pushed the stem of a flame-red rose into her anus to add a humiliating touch of ridicule to her position, he mounted her and made a leisurely use of her while the rose bobbed up and down between her spread cheeks in time to his pushes. By the time he came she was frantic with lust, and he allowed her relief with his fingers, bringing her to a second orgasm perhaps more intense than the first.

Having finished and feeling too exhausted for another round, he decided that it was best to leave her tied. Pulling out a share of the bedding from beneath her and ignoring the angry glare of her eyes, he made himself as comfortable as possible on the rug and presently fell asleep.

By the following evening Sigismund felt ready for Bethan, despite the various scratches that marked his body. To receive her the great bedroom was furnished in greens and golds as rich and varied as the leaves of the trees, with furniture of unpolished oak and a magnificent carpet the colour of summer grass. A buffet stood to the side, laden with ale skins, hunches of cheese and a cauldron of venison stewed in forest herbs. He was masturbating lazily over the thought of her full, soft curves and was erect when she entered the room.

Bethan's eyes went straight to Sigismund's cock and she licked her lips in anticipation. Pushing her kirtle down and off, she revealed her lovely body. At the sight of her huge breasts and broad hips Sigismund found himself licking his lips in return. They came together, kissing and touching without reserve, exploring each other's bodies. Bethan's hand was soon on his cock and he made no resistance as she eased him gently down and straddled his body. Still holding his cock, she guided it to her quim and briefly rubbed the head among the wet, fleshy folds. Sigismund groaned in pleasure, then once more as she lowered her body onto his and his erection was engulfed in warm flesh. He let her ride him, admiring the way her breasts bounced with the motion. After a while she began to masturbate as she rode him, rubbing at her clitoris while cupping both huge breasts beneath an arm and teasing a nipple. Sigismund watched in delight as she came, and when her vagina contracted on his cock the sensation became too much. He too came, filling her with semen as she cried out her ecstasy.

Having finished her orgasm she dismounted with a happy smile, thanked Sigismund and went to the buffet. He joined her as she devoured a large helping of the stew and sank a quart or so of ale. All the while she chatted happily, complimenting the food and the sex, remarking on other

fine meals and men she had enjoyed and assuring him that
their children would all be powerful warriors and beautiful
women. At length she finished and turned to him with a
smile. There was grease running down her chin and over
the upper surfaces of her breasts, and as she rose Sigismund found his face inches away from the plump globes.
With a growl he buried his face between them and began
to lick the juice from her skin. Bethan responded by
hugging his head tight between her breasts and reaching
down for his cock. With his face smothered in the fat
pillows of her chest he was quickly erect, and she mounted
him on the chair, clinging to his neck and leaning back so
that he could fondle her breasts while they fucked. Before
long he had come, as had she, using a phallus-shaped
salt-cellar to rub at herself while he was in her.

Bethan returned to the buffet as Sigismund brushed the
spilled salt from his crotch. Once more she talked happily
of this and that as she ate, and after a while bent forwards
across the table to reach for a particularly choice morsel.
The pose left her big bottom thrust out with the cheeks
high and wide, a sight Sigismund found impossible to
resist. Rising from the bed, he took her by the scruff of her
neck and pushed her face down into the cheeses, then
began to rub his cock in the deep crease of her bottom.
Bethan laughed at the rude treatment and wiggled her
bottom, sending the blood coursing into Sigismund's cock.
Before long he was erect and he entered her from the rear.
She played with her breasts as they fucked, kneading and
stroking the dangling globes and panting out her lust into
the mess of food beneath her face. Sigismund found her
bottom a true glory, two big pillows of soft girl-flesh
parted by a deep crease. After a while he hauled her cheeks
apart so that he could admire the rich growth of fur
between them and the pouting pink dimple of her anus.
Her vagina was slick with come and juice, making it easy
to slide himself in to the very hilt yet making purchase
difficult and he was grunting with the strain before he came
inside her. As he withdrew, Bethan gave a long sigh and
then held her position. Mindful of her needs, Sigismund

sank down behind her and applied his tongue to her quim, licking her with his face smothered between her ample bottom cheeks until she too reached orgasm.

Once more she went back to talking and eating, while Sigismund refreshed himself with a skin of ale. Having come three times he was in a mood to relax, and perhaps to enjoy a longer, slower session of lovemaking in due time. Bethan, however, was quickly eager for more and after finishing the last of the stew she crawled onto the bed and wiggled her bottom at him. Even after three orgasms Sigismund found the sight irresistible, having always considered a crawling position to show a woman to her best sexual advantage. Her mass of brown hair was cascading down over her body, while with her bottom high and her breasts dangling nothing whatever was concealed. Sigismund came around the bed and took her by the hair, pushing his cock close to her face. Bethan took it willingly and began to suck while he concentrated on the feel of her lips and tongue and the sight of her plump curves. When erect he mounted her from behind and began to fuck her while she masturbated to the rhythm of his pushes. She came first, then again as he did, leaving him to sink thankfully down onto the bed.

Bethan brought Sigismund an ale skin, which he accepted gratefully. Once he had drunk his fill she took it herself and drained the remainder down her throat. Hurling the skin to the floor, she cocked a thigh over him and settled her bottom onto his face, smothering his protest between her ample cheeks. With his face engulfed in ripe, female bottom, Sigismund could only lick, and as he did so Bethan reached for his cock. After a while she leaned forwards, taking him in her mouth while he continued to lick her from behind. Three times she came beneath his tongue before he managed to reach orgasm himself, only for Bethan to sit up once more and demand her bottom licked while she masturbated herself to yet another climax. Determined not to show weakness, Sigismund obliged.

A further five times that night Bethan demanded his attention, until Sigismund had begun to wonder if she did indeed draw her strength from the earth itself. As dawn rose she was blithely telling him that she intended to bear at least a dozen children while she coated the last crust of bread with a liberal layer of butter. Sigismund managed a grunt in reply. His thoughts were on the soreness of his penis and the aching, drained feeling in his testicles.

Sigismund awaited the arrival of Lioqué with a degree of trepidation. The scratches on his back had become irritating, while his cock was still sore and his body ached as if he had been through a battle. Nevertheless, in the interests of fair play he had ordered the room decked in drapes of rich, deep blue, furniture of black wood waxed to a soft sheen and a rug depicting sea monsters attacking a ship. The buffet consisted of a single gigantic lobster surrounded by oysters and scallops in their shells, with several flasks of the pearl grey wine of Aplicia. Despite the appeal of Lioqué's sweet body and shy manner, he was sipping at a goblet when she entered, with his cock lying flaccid in his lap.

She greeted him with a smile and at his invitation poured herself wine. Sitting beside him on the bed, she threw a coy glance at his cock. Sigismund managed a grin in reply, reacting despite himself. Lioqué immediately rose from the bed, set down her goblet and walked quickly to the door. Opening it, she held a brief conversation with his attendants, then came back. She was in a blue gown, beautiful yet reaching to the floor and so making a secret of the contours of her body. This she removed, and folded it neatly on a chair. Beneath she wore petticoats and a chemise, each of which she removed and folded, until she was bare-chested and wore no more than knee stockings and a pair of voluminous bloomers that were stretched taut over her chubby bottom. These she eased slowly down with her back to Sigismund and her bottom pushed slightly out, revealing the full glory of her rear view in a manner that he could not fail to appreciate, the more so because she made it seem more accidental than deliberate. Leaving the bloomers around her knees, she seated herself. She removed her boots, pulled the drawers free of her ankles and peeled each stocking away to go fully naked.

No sooner was Lioqué nude than a respectful tap sounded at the door. She opened it no more than a crack and took an alabaster pot from somebody out of sight. Walking purposefully towards him, she removed the lid of the pot and dipped her hand in, bringing out a thick wad of glistening paste. Sigismund smiled and took a sip of wine as Lioqué sat down by his side. He sighed as the paste was applied to his genitals and his smile grew to a broad grin as she gently began to massage it into his balls and cock. She was sitting with her back to him, and after a while he reached out and began to fondle her bottom, feeling each round, well-fleshed cheek in turn. Lioqué allowed him to explore her bottom and continued to work the greasy paste into his genitals. His cock had soon begun to grow and her motions changed, until she was masturbating his shaft with long, easy strokes of her hand.

Lioqué's attention seemed as therapeutic as it was erotic, even in the way she was allowing her bottom to be fondled, as if such intimate contact were simply a part of nursing him. Nevertheless, with his cock a thick, glistening rod of flesh, rock hard in her little hand, his full attention was focused on her body. Sensing his need, she mounted him, his cock sliding easily into her wet vagina. She began to move on him with slow, smooth motions, taking his cock in to the very hilt each time and then rising so that the tip once more penetrated her vagina. Despite the intimacy of the act, Sigismund still felt that she was nursing him as much as she was enjoying his sex. Having his cock nursed by a beautiful, naked girl was a new experience, and one he was quickly coming to appreciate to the full.

Slowly Lioqué's pleasure began to show more openly. First she took a breast in each hand and began to stroke them, teasing the nipples to erection. As she did so her head was thrown back and her eyes shut, with the expression on her face slowly changing from serious to ecstatic. With both her nipples hard buds of flesh peeping out from between her fingers she made an entrancing sight, and Sigismund's eyes were locked to her chest. She had began to sigh, and to squirm herself onto his cock with slow, round motions that made her bottom cheeks rub against his thighs.

He admired her body as she rode him, finding her face ever more beautiful as her pleasure grew. Her hair was a mass of gold, shimmering in the light as she moved. Her breasts were ripe and round, their size exaggerated by the narrowness of her waist. Her skin was smooth and pale, her flesh soft yet never loose, while her undressing had already displayed the perfect peach of her bottom.

She had began to buck, and one hand left her breasts, travelling slowly down over the gentle swell of her belly to her sex. Sigismund watched, enraptured as her fingers wriggled in among the golden curls and pulled open the plump sex-lips to expose her clitoris. She began to touch herself, patting the little bud gently as her sighs turned to soft, urgent moans. He knew she was going to come on his cock and was bracing himself for the ecstasy of her vaginal contractions, determined to flood her with semen at the very peak of her pleasure. Her squirming had become desperate as he found his rhythm inside her and then she was coming, and as his cock erupted semen into her body so her vulva erupted over his, urine spraying out onto his stomach, bursting into a spatter of droplets, soaking her thighs, his front and the bed in equal proportions.

Sigismund lay back, urine running from his chest and dripping from his beard. Lioqué dismounted slowly, biting her lip in bashful reaction to the consequences of her ecstasy. Saying nothing, Sigismund rose from the bed, shook what liquid he could from his body and strode to the door. Kicking it wide, he bellowed for Torquil.

'Damn this!' he roared as the councillor appeared. 'Send me fresh bedding, and no more of these hoity-toity wenches. I'll have a servant girl, a fat one!'

The moral being, of course, that the sexual experiences we are told to believe are the best very seldom are. What would it really be like in bed with that sex symbol of screen or stage? Boring, I suspect: too much ego, not enough desire to please.

Not that intense sexual experiences even need to involve contact at all. Sophie, the petite, mischievous blonde who appears in In for a Penny, *is a case in point, providing more pleasure to people who have never met her and who have no idea who she is than to any boyfriend . . .*

Going Bare – Sophie Cherwell

I've always loved to show off: it's so daring, so dangerous. Nowadays it's easy. I'll go to a club in a little rubber bikini, and if they'll let me I'll end up stark naked. Sometimes I'll end up stark naked anyway, and get thrown out. That's me, and I'm proud of me, but it wasn't always so easy.

I used to be really envious of girls who had the courage to show off. All my friends used to be really prissy, always going on about the sanctity of their bodies. One even wanted to be a glamour model, but wasn't prepared to do more than take her top off. She thought the men in the business were sleazy and dirty, as if she was some kind of angel. I could have told her she wouldn't get far.

That wasn't what I wanted. I didn't care about the money, I just wanted to show off. That was somehow worse, as if being paid for it made it all right, and I didn't tell anybody, especially not at college, where everyone was into religion or feminism and basically really stuffy. I knew not everyone was like that, and it was when Dad was driving me back from college with all my stuff that I discovered just how daring some girls could be.

We were on the A3, and Dad was driving as if he was in a daydream, thinking about which country pub to stop at for lunch. I was staring out of the window, just watching the countryside go past, when a mini-bus overtook us. It was the day of some big rugby match, and there were lots of cars and things showing colours. So was the mini-bus, but that wasn't all that was showing, I realised as it pulled level and a big, hairy bottom was suddenly stuck out of a window. His balls were showing and everything, and I must have looked really shocked, because I saw the faces of the other people in the bus and they were all laughing at me. A moment later another bottom had been stuck out, as big and hairy as the first, then a third, smaller, rounder one with a neatly shaved pussy sticking out from between the thighs instead of a pair of hairy balls.

I just gaped. I'd seen everything, her whole bare moon, all plump and naked with the little tight hole at the centre and her pussy too. Then they had passed and for a moment I saw her face in the back window, a pretty, smiling face, framed in brown curls with her eyes sparkling in delight. That image has stayed with me ever since, not so much her bare bum, but the sheer joy on her face as she showed her most intimate secrets, details of her body that should have had her blushing just to think of them being seen. Dad laughed and said something about 'rugger buggers' and that broke the spell. I couldn't stop thinking about it, about how much fun she'd been having and how daring she'd been, and wishing I could be the same.

It wasn't that I was embarrassed or ashamed; that wasn't the problem. I was proud of my body, especially my bum, which one boyfriend had described as a 'perfect little peach'. My boobs are nice too, at least I think so, quite big and very round, with little pert nipples. I'm only five foot, and lightly built, but that just makes my boobs look bigger in proportion, my bum too. So I felt I had something to show; I just didn't seem to have the opportunity to show it.

The mooning incident made me bolder, and that summer I stripped naked outdoors for the first time. We'd gone up to Mundesley, and I absolutely fell in love with the beach. Not the actual beach by the resort, but further south, where it stretches on and on, with the sea to one side and the dunes to the other, often without another person in sight. I'd bought a bikini, a little purple number that left most of my bottom showing and a good deal of my boobs too. Mum didn't really approve, and told me I ought to cover up or men might get the wrong idea.

I didn't actually want men to approach me – not then, at sixteen. Well, not many of them anyway, and not just any old men. What I wanted was to be seen, not to be touched, to tease really. I knew it could be dangerous too, but I so badly wanted that thrill, the gorgeous feeling of going bare, with the sun and the wind on my naked flesh. Also the thrill of danger was part of it, I couldn't deny that, but I did determine not to take any stupid risks.

My chance came on the fourth day we were there. We'd been to see Great Yarmouth, and then stopped for tea at a place called Horsey on the way back. Dad wanted to have dinner at Sea Palling, a place a little way further on, and was looking at the map, wondering how to pass the time. There was a little museum not far away, which they wanted to visit. Looking at the map, I could see how lonely the coast was, and I saw my chance immediately. I said I'd rather go down to the beach, and would walk along to meet them at dinner time. After a bit of fuss they agreed, and I set off, determined that I was going to go in the nude.

The beach was everything I could have hoped for, a broad band of golden sand stretching away to north and south. There was one family there, but they were already packing up. I started walking, and was soon out of sight. It was so lonely, and I felt safe and daring at the same time. The first thrill came from changing. My bikini was in my bag, and instead of taking my knickers and bra off under my clothes and putting it on, I took all my clothes off before I even bothered to get it out. The feeling of being naked as I scrabbled in the bottom of my bag for the bikini was great. It felt so vulnerable, just to know I'd be nude until I found it and that anyone looking was going to get a good eyeful.

With the bikini on I continued to walk, trying to pluck up the courage to go further. What I'd done could have been misinterpreted by a watcher, who might just have assumed I was a bit clumsy. Now if I stripped it would obviously be deliberate. I knew I was going to do it, but I teased myself for a while. First I walked with my bikini bottoms pulled tight up my crease, so that the whole of my bottom showed, all bare and pink in the sun. That felt daring, and I wanted more, but I held myself in, waiting until I could wait no more, then stopping.

I took hold of my bikini top, my fingers trembling. One quick tug was all it needed and they'd be bare, but I held back, waiting, then suddenly tugging up and they were out, all round and pink and girlish, but above all, bare. It was so nice, more daring than ever, and I was thinking of what people would think, of their lust, their disapproval, their envy, all because I had my boobs showing.

That's the way I stayed, for a good half mile, just enjoying being topless. A nagging little voice in my head was telling me that it wasn't much, that lots of girls went topless. Maybe, but not me, and that was what mattered, my feelings, not what other people did. That was what made me pull my bikini pants down, a sudden rush of rebelliousness. I stopped, and before common sense could get the better of me I'd stuck my bum out and pushed them down, imagining the exposure of my bottom as an impudent gesture to the whole disapproving world.

For a moment I felt scared and pulled them quickly up again, looking around to see if I'd been caught. There was nobody there, and with my teeth set in determination I pushed them back down, off my bum, over my legs and away, kicking them up in the air to leave me starkers, naked, baby-bare, with my boobs and bum and pussy all on show to anyone who cared to look.

That was it, my first time, and if it doesn't sound a big deal, then remember that I was a sixteen-year-old girl who'd been brought up to believe that her body was a temple. Sex was something that happened after marriage, with my husband, in bed with the lights out. Going bare was a big deal for me, and as I walked along that beach with my tiny bikini dangling from my hand and not a stitch on I felt incredibly good.

At the time just being in the nude was enough, but afterwards, looking back on what I'd done in the privacy of my room, I felt I needed more, and that was how I learnt to masturbate. I'd read about orgasms, and I thought I had them, when really it was just that jumpy feeling you get when a boy's got his hand down your knickers. It's not the same, as I found out.

It was after our holiday, and Dad was back at work, and Mum was out shopping with the others. I was alone and I knew I had a good hour of peace, so I decided to strip off and try to recapture something of the way I'd felt in Norfolk. I even took a towel so that I could pretend I'd been about to have a bath if they did come back early.

I took my clothes off really slowly, imagining that someone was looking all the time. My skirt came off first, leaving me in the big white knickers my Mum always chose and my top, with the tail covering about half my bum. That felt cheeky, so I pulled down my knickers, just far enough to show my bum and make it obvious to my imaginary watcher that I was being rude. My top went next, and for some reason I didn't make a big deal over my bra, but just unsnipped and shrugged it off. Having my knickers rolled down to show my bum and pubic hair was good, and I stayed like that for a while.

It was exciting, and it felt as if they'd just been rolled down to make my bum show, perhaps for someone who wanted to get off on seeing me like that. I knew they were coming off, and soon had them whipped down. Again I stood still, in just my shoes, with my knickers a little puddle of white cloth around my ankles. At last I kicked them off, spent another brief moment enjoying the feel of being in shoes, socks and nothing more, then took those off too.

My body was bare, in the middle of the day, in my room. I began to stroke my breasts, still imagining a man watching and getting excited over my bare flesh. I imagined that he would have told me to get my clothes off, bit by bit, until I was naked. He'd have his cock out and be stroking it, watching my body as he ordered me to play with myself. My nipples would pop up and he'd smile, leering at my pretty, clean breasts. He'd be dirty too, and make me turn around and pull open my bum-cheeks, showing him the little pinky-brown hole in between them.

My pussy would come last, pulled open for him, then fingered as he tugged at his big cock and rubbed me with his thumb.

I did the motions as I imagined it, first my boobs, then my bum, then my pussy. My breathing was coming fast and I was getting really excited, and my pussy had started to jump and tighten as I put my finger in. I rubbed myself with the knuckle of my thumb, my flesh twitching with what I fondly imagined to be orgasms each time I touched the little bump at the top of my cleft.

It just happened. I was thinking of the man's cock and how excited he'd be over my naked body, and of how it might have happened if he'd caught me stripping on the beach. He'd have made me show and made me touch his cock, he'd have made me play with myself so he could get off over me. Suddenly I was there, my whole body tightening as everything seemed to come together around my pussy, which for one glorious instant was the whole centre of absolutely everything. I fell to my knees, my spine arched tight and my mouth wide, my eyes shut and my fingers diddling away frantically as it went through me, over and over until I could stand no more and slumped forwards, face down on the carpet with my bottom in the air, imagining at that last instant how it would feel if he mounted me and took me from behind.

After that I took to doing it regularly, whenever I had the chance. I thought of lots of things while I did it – boys I knew, men I fancied, all sorts of rude situations – but most of all I thought about going bare in public, and that was always best. Because of that I wanted to do it for real, more and more, but in the middle of Croydon there just wasn't anywhere safe. I might think of being caught and molested when I masturbated, but in reality the idea was terrifying.

What I needed was a friend, someone who felt the same way. That way I could have someone to share my pleasure, also to watch out for me. It couldn't be a boyfriend, because they'd want to possess me, to show me off rather than let me show myself off. Not that it stopped me being rude once or twice, snogging in parked cars with my boobs out, knowing full well that there might be some dirty old man watching from the undergrowth. That was a thrill, but I preferred the idea of being seen by someone who'd be really shocked; turned on, yes, but shocked too. What I wanted to do was to go flashing, to give someone a peep of my boobs or my bum and see their mouth open the same way mine had when I'd seen the girl in the mini-bus. That brief view of her bare bottom and happy face had really affected me, and I wanted that same power myself.

I found my friend in one of the guys at college, Chris. He was small and very effeminate, and gay. Once I got to know him I found out that he felt he was in fact female, in spirit anyway, a woman trapped in a man's body, if you like. He was shy at first and reluctant to make friends, but I'm bubbly and he found me easy to get on with. At first I was a shoulder to cry on, but after one drunken and emotional evening I admitted what I was like, and really it went from there.

Like me, he wanted to display sexually, but it's not so easy for a man. For the first time I realised the amount of freedom for erotic display that women take for granted. By and large women's clothes are designed to display their bodies, men's for function, like work clothes, or to project an image, like a suit. Chris wanted to be looked at, to show off, as a woman, and would have been perfectly happy with levels of display that I took for granted. It was a real eye-opener for me to discover how envious a man could be of female prerogatives, even things that many women actually find a bit of a nuisance. Still, the grass is always greener, I suppose.

Chris wanted to be a girl, which I found a real giggle, so I started to help him cross-dress and how to make up and other girlie things. In return he let me show off in ways that I would never have risked on my own. He was good for my confidence too, because he loved my body; in fact he said he'd like one just the same. Not only that, but he gave me a male perspective on how a girl should show off, and what movements and positions were the most sexy.

In no time I was going out with no bra, or in skirts so short that my knickers showed when I bent over. I even went knickerless, which felt wonderful, knowing that if I bent down any men looking were going to get a prime view of my bare bum, maybe even a glimpse of my pussy. In fact it was as much fun shocking other women, particularly old ladies, with a flash of cheeky pink bottom in the street.

One thing Chris explained was that a lot of men got a bigger kick out of it if they thought they'd caught a girl out in some way, seeing something she didn't want to be seen. As he said, when a girl's in a little skirt, you always know that she has chosen that little skirt, and that unless she's half-witted she must realise that it shows her knickers when she bends. On the other hand, a girl in a long skirt gives the impression that she wants to conceal herself, and so if the skirt gets blown up and her knickers show, then it's much sexier. That appealed to me, and I started to think of ways I could make it look completely accidental.

Sunbathing was one, because it means showing a lot of flesh for a reason that isn't sexual. Women get resentful if they're watched sunbathing, and the more flesh they're showing, the more resentful they are towards leering male onlookers. Also, the more resentful the women, the bigger the kick for the Peeping Toms. I'd never really thought of it that way, maybe because I love to tease, but Chris assured me that that was how it worked for a lot of people.

The idea was to go somewhere that we might have thought would be safe from prying eyes, but wasn't. Chris already had it worked out: the roof of the building his room was in, on a Sunday. It was overlooked by two big office blocks, which it was not unreasonable to think would be empty at the weekends. In fact one had resident security and both had weekend cleaners. It was ideal, and also the perfect chance to give Chris his first outing as a woman.

We had great fun with the makeover, shaving his legs, putting his make-up on, fitting a long brown wig. I had persuaded him not to go for a tarty look, sure that something more natural would be more convincing. The finished product was impressive. He was small and had a really feminine face anyway, but with the makeover and with his little cock taped down between his legs I could almost believe he was a she. I was sure anyone watching from one of the office windows would be fooled, and so Chris became Cindy and we climbed out onto the roof.

It was sunny, with the flat area of lead we wanted to use almost too hot to stand on. We made a big deal out of spreading out our towels and undressing, going down to the bikinis we had on underneath our clothes. Chris, or rather Cindy, was in a dress, which I unbuttoned before peeling off my jeans and top with all the assurance of a girl undressing for a bath. Never once did we look up at the offices, even as we applied our suntan cream, helping each other with the tricky bits.

I already had that little daring thrill as I lay down on my towel. Peeping through my eyelashes, I could see the office blocks rising above us, side by side, the windows glinting in the sun. It didn't take long to get noticed: first a security guard, who called two mates, then a janitor in the other block. I was being watched sunbathing and it sent a thrill right through me, knowing that I was being ogled and that the watchers imagined us not to know.

My real need was to strip naked, but I knew it was best to take it slowly. Over the next hour I gradually showed off more, first rolling onto my front and unclipping the strap of my bikini top, then tugging the bottoms up to show a bit more cheek. Cindy did the same and we shared an excited grin. It was like acting. My top went next, shrugged off with mock petulance, as if it was a nuisance that I needed out of the way. In doing so I gave a brief flash of my boobs, then rolled over once more, showing them completely. I knew people were staring, and it was really getting to me, with the thrill of danger added to the thrill of being daring.

Cindy couldn't show her chest, of course, but she took her top off anyway and then pushed down her bikini bottoms. Her bottom was smooth and pink, and remarkably girlish, if a bit skinny. Still, skinny girls are in and I was sure the watchers didn't mind. With her nude I more or less had to follow suit, so I rolled again, down came my bikini pants and we were both naked, laid bare in the sun.

I could just imagine the men getting worked up over our naked bodies, and the fact that one of us was really a boy made it all the better. It was hard not to giggle, just thinking of the macho security guards getting hard-ons over another man's body and of how angry they'd be if they knew. I wanted to see, and even though I was nervous about showing my pussy I rolled, turning face up with everything on show and peeping through my eyelids.

Immediately I saw a movement, the janitor getting quickly back. Not for long. His head appeared, his face red against his greying hair, his pop eyes staring right down at me, from no more than fifty feet. My flesh seemed to crawl under his gaze, it was so filled with lust, as if he was groping me with his eyes. It was strong, almost too much, and if Cindy hadn't been there I think I would have panicked. As it was I willed myself to stay still, struggling to keep my breathing even.

For what seemed like an age I lay there, not daring to move, watching him watching me, or rather us, because his eyes were flicking from my body to Cindy's and back, all the while making a nervous, jerking movement and at last I realised that he was masturbating over us. I told Cindy, trying to make it look like a casual comment as I knew he'd see my lips moving. Cindy giggled, an excited, aroused sound. I lay still, watching, seeing the man's face get redder and his jerking more frantic until suddenly his eyes shut, his teeth gritted and I knew he'd come, wanking his dirty cock over my body and my friend's.

I was really aroused, not from sex so much as from the raw power of seeing what my body could do. As he came he moved quickly back, then reappeared, and by instinct I opened my eyes and pretended to see him for the first time I jumped up, covering my boobs with one arm and my pussy hair with a hand. I gave him a string of abuse, calling him a wanker and a Peeping Tom and more as I covered myself with the towel. He vanished and I turned my attention to the security men, but they only laughed at me.

Inside it was our turn to laugh. The janitor had come over Cindy's body as much as mine, and the security men had been ogling her pretty freely as well. It was hilarious and we absolutely fell about laughing. I was randy too, so randy, and Cindy's little cock was rock-hard. We brought each other off, the only time in our friendship, doing it out of sheer mischievous joy, in a sixty-nine with his cock in my mouth and his tongue on my pussy.

We felt so pleased with ourselves after that, but it was like a drug, with the experience creating a need for more. Twice more we sunbathed, but never with such an extreme reaction, while Chris was growing ever more confident and ever more skilled as Cindy. He told me how men cruise in parks, hoping for sex, mainly gays, but some simply eager for anything on offer. The knowledge scared me, and I was thinking of stalkers and rapists. He was keen, though, really keen – desperate, even, wanting so badly to suck a man off when that man thought he was a woman. The idea thrilled me, and before I had really come to terms with it I had agreed to go with him.

We chose Wimbledon Common, towards dusk. Cindy explained how she intended to start hormone treatment to make her breasts grow as we drove up, and the conversation seemed so strange yet so natural that I began to feel detached from the real world, and bolder too. We set out across the common, giggling at the prospect of what we were going to do, and I felt so good, a real show-off, a real little flirt. Cindy was in a frock, making the best of her fake bust and long legs. I was in a loose top and a floaty, knee-length skirt, no knickers, ideal for flashing.

I felt so good I gave a twirl as soon as we got into the woods, making the skirt rise and revealing the fact that I was knickerless to anybody who might have been looking. Cindy watched with a smile, and when I'd stopped she quite coolly took the hem of my skirt and tucked it into the waistband, then doubled it up, leaving my whole bum bare. That was so good. I was walking through the woods, very public woods, with my bottom showing. My heart was absolutely hammering, and I was dreading and praying for us to be seen, all at the same time.

When the man came it nearly gave me a heart attack. He just stepped out of the woods, suddenly. I stopped dead, too shocked to even cover my bum. He looked like an owl, with big, staring eyes behind thick glasses and a round, heavy body concealed beneath a greatcoat. He never said a word, but just stared, not moving, his eyes fixed on us. It was creepy and I would have run, but Cindy was made of sterner stuff. She glanced around, then smiled at him and nodded at his crotch.

It was my turn to stare as he opened his greatcoat. His cock was already out of his fly, his balls too, the way they were sticking out so rude, the dark, wrinkly skin looking so dirty, yet so compelling too. I didn't want to touch, but I did want to look. Cindy was braver, and dirtier. She just went down, on her knees in front of him, and took the whole obscene, rubbery mass in her mouth. The man's leer grew broader and he turned to me, motioning for me to turn around.

I showed him my knickerless bum, looking back over my shoulder as Cindy gave him his blow-job. It didn't take long, his cock coming quickly to erection while his eyes feasted on my bare bottom. After a while I added my boobs to the treat, pulling my top up, then actually off to give him a good view. He came then, down Cindy's throat, grunting out his passion and calling us whores and bitch girls and worse things.

As soon as he'd come he ran off, so suddenly that it had me looking round, expecting half a dozen police to be after us. I quickly covered myself as Cindy spat her mouthful on the ground and tidied up with a handkerchief. She was elated. He'd come in her mouth, all the while believing it was a girl sucking him off, or at least if he had suspected he'd given no sign. I was sure he hadn't known, and told her so, laughing happily along and thoroughly pleased with myself too, not just for my little piece of flashing and showing off, but for my courage in going through with it.

We did similar things several more times, and I always enjoyed it. It was dangerous, though, and I began to feel that it was chancing my luck to go on, while the initial kick

158

was fading anyway. Cindy was different; she just loved to suck, with a seemingly endless appetite for men's cocks. She liked come, too; in fact she loved it, often licking up any that got spilled and often swallowing it. I knew men liked to come in girls' mouths, and I'd let a couple do it, including Cindy actually. Spunk is too slimy and too salty for me, and I've always looked on having it in my mouth as a favour, a big favour.

Some of the men weren't content with me just showing off, and wanted more. I wouldn't, or at least no more than a squeeze of my boobs, until what I knew was going to be the last time for me. The guy was younger than most of them, fat but muscular too. He was a talker, which I always preferred, as the ones who wouldn't speak gave me the creeps. As always he was happy with the idea of a blow-job from Cindy, and he complimented me on my figure when I'd got it out for him, but wanted a feel too. I let him, making him promise not to try and finger me, but giving him free rein with my boobs and bum. He was good, groping away as Cindy sucked and felt his balls, and paying particular attention to my nipples. That actually made me randy, and for a special treat I took hold of his cock and tugged at the base of the shaft, getting him off into Cindy's mouth.

I'd already said I wanted to stop, and that was my swan song. It was getting too cold for me anyway. That didn't bother Cindy, but then she never had to get her kit off. So I suspended my exhibitionism for the winter and got my kicks out of listening to Cindy's stories of night-time liaisons and the cocks she had sucked. It had done a lot of good for my confidence, and I knew that next summer I'd be topless on the beach if I could get away with it, and that I'd thoroughly enjoy the attention.

Cindy and I – I couldn't think of her as Chris any more by then – stayed the best of friends, and I like to think I helped her with what could never be an easy thing to do. She certainly helped me. One other thing I was pleased with was that I'd had a lot of fun but without getting myself a reputation. I'd been no worse than the next girl, as far as anyone knew, except Cindy, and she wasn't talking. It's always struck me as really unfair, and stupid, that men want all the nookie they can get, but when a girl gives it they brand her a tart and other nasty names. At least, that's the way it was with my friends in Croydon. I'd started to go in to the centre more, and to clubs where they took a cooler attitude. There I could dress sexy and be myself. Still, I had to keep my gear at Cindy's bedsit.

Despite my growing self-assurance, I still liked the idea of being seen as if by accident. It suited my sense of daring, and of being a tease without ever being thought to have done it on purpose. Dancing in a pair of tight blue velvet shorts and a minuscule top was nice, but everyone knew I was showing off, and a lot of them were too cool to notice, or at least pretended to be. I was also one among a lot of other girls, many showing as much as me. What I wanted was impact. OK, I wanted to be the centre of attention, but why not?

I got my chance the next spring. It was April and we'd taken a cottage in Norfolk for a week, rather to the south of the area we normally visited. The weather was good, or good enough at any rate, and I was looking forward to a chance to strip off in the open again, maybe even to masturbate like that. The idea thrilled me so much, and the very first evening I went for a walk to explore. I was with my little sisters, so I couldn't do anything, and anyway I soon realised that there was a problem. With all the little waterways and drainage channels, it was almost impossible to get away from the main paths.

After dinner I got a map out, and soon realised that what I'd thought was a problem was in fact a bonus. It might be hard to get across the waterways, but once on the other side I'd be really lonely. If I was prepared to get my legs wet I'd be able to get to places that were completely cut off. In fact the idea of getting wet rather appealed to me, as it would make an excellent reason for getting my clothes off.

It wasn't until the middle of the week that I managed to do it. I'd chosen my place from the map, a long thin wood trapped between a broad and a channel, apparently just vacant land, with no access at all. I had a look and I was right; the only way to get to it was by wading as, with a thick bank of reeds along the shore, even a boat would have had trouble landing. Landing, yes, not seeing.

With everyone doing their own thing for the afternoon, I put on a pair of loose canvas trousers, easy to get on and off, but tough enough not to have to worry about nettles and things. Just walking away from the cottage felt daring, knowing what I was going to do.

It was half an hour's brisk walk to get there, and I was hot when I arrived and more eager than ever to take my clothes off. My sense of daring was sky high, and I even took my trousers off in the field before wading the ditch, my heart absolutely hammering because there were dead flat, open fields on all sides and a farm visible not a quarter of a mile away. I did it, though, down to my knickers, and waded in with my plimsolls on, feeling my feet sink into the lovely squishy mud at the bottom. It was deeper than I'd expected, with the mud coming up to my knees in the middle and the water so high I had to hold my top up to stop it getting wet. In the end I dropped my top and deliberately dipped down, leaving the wet cotton stretched over my boobs as if I'd been in a Miss Wet T-shirt contest. My knickers got soaked too.

I felt really triumphant on the far side, and more daring than ever. My knickers were wet and heavy, clinging to my bum, with my pubes showing through the front. The top was the same over my boobs, showing just about every detail, even with my bra on. That felt nice, and I walked like that, just enjoying the feel of it. Soon my bra was off, improving the wet T-shirt feel, then that was off too, and I stuffed it all into my canvas bag and hung that from a tree. I went exploring, in just plimsolls and wet panties, the thrill rising as I went further and further from my clothes. It was lovely, and as I got more excited and my courage rose, I went closer to the edge, until I was looking out over the fringe of reeds across the broad.

My boobs were visible above the reeds and two pleasure boats were in view, but I held my place, knowing full well they could see me. Sure enough, one of the distant figures turned their binoculars towards me, then another, and I nipped back into the trees, knowing I'd given them a show and thoroughly pleased with myself.

The inside of the wood was wet and rough, with a lot of mud and fallen wood, or I'd have sat down and masturbated then and there. I put it off, and deliberately went back to my clothes, took off my knickers and hung them up on a twig, like a little pink flag to announced the fact that I was nude.

For nearly an hour I stayed like that, just running around, bare except for my plimsolls and absolutely loving it. Twice more I let myself be seen, until at last my excitement got the better of me and I could hold back no more. I did it in a big, slimy pool of mud, my bare bottom sat full in it, with the squashy, warm black muck oozing up between my bum-cheeks. I smeared it on my boobs too, just for the feel of it, and slapped a handful on my belly, then my pussy and I started to rub. My favourite way is to slide a finger up my hole and use the knuckle of my thumb; a bit awkward, maybe, but nice too. In no time I was moaning aloud and using my free hand to smear more mud over my front, paying special attention to my boobs. I came like that, crying out in my ecstasy, so free and so high, just on the feel of going bare.

It took a while to clean up, and I had to go back with no knickers. In the hope that they would dry before I got back I wrung them out and walked with them in my hand. That was how I was as I followed a piece of flat land between two banks of reeds, perfectly decent, except for a pair of dripping knicks in one hand. All I could see were the reeds, a thick fringe to either side with more beyond and a church tower and two wind pumps in the distance.

I heard a sound first, the throb of an engine, then conversation, and I turned to find a pleasure boat no more than a few yards away, obviously on a channel that was completely invisible to me. It passed within feet, and as the faces of the passengers looked out at me I wondered if it was the same one I'd been showing off to in the woods. That made me blush, as did the fact that they must all have realised I had no knickers on.

That was all, but it might have been so much more. I'd thought I was completely alone. I might even have been walking topless, nude if I'd really felt daring. It hadn't been a track, just the edge of a newly repaired dyke. The boat had looked right down on me and they would have seen everything.

I had to do it. I'd never have forgiven myself if I hadn't. My first thought was to go there and sunbathe, nude, which would have been nice, and given me that sense of invaded privacy. The next idea was to actually let them see me masturbating, but it would lose the feeling of injured innocence. After all, good girls don't rub their pussies off in the great outdoors. They do something else, though; sometimes they get no choice.

Next day I couldn't get away, and I was in a fidget all the time. The one after was our last, and I managed to get out in the afternoon. I think Mum and Dad imagined I was going to see some local boy, and I didn't try to dissuade them. To get to my special place I had to wade. In fact, I'm not sure I'd have had the guts otherwise. I did it in my knickers again, but I'd brought a spare pair and put those on in a genuinely sheltered place, spending a little time bottomless just to get myself worked up.

The feeling of daring that I'd come to crave was stronger than ever as I chose the place for my exposure. It was ideal, a little triangular piece of grass between high reeds, apparently sheltered from every side, but in practise visible to the boats on the channel. Climbing the dyke, I found a spot where I could see the channel, which angled in to the cut I was by, so that I'd come into view of the boat as it came around the corner.

I knew what I had to do, and was determined not to back out. Crouched low, I waited until I saw a boat in the distance, a big white pleasure boat. It seemed to be full of old folk on some sort of outing, which was perfect. I ducked back, my heart hammering as I scrambled down to my special place. For a minute I waited, my back to the channel, my thumbs in the waistband of my trousers.

The moment I saw the top of the boat I pushed it all down, trousers and knickers, right to my ankles, exposing my bare bum to the world. I got in a squat, sticking it out, knowing the position showed my pussy and bumhole as well as the two chubby pink cheeks of my bottom. They could see me, they had to be able to, but I didn't look round, and with my eyes closed in utter, shameless ecstasy for my own dirty behaviour, I let go of my bladder. I felt it go, a thick stream of pee, gushing out below me in full view of who knew how many people, some shocked, some excited, some disgusted, but everyone one with a prime view of my bare bum and what I was doing.

It was the best feeling short of orgasm I'd ever had, and I just couldn't stop myself. I know it was filthy, the rudest conceivable thing to have done, but it was impossible to resist it. Besides, I needed to go. I felt the pressure in my belly, and with a little moan I let my bumhole open, squeezing out one big, fat lump, in full view. It fell and another followed, and I could hear their buzz of conversation.

If I pulled up my knickers I was going to mess myself, so I turned, pretending I'd just seen them, gaping in mock horror, my mouth and eyes wide. Some were watching openly, some pretending not to, a line of faces, everyone of whom had seen what I was doing. I couldn't stop and I couldn't move, I just had to stay still, performing the most intimate of bodily functions in front of them, what girls do every day, but never, ever let anyone watch.

My pile grew under me as the boat passed, until at last it was all out and my hole closed behind me. I was clutching my knickers, my head swimming in ecstasy for what had to have been the rudest, most daring piece of showing off ever. I was going to come, and I didn't care where I was. If another boat came, all the better. I did it like that, knickers down, dirty bum stuck out squatting over what I'd done, what they'd seen me do. My finger went in, up my pussy, then out and up my sticky, slimy

164

bumhole instead. The ball of my thumb was on my clitoris, and I fingered my bottom as I masturbated, in and out, squashing and squelching in the mess until my orgasm hit me, my balance went, and at that last moment of perfect ecstasy I sat down in my own mess.

Selfish, true, the pleasure she gives to others being entirely incidental to her own fun. Still, real altruism is almost unknown and even then seldom what it seems. Consider, for instance, how the lucky fellow in the next story must have felt about Natasha, the brat herself, average height, enviably pretty, perfectly groomed . . .

The Lady and the Tramp –
Natasha Linnet

It wasn't so much that I felt I needed therapy, but that everyone else was getting it and so I felt left out because I wasn't. We were doing lunch at the *Café Epernay*, Jocasta and Ami, and Sophie and I. Jocasta was telling us about how her therapist had helped her regain her self-worth after she'd split up with her latest man. The others were agreeing with her and comparing her experience with their own. I could only sit and listen, and I hate that.

Ami was taking aromatherapy and shiatsu and she swore it was the only thing that had kept her together in her new job. Sophie was studying primal scream therapy and something else, with a Japanese-sounding name that I didn't catch. When I asked she said it was actually a discipline from Laos, at which the others nodded knowledgeably. When I admitted that I wasn't doing anything, they were all full of advice, telling me how good it would be for me and recommending various practitioners.

As a freelance wine writer I felt I had as much job-related stress as any of them, what with deadlines and fussy editors and never knowing where the next commission was coming from. On the sex-life front it wasn't so bad, with plenty of nice rude attention from Percy. Not that I was going to admit getting my kicks from being punished by a dirty old man, not to the three of them and certainly not to some shrink. Unfortunately, that meant that they thought I wasn't getting anything at all, and they all felt I should be, so I ended up accepting the details of Jocasta's whole-being therapist.

This was a Ms Gabrielle Salinger, who was apparently so exclusive that she only accepted new clients by recommendation. My appointment was on a Tuesday afternoon, at her clinic in Victoria. I didn't expect much, only really to be able to say I was seeing her. Certainly I wasn't going to tell her what I was like, because I was certain she wouldn't understand. Besides, I'd come to terms with my enjoyment of being spanked and dominated, even if it had taken me a while, and I didn't want it spoiled by her. I was a bit worried, thinking that she might really be as good as Jocasta said and manage to get it out of me. I needn't have bothered, because she was far too full of herself to think that she couldn't see through me. My reticence was put down to repression, which fitted in nicely with my supposed lack of a boyfriend.

Her big thing was about raising women's sense of their own worth. Apparently my repression was the result of low self-esteem, which is about as far from the truth as it is possible to get. I know I'm gorgeous and clever, and if that makes me a spoiled brat, then that's what makes it so hot to take a spanking. Having analysed me, she did her best to boost me up, telling me all about my value as a woman. It was nothing new, just couched in fancier language, but I was feeling as good about myself as I ever have when I left, if for the wrong reasons.

Mind over matter was important, she had said, doing something because I wanted to, regardless of my insecurities. She had advised trying to take the lead in my relationships, and suggesting I ask a good-looking man out. It was ironic, because that was how I used to behave before I got into spanking, and it was never nearly as much fun. I always used to get considerate, easily dominated ones, men who'd let me control the sex from start to finish. In fact I'd thought that was what I'd wanted, even though it was somehow never fully satisfying. Since then I'd learned that my best orgasms come with a hot bottom and strong feelings of shame and exposure.

Time was getting on, so I ate in a little café off Grosvenor Place, ciabatta with sun-dried tomatoes and a little Munster, washed down with Salice Salentino. As I ate I thought about what Gabrielle had said, about my difficulty in trusting men and opening up to them. It just wasn't true. I'd never been the sort to say no when I meant yes, nor to run away from an opportunity and then wish I'd taken it. When I made my decisions I stuck with them, and I never regretted my choice.

To prove it I promised myself that the next man who propositioned me would get what he wanted, or woman for that matter. It was rather a nice idea, bringing on a pleasantly naughty feeling that grew stronger as I finished my wine and sipped a glass of grappa. Maybe it would be one of the waiters, both young, muscular Italian boys who could be guaranteed to provide plenty of lust if not a lot of style. No, an older man would be better, someone who'd take his time and want me to do something rude before we got down to the full-blown sex. If I was lucky I might even catch a spanker. Percy tells me that bottoms don't come more spankable than mine, especially in trousers, and I was wearing loose white combats, just nicely tight across my rear.

The thought made me feel naughtier than ever, and as I left the restaurant I was wiggling deliberately, hoping to attract some male attention. One of the waiters whistled, but I decided not to count that. Strictly speaking it was just a mark of appreciation, not an actual proposition. Besides, Italians are like so many of their wines, all show and no substance. What I wanted was an Englishman, cool and reserved on the exterior but seething with kinky desires.

I got one, but not quite in the way I'd anticipated. My thoughts had started to drift, thinking of how it felt to be laid across a man's lap and held firmly in place, then spanked on my bare bottom. The idea of waiting for someone to proposition me was getting rapidly less appealing. After all, it might have taken ages, and the chances of attracting a spanker were actually pretty slim. A much better bet was to give Percy a call. He could be relied on for dinner, smacked bum, maybe six of the best with a cane and a nice orgasm to finish. All I needed to do was call him.

Five minutes later I'd arranged a date, meeting at a pub we knew in Pimlico later that evening. From there it would be to a good restaurant, back to his flat, and knickers down in no time. For now I had about two hours to kill, but it seemed best to go down to Pimlico and get a couple of drinks in before he arrived.

As I crossed Grosvenor Gardens towards the station I saw the drinking school, four tramps with big bottles of cheap cider, three on a bench, one standing. I hardly noticed them, save to step out a little way to avoid the swaying body of the standing one. Not wanting to step into the traffic, I still passed pretty close, and as I did so his eyes met mine and his face broke into a gap-toothed leer.

'Nice tits, love. How about a wank?'

He said it in a drunken slur, but I caught every word and snapped back a curt 'fuck off' without breaking my stride. Then I was past, ignoring some mumbled remark about being a stuck-up bitch.

I walked on, my mood broken by the incident. It was annoying, because I'd been so turned on and now I was angry, and over what was really a pretty trivial incident. After all, it wasn't as if even in his wildest dreams he could possibly have expected me to accept the proposition . . .

Only then did I remember exactly what I'd promised, and why. He had propositioned me, there was no denying it, and I'd intended to prove that, whatever Ms Gabrielle Salinger might think, I was quite capable of exerting mind over matter. I'd said I'd do it, and I would have done, but not with a dirty old tramp. That hardly counted; it was just too gross. No, I'd wait until somebody attractive made a move . . .

Which would prove exactly what she'd said, that I couldn't exert myself, that I gave in to my insecurities. Well, yes, but being insecure about wanking off a tramp was hardly the same thing. I mean, what woman wouldn't be? The whole thing was silly anyway. It didn't prove a thing.

It did. That was the trouble. I'd played the same game when I was little, only not in a sexual way. Just to prove how strong-minded I was I'd set myself a task, at random, and go through with it. Sometimes it had been daring, like raiding the pantry for biscuits at school. Sometimes it had been physically risky, like balancing on a log to cross a river. Not big things, maybe, but I had built up my self-respect on them. It was the same now. When I decided to do something, I did it. Not wanking off some old tramp, though, surely?

I told myself to grow up, and walked on, only to stop at the ticket barrier. If I went past that would be it, I'd have broken my word and proved Ms Salinger right. That rankled, and if she didn't know it, then I did. The question was, would it be as bad as taking the old bastard who'd accosted me in my hand? Of course, that assumed I actually ended up doing it; all I'd said was that I'd accept the proposition. Yes, that was all I had to do, go back and tell him I'd do it. He wouldn't believe me and would probably call me a stuck-up bitch again, but I'd have done it and honour would be satisfied.

There was a big lump in my throat as I walked back up Grosvenor Gardens. It was going to take courage, there was no denying that, and then there was the horrible thought that he might be so drunk that he'd just pull his cock out and demand it attended to. If he did I'd have to ask that we go somewhere private and hope he got arrested before I had to do it.

I was hoping he'd gone, but he hadn't. He was standing as before, swaying gently, his cider bottle dangling from one hand. My fingers were shaking and I was so nervous that I felt sick, but I forced myself to go on. I walked past the first time, but set my jaw and turned back. I wasn't going to do it in front of his friends, so I drew his attention with a cough and beckoned him to the side. He responded with a bleary-eyed stare, blank at first, then aggressive as he recognised me.

'What d'you want, bitch?' he drawled as he came towards me. 'Come to tell me to mind my manners, have you?'

'No,' I answered, forcing the words out. 'I've been thinking about what you said earlier, and yes, I would like to, if you want.'

'Like to what?' he snarled, rocking back on his heels.

'What you said,' I went on, cursing him inside for making me actually say it out loud. 'You remember, you asked for a hand job.'

He looked at me. His expression was hard to read through his beard, but I was sure he didn't believe me. Unfortunately I'd forgotten something.

'How much?' he demanded.

It had never occurred to me, not for one second, that he might think I wanted money. I mean, why should it? I was carrying a Prada bag; my whole outfit was designer wear; even my shoes must have cost more than his benefits for a month. The idea that he might think I was a prostitute when I propositioned him had never occurred to me. Prostitution is just not part of my world.

'Fifty?' he snarled. 'I've got it, don't think I haven't.'

'No, I don't want your money,' I answered, still trying to get my head around the mistake.

He looked at me, right into my eyes. I hoped he was trying to work out if I was serious and would decide otherwise, although it looked more like he was wondering if I was sane. For a moment he opened his mouth, and I stepped back, expecting the torrent of abuse as he decided that I was winding him up. It never came. Instead he reached out, took me by the elbow and began to steer me back the way I had come.

'I know a place,' he grated, 'down by the river.'

I didn't know what to say. People were giving me peculiar looks, and I pulled away from his hand. That was all, because I knew that if I backed out now I was going to feel even more pathetic. He smelled of cider, but I'd expected worse and was trying to tell myself that it wouldn't take long. Just a few quick jerks of my wrist and it would be over. I didn't even have to watch, and I could pretend it was a boyfriend and not him. He'd come and then I'd be vindicated and feel strong again, just as I always had before.

He didn't talk at first, not until we'd got into the quieter streets beyond the station. Then he began to mumble, so faintly that I could hardly hear him at first, but then more clearly. He told me how he liked to watch girls, preferably ones in tight clothes that showed off the shape of their bottoms and breasts. It was so crude, just the way he talked.

'. . . right up your cunt-slits, that's the way I like it,' he drawled. 'A nice tight pair of trousers, pulled right up the fanny. Skirts is good too, little ones so I can see up them. You girls don't even know you're showing your pants, sometimes. Sometimes you don't have any pants, I know.'

With the last comment he gave me a dirty wink and offered his cider bottle, which I refused, getting called a stuck-up little bitch again for my trouble. He took a long swallow, supporting himself against the wall as he did it.

'Have you got pants on?' he asked, craning around to peer at my bottom.

'Yes, of course,' I answered quickly.

'What colour?'

'White, or they'd show through.'

'They show through, anyway, darling!'

He laughed and slapped my bum, hard enough to make my cheeks bounce and send that familiar tingling sensation through my bottom. Feeling me was no part of the deal and I would have said something, but the look on his face told me that he'd only laugh at me. He laughed anyway, looking at my bum, and as I peered back over my shoulder I found what I had been dreading. On my bottom, right across the right cheek, my immaculate white trousers were marked, marked with a big, grey handprint.

I called him a dirty bastard, but he just went on talking, making remarks on my figure in the crudest possible language, and I think really intending it as a compliment. He said he'd been staring at my boobs as I walked towards him the first time, and wondering how they'd look bare and how they'd feel in his hands. He'd been able to see my nipples too, really clearly through my top. That was what had made him proposition me. They'd been erect because of what I was thinking about, an irony that wasn't lost on me.

Twice, when nobody was near, he put his hand inside his greatcoat, obviously having a quick feel of what I suspected was an already erect cock. We went a long way, right down to a little patch of green by the river. He took me to a bench in among some bushes, completely shielded even though I could hear people talking as they went past, no more than a few feet away. It was so risky, and my heart was hammering. I wanted to put it off too, even though I knew I was going to do it.

'Isn't there anywhere better?' I demanded.

'Don't worry, love, I always do it here,' he answered.

I swallowed hard, thinking of him sitting there, masturbating with his great dirty cock in his hand, thinking dirty thoughts about the bums and boobs of the girls he watched on the streets. He sat down, leering at me and patting the bench beside him. It was filthy, stained, and I had a horrible suspicion I knew what with. I shook my head. As it was I looked like having to spend the evening wandering around London with a dirty bottom, and I didn't want to make it worse than it already was.

The only choice was to squat down in front of him, the way some men like their blow-jobs. I like to be licked the same way, with my partner kneeling. There's an extra kick out of having someone in such a subservient position. I was going to do it anyway, rather than dirty my combats, and I felt a submissive flush as I sank down. He gave me his gap-toothed grin and spread his knees to accommodate me, then pulled open his overcoat.

I could see his cock in his trousers, a long, thick lump sticking out to one side. He was hard, for me, and I couldn't keep my eyes off it. The sick feeling in my throat got quickly worse as his hands went to his fly, took the zip, eased it down and opened the button of his trousers. A thumb went into his greyish underpants, levering them open, over the head of his cock. It was dark red, big and bulbous, glossy with pressure, the skin stretched taut in his excitement. His other hand went down his pants and he

174

scooped it out, all of it, a good seven inches of thick cock and two huge balls in a wrinkled, hairy scrotum. His shaft was slightly bent, his skin a sort of ugly reddish grey, gnarled and thick with veins, giving an extra touch of the grotesque. The smell of cock was heavy in the air, really strong. It was actually frightening me, and I wanted to delay the awful moment I took the grotesque thing in front of me in my hand.

'What's your name?' I asked, feeling that if I was going to masturbate him we should at least be introduced.

'Richie,' he answered, taking hold of his ghastly cock and pushing it towards me. 'Ain't I got a nice one?'

'Tasha,' I answered, immediately wondering why I'd given the name only my close friends use. 'It's . . . it's big, yes.'

'You're pretty,' he said. 'Come on, love, wank me.'

'All right, all right.'

'I love to watch while I wank,' he drawled. 'I do it under my coat. I love to see wiggling arses and bouncing tits. Yours are lovely and big, that's what I first noticed about you. You going to get them out for me then?'

'No, I'm not! I promised you a wank, and that's what you're going to get.'

'Stuck-up bitch.'

I swallowed and closed my eyes. My hand was shaking but I forced myself to reach out. I found it, my fingers touching the hot, damp skin, curling around it and closing on the hard shaft. He gave a grunt as I started to toss him, holding the thick skin and sliding it up and down the shaft, my hand bumping on his gathered foreskin with each tug.

'Fucking great,' he mumbled and moved forwards, closer to me.

Setting my teeth in determination, I sped up, jerking hard at his cock and aiming it back to avoid an accident. He groaned again and shifted, making me open my eyes in case he was going to try and grab my boobs or anything. I saw my hand, tiny and pale on his cock, my slim fingers and neatly manicured nails making an obscene contrast to what I was holding and the way it stuck out from his grubby old trousers. Now that I was looking, I couldn't take my eyes off it, watching myself masturbate a tramp.

I wondered what my friends would have thought of me, with their professional thirty-something boyfriends and clean, healthy lifestyles. They wouldn't have done it, none of them, ever, and I knew they wouldn't believe anyone who told them I had. I was, though, squatting by a dirty bench in my immaculate white outfit with a tramp's penis in his hand, wanking him, willingly.

Little bubbles of fluid had started to come out of the tip of his cock and I knew it wouldn't be long. He was groaning and pushing up into my hand, getting urgent. His eyes were glued to my chest, watching my boobs bounce to the motion of my hand. He'd wanted them out, bare in front of him to give him something to get off over, my naked chest. A voice startled me, sending my heart into my mouth even as I realised that it was just a couple on the far side of the bushes.

I began to tug harder, frantic to make him come and sure that we'd be caught if it didn't happen soon. He didn't seem to care, and I wondered if it wouldn't be best to show him my boobs after all. It wouldn't have taken much, just a tug to lift my top and show them. It had to make him come faster, and suddenly I was scrabbling at my top with my free hand, lifting it, pulling my bra cups free, one by one to spill my breasts into the light.

'Dirty tart,' he grunted.

'Just do it!' I snapped.

'Talk dirty,' he urged. 'I like that, real dirty.'

I bit back the answer that came to my lips.

'You do,' I said. 'Tell me what you like. Tell me your favourite fantasy, or how you like to watch girls.'

'No, you, I want to hear what you do with your posh boyfriends, or when you're on your own. What you wear in bed? Diddle your twat, do you?'

'No, look . . .'

Again a voice sounded from beyond the bushes, then a woman's laughter.

176

'Oh, all right!' I snapped, desperately trying to think of what to say. 'I wear silk pyjamas, sometimes a nightie. I do it with a vibrator, on my bed.'

'What, stripped off?'

'No, with my pyjamas down. I like to keep some clothes on.'

'D'you feel your tits?'

'Yes, or I like to kneel and rub them on the coverlet . . .'

I stopped, amazed I'd made such an intimate admission. My wrist was getting sore and I changed hands, wanking clumsily with my left so that his cock jerked from side to side as I pulled. His eyes were still locked on my bare boobs, which were bouncing about like anything. I had to make him come, to say something to get him there, something dirty enough, something to make him feel special.

'I love to get them out,' I said. 'They are big, aren't they? Look at them, Richie, all bare, just for you. Look, my nipples have gone all stiff. I bet you like that, don't you? That's why I asked if you wanted a wank. You turned me on and I wanted to show them to you, all bare and white and creamy. If we weren't outdoors I'd let you spunk on them, Richie, all over my lovely round boobies. I'd suck you too, right in . . .'

He grabbed me by the hair. I squealed as my face was jerked into his crotch, his cock pressing against my face, his balls on my chin. I did it. I put his big, dirty cock in my mouth and started to suck it, feeling utterly filthy, utterly disgusted with myself but unable to stop. I grabbed his balls, feeling the fat shapes squirm in his scrotum. His grip tightened, forcing his erection deep into my throat and making me gag. I pulled back, took the shaft, sucking the thick, oily foreskin and masturbating him urgently into my mouth. I felt it jerk and prepared to swallow, wanting to do it yet burning with self-disgust.

I wasn't allowed. He jerked my head back hard by the hair, his cock flew from my mouth and it all came out, a thick jet of sperm erupting from the tip, full in my face. I gasped in protest, closing my eyes and screwing my face up as it splashed over me, right on one eye, then in my open mouth, more in my other eye and down over my cheek and nose. Then once more his cock had been pushed to the hilt in my mouth and I felt the last of his sperm squeeze out into my throat.

He pulled back, chuckling as I spluttered and gagged on his come, still holding me by the hair. I was blinded, furious and filthy, my make-up ruined, probably my top too, because I could feel a piece of his come hanging from my chin. When I finally managed to get my breath back I managed to call him a bastard.

I stood up, trying to wipe the sperm out of my eyes. It wouldn't come, not properly, but I opened my eyes anyway, enough to see him, cock still out, taking a swig from his cider bottle. He offered it to me and I gave him a dirty look, wondering what the hell I was supposed to do.

There was nothing to clean up with. I'd thought I had tissues in my bag, but the packet was empty. There was only one thing to do, and as I nipped in among the bushes I was already struggling with my belt, my back to Richie. It was so awkward, using my shoes to stand on, one by one as I struggled to get my trousers off, then my knickers. They were wet with my juice, which set me blushing more than having to show him my bum. Bare from the waist down, I hastily wiped the worst of the sperm away with my panties.

He was staring at me, grinning at my distress, also at the way I looked. I glared at him as I pulled my trousers back up, fully aware that it would be fairly obvious that I was knickerless beneath. When I took my mirror out I found just how bad it was. My mascara was smeared everywhere, my lipstick a mess, at least what wasn't in a thick ring around his cock. Even the green from my eye pencil was smudged. I dabbed what I could away with a corner of my knickers, Richie watching and drinking cider, still with his now flaccid cock hanging out of his fly. I told him to put it away and he called me a stuck-up bitch again but did it.

A glance at my watch, which showed that it was time to meet Percy. In fact I was likely to be late, which would give him a great excuse to cane me. At that thought I realised just how turned on I was.

178

Perverse? Perhaps. Certainly a lot of what is or is not acceptable depends not on what you do, but on who you do it with. Give a helping hand to a handsome young man and you're a lucky girl; give it to a down and out and you're a pervert.

The next story is from my colleague Wendy, who has appeared in several of my books, notably Plaything. *Wendy is compact, curvaceous and quite bold. In her case there is no possible doubt about her choice of partner: it's perverse . . .*

Suction – Wendy Smith

It was the middle of my month, but I hadn't expected to get turned on. Still, sometimes it happens like that. It was just a little thing that kicked it off, no more than a glimpse really, but it was enough to bring back one of my rudest memories and with it a favourite fantasy.

I was scrambling down to the beach and I passed a woman, about thirty, I suppose, and quite fit-looking. She had been snorkelling, and had her things in a string bag. She picked it up and it caught on a rock, and for just an instant the mesh was pressed to the upper part of her thigh, making the flesh bulge out in a criss-cross pattern.

A minor thing, sure, tiny really – but not to me, not ever. The memory it provoked is of something that happened at college. A girl there, Elizabeth, got into an argument with a boy and he stuck her in a litter bin, one of those big ones made of wire. She was in a short dress, anyway, which rode up, but by bad luck her knickers got caught on a piece of wire and pulled down. That left her sex pushed hard against the wire mesh, with that same criss-cross pattern of little fleshy bumps. Every detail of her pussy had been showing, even her clitoris, stuck out through a diamond of wire, along with a fair bit of thigh and bottom-cheek.

The image has stayed in my mind ever since, inspiring some really dirty fantasies. True, they're all rather abusive, but they're only fantasies, and I'm always the victim anyway. Most of them involve being put in litter bins, usually after being stripped or half stripped. Others involve being made to sit in various disgusting messes, or having my face pushed in them. Sometimes I just lose a food fight and maybe end up sat on with a handful of cake down my knickers. At worst I can't pay in a restaurant and end up upside down in a bin full of really disgusting slops while the staff take turns with me. That one means they'd have to enter me by kneeling on the rim of the bin and pushing their cocks down into me, which might not be so easy, but they always seem to manage in the fantasy.

Once it was in my head, that was it. I kept getting images of Elizabeth in the bin and remembering her outrage and shame. It wouldn't go away until I'd come, maybe not then, but I didn't mind. After all, the beach was mainly rocks and not many people were about, so it would be easy to find a quiet place and slip my hand down the front of my shorts for a quick wank. Last year I'd been much ruder, and got away with it.

Thinking of the previous year added to my frustration. Penny had been with me, and we'd ended up being very rude together indeed. This year I was setting up the field course alone, and although Brittany is lovely and I wasn't bored, or even lonely, the occasional long, slow wank was no substitute for her tongue and fingers.

So I was going to do it, and I wanted to be rude. I had to watch the tide, and get the specimens I needed, but I still had plenty of time. The sensible thing to do seemed to be to get all the *Littorina* I needed and put them in a rock pool, from which I could collect them when it was time to go. Meanwhile I'd be able to think of some deliciously naughty way to bring myself to orgasm, preferably involving getting messy.

I thought of tar first. There was plenty about, as there always is on channel beaches. A few lumps down my shorts would have been nice, all sticky and lumpy and heavy. Once I was turned on enough I could find somewhere really private, strip off and smear it over my body, especially on my boobs, then come like that, all filthy with tar. Unfortunately it would ruin my clothes and take a hell of a lot of getting off, especially if I got any in my hair.

Not only that, but anyone who saw me while I was collecting would think I had had a really dirty accident.

Seaweed was my next thought. It would feel lovely and slimy on my skin, and I could sit in a pile while I came and rub my bottom and pussy in it. I was tempted, and I even investigated some, only to abandon the idea because all of it was crawling with sandhoppers. I may be a bit of a masochist, but there are limits. Sandhoppers bite, and the thought of spending the next two days with my boobs and bum swollen and sore was too much for me, never mind what they would have done to the fleshy centre of my pussy. Penny might have done it, not me.

Sand is too gritty, and hurts without being sexy, unless it's very fine. There was no mud, which was a pity, as a good roll in some really filthy mud would have been just the thing. The cliffs were hard, igneous rock, so there was no nice sticky clay either. That didn't leave me with much, except going back to the car park and plonking myself in the big litter bin, which might have been a nice fantasy but was hardly practical.

It looked like it was just going to be a quick strip and a rub, which was a bit irritating, when I had a very inspired and very naughty idea. I'd been collecting the *Littorina* in transparent plastic bags, and one, a *saxatalis* with a bright orange body, was crawling up the inside. I could see its foot, with the muscular ripples travelling up as it crawled. Immediately I thought how it would feel on my pussy, right on my clitoris, with that same muscular movement sucking and squirming on my flesh.

I had to try; it was too good to miss. Not with a *saxatalis*, which are so small that I'd have to keep putting it back. I needed something bigger, much bigger. Being a biologist, the answer was obvious. I needed an ormer. *Haliotis tuberculata*, a big gastropod with a sucking foot sometimes six inches long. They don't go as far north as the English coast, but in Brittany there was a fair chance of finding one. The idea put a smile on my face, mischief mixed with not a little guilt, as it was a pretty rude thing to do. As I began to look it felt as if everyone within sight knew exactly what I was doing, which was at once terrifying and thrilling.

The French eat them, poor things, so it wasn't easy. In fact, it took ages, turning rocks right down by the water line and putting them carefully back. Finally I found what I wanted, an absolute whopper, big enough to cover the palm of my hand. I christened him Herbert, having decided he was male and feeling that we ought to be introduced. Not that I expected him to get anything out of his experience, but he wouldn't come to any harm either and I would at least put him back where he wasn't likely to be caught.

Holding him up, I was sure it was going to be a good experience. His foot was big enough to cover most of my vulva, and one single, rippling muscle, with the waves moving as he tried to walk on air. To be fair I needed to do it with my middle under water, and for very obvious reasons I needed to do it somewhere I was not going to be seen.

I had plenty of choice. The shore stretched away in both directions, a great shelf of rock cut into a multitude of shapes by waves and currents. All I had to do was walk a few hundreds yards to be out of sight of the beach, and then find a pool that would be comfortable to sit in. I did it quickly, worried that the feelings of shame that were running just under the surface of my arousal might get the better of me.

My pool was a beauty, nearly round and worn, so that I could settle my bottom on smooth rock and rest my back in comfort. I put Herbert down and gave a finally guilty glance to make sure I wasn't observed. It was safe, and the next moment I was struggling with the belt that held my shorts up. It gave and I pushed them down, taking my knickers with them. Bottomless, the full naughtiness of what I was doing sank in, but I was determined to do it, and do it nude.

I hurriedly pulled up my top, unclipped my bra and let it fall, piling my clothes together on a dry area of rock before kicking off my shoes. That was it: I was naked on

183

the beach, naked and naughty, about to bring myself off in such a rude way. I climbed into the pool, enjoying the tepid water which had had most of the day to warm in the sun. Spreading my thighs, I opened my pussy to the water, grinning from ear to ear and shaking my head in sheer amazement at my own actions.

Not that I was going to chicken out. I picked Herbert up and gave him a kiss on the top of his shell, then dipped him under the surface and between my legs. Of course it might not have worked, but the moment I touched Herbert to my pussy I knew it would. Just the feeling of his foot sucking onto my vulva made me gasp out loud. It was extraordinary, like having the whole centre of my sex sucked on, and by a mouth that was all muscle and moved with a steady, firm rhythm.

It had me cross-eyed with pleasure, straight away. I always get that when I'm really excited: my focus just goes completely. Not many people do that to me with the first touch, but Herbert did. He had begun to crawl, squirming his fat, powerful foot up my pussy, each wave sucking on my flesh. I could feel them coming, travelling slowly up my lips, sucking out my clitoris, then on, higher, only for the next one to come in turn.

Everything was centred on my pussy, my whole being focused on that wonderful sensation. Normally I like to play with my tits while I wank, sometimes to stroke myself all over, especially my bum. This time it was all at the centre, with Herbert moving slowly up, sucking out my clit again and again, relaxing and sucking, relaxing and sucking . . .

I really screamed as I came, calling out Herbert's name, which felt so silly the moment my orgasm had begun to die down. Not that that happened quickly, because unlike with my own fingers, I had no control over the point at which my clit got too sensitive to touch. Herbert just sucked and sucked, and if it was torture, then it was ecstasy too.

When I'd finished I levered him off, very gently, and found a nice safe crevice for him, below normal tide line. Only then did I start to think of myself, climbing out of the pool and onto a ledge of smooth rock protected by a line of reef. I sunbathed, nude, allowing myself to dry slowly, until the water, which had been slack, began to move. Knowing that the tide had turned, I dressed quickly and began to walk back, collecting my samples on the way.

As I crossed the beach a French boy propositioned me, quite openly, pointing to the size of the bulge in his trunks. I turned him down politely. After all, he might have a big cock, he might even have been prepared to lick, but he would never, ever be able to do what Herbert had done.

Still, Herbert won't tell all his friends what she's like, he won't pinch the last of the milk in the morning and he won't get her pregnant. Men tend to do all those things, especially tell their friends. It's natural to want to boast, I suppose, but what has always annoyed me is that a girl is frigid if she won't and a slut if she will. You can't win!

Boasting about sexual prowess and conquests is human nature, and girls can be as bad as men. Sometimes it can get out of hand, as the next story shows, from Caroline, a slim, freckled girl with long red hair who appeared A Taste of Amber . . .

Against the Book – Carrie Gibson

There were eighteen in the shooting party, all men, and a
pretty typical lot they were. Most were City types, with two
block corporate hospitality bookings, along with a racing
driver and an ageing pop star. There was Anderson, too,
who was helping Daddy to play host. Anderson was Vicky
Belstone's boyfriend, and if he kept her happy, then he had
to be serious fun in bed. We got on really well too, and I
was tempted, although a little guilty at the same time.

Not that it would have been easy anyway, because I
never seemed to have a moment alone. I'm used to the
shooting party guests trying to get into my knickers, and
now and then I'll let myself go. This time all of them
seemed to be keen. I'm not so vain that I think every man
fancies me, so it seemed a bit odd. When I finally found a
chance to speak to Anderson alone I found out why.

The party was shooting a line down by the low copse,
and he had come back for more cartridges. I walked across
the lawn, trying to drop hints without being too obvious,
just jokingly trying to suggest that a spanking might do me
good. He caught on straight away, laughed and apologised, not because of Vicky, but because the party were
taking bets on who could get me into bed first.

I was furious. I'm not a prude, and I don't see sex as
something holy that should only take place between
married couples, after dark and with the lights out. I've

been with other girls and I've had my bottom smacked and I've even been on a collar and lead. None of it makes me feel bad, or used, or anything like that. This was different, not because of what they wanted to do to me, but because it was just so bloody arrogant of them!

Austin Myers had started it, and I wasn't surprised. He was something big in the City, and really flash, always boasting about how much he earned. Apparently they'd all got drunk together after dinner on the first night of our stay. The conversation had got round to me somehow, and Myers had boasted that he'd have me in bed before the end of the week. In fact, what he'd said was that he'd have me trying to get out of my knickers so fast that I'd trip over my own feet.

He wasn't the only arrogant one, not by a long chalk, and when some of the others had suggested that they stood a better chance, he offered to take bets. By the end of the evening and a serious quantity of Daddy's brandy, Mickey Jarett, the racing driver, had opened a book, with odds on each of the men's chances of success. That explained why they'd been so attentive, and I was glad I hadn't taken any of them up on it.

To win they didn't have to actually fuck me. A suck counted, or even one in my hand, anything which involved me making them come, although there had to be some sort of proof. Obviously I had to be willing, at least I hoped I did, but I could see more than one of them getting pretty pushy, or maybe trying to get me really drunk and then having me like that. Not that it would be simple, because as I had already noticed it was not easy to get me alone. Several were quite capable of coming to my room unexpectedly, Myers especially, who had put a thousand on himself to win.

Anderson said he'd be happy to play with me, and that Vicky wouldn't mind anything short of penetration. He offered to oblige, or fake it, and even to put some money on for me at his odds of four-to-one. I was tempted, but not enough; I wanted to get Myers back for being such an arrogant little prick, and just denying him the pleasure of my body failed to satisfy.

We talked as far as the style before I turned back. I was seething, and pretty humiliated too. My first thought was just to give them a piece of my mind, especially Myers and Jarett. I could even tell Daddy, and while I wasn't sure if he'd actually throw them out when they'd all paid so much, I could count on him to give them a lecture. The trouble was that they'd only think it was amusing and my anger and shame would just add spice to the resulting funny story.

Holding myself aloof all week wasn't much better. The odds of nobody succeeding were ten-to-one, and I could get Anderson to place my bet, so it was tempting. On the other hand, in a way, it would be playing along with their game, and it wasn't revenge, not real revenge. I wanted Myers to feel the way I did – Jarett, too, but mainly Myers.

I spoke to Anderson that evening, before we went down to dinner. He said that after the shooting the betting had got pretty heated, and that there was a lot of money riding on the outcome. He also had a couple of suggestions. One was to drop a hint to Myers that I was into female domination. Once I'd got him tied up I could thrash him at leisure, then refuse to finish him off. It was tempting, but I could see it backfiring badly. The same was true for nipping up to London and hiring a rent boy to take my place in bed, then inviting Myers to come to me. Anderson did persuade me to listen in to their after-dinner conversation that evening.

It was easy enough to do. I just excused myself early, saying I had a headache and declining all offers of a walk in the grounds. Instead of going to my bedroom, I nipped into the smoking room and tucked myself up in the sideboard, closing the door behind me. Anderson had agreed to ensure my safety by putting the trolley with the cheese and cigars in front of my hiding place, but I was still tense as they began to come in to the room.

All evening they had been really persistent. Myers had even tried to come into my room while I'd been changing for dinner. Not that I felt as bad as I had earlier. It was getting to be a bit of a game, and it appealed to my sense of mischief, so despite my nervousness I was also pretty excited as I waited for Daddy to retire.

It wasn't long, Daddy quickly excusing himself and leaving Anderson to play host. I was in total darkness, and most of their voices sounded much the same, but I could recognise some. Micky Jarett was easy, with his Liverpool accent, Myers less so, despite his arrogant drawl. Anderson was easy too, sounding like a younger version of Daddy, quiet, but with an easy assurance. The only other one I could be sure of was Davey Sams, who'd been the drummer with one of the big groups in the sixties. He was the oldest man there by quite a way, and different from the others, while his accent came straight from London's East End.

It didn't take long for them to get on to the subject of the bet, with several of them claiming to have more or less been invited into bed with me. Myers was the worst, claiming I was desperate for him and that it was only because the others were around that he hadn't already had me. The odds varied, and I learned most of them, which I imagined must have been rather like hearing yourself priced at a sale of slaves. Mickey Jarett was quoting himself at three to one. Most of the city boys were at longer odds, with Davey Sams quoted at thirty to one. Myers was favourite, at five to three.

'She wants it,' he was saying. 'You ought to see her wiggle that little arse at me, right in my face, like a little peach. She's choking for me and, if you bastards wouldn't keep cramping my style, I'd have had her by now.'

'Your style? Let me tell you, boy, twice she's given me the come-on, but you're always bloody there!'

'In your dreams, John.'

'It's me she wants. You lot just can't handle that, can you?'

'Sure, mate.'

'Yeah, right, well here's another twenty on myself Mickey?'

'Got it, Geoff.'

'What happens if Carrie chooses somebody else, not one of us?'

It was Anderson speaking, his question causing a brief pause in the conversation.

'Some chance,' Myers laughed. 'What, with me around?'

'And eighteen others,' someone else added.

'No, no, all bets taken,' Mickey cut in. 'She might well be into a bit of rough. Let's see, the two younger keepers, I'm offering ten to one. The head keeper, twenty-five, them two old buggers who helped with the beating, a hundred each.'

'What if she's a lezzie? She might make it with the cook?'

'What, fat Annie? Two hundred to one.'

'That greasy old git of a gardener?'

'Same odds, two hundred to one.'

'The big fat butler!'

'Fifty.'

'Goldsmith's gay,' Anderson's calm voice cut in.

'Five hundred then!'

'Her dad!'

'Yeah, Austin, sure. A thousand to one.'

'Here's a tenner on the cook, Mickey!'

'Taken. Anyone else reckon the cook?'

'No, no, not the cook, the cook's dog, that dirty little brown and white mongrel. It's always trying to fuck people's legs, I bet it'd be straight up if it caught her kneeling!'

'Got to be cautious on that one. A hundred to eight, and leg fucks don't count.'

'What do you give on the horse, then? Not her mare with the stupid name, that big brown bugger her dad rides.'

'Well, he's got twice the dick of anyone else.'

'More like ten times!'

'Speak for yourself, mate.'

'Hang on, hang on. OK, she's a country girl; who knows, she might be kinky that way. Ten to one on the horse. Twenty to one the field.'

Each suggestion was greeted with gales of laughter and left me red-faced with humiliation. It was bad enough them picturing me with the cook or the gardener, but the mention of Icarus, Daddy's hunter, was really

191

embarrassing, never mind the dog. Somehow the suggestion that it might be Daddy was worst of all. One or two of them even put money on, just showing off. It had me burning with embarrassment.

Everyone was laughing, at my expense, and Mickey was taking the bets down. I could hear the chink of glasses too, and Anderson's voice as he did his best to keep the drink flowing, which didn't seem to need much effort.

'Shame she went off,' someone said after a while. 'We could make her choose and fuck her on the table.'

'In your dreams, John.'

'What, a posh bird like her? No way. Some of the tarts I've known, sure, but not little Carrie.'

'The posh ones are the worst. I've known some right dirty little bitches.'

'Not Carrie. Sure, I reckon she goes, but not like that. You've got no style, that's your problem. Dim lights, nice quiet music, a bottle of champagne, that's the way into her knickers.'

There was more, lots more, most of it dirty, most of it humiliating, but nothing quite so bad as the suggestions for outsiders. Nor had listening to them given me any ideas about what to do.

I was no wiser the next day. Anderson suggested letting him put a hundred on old Worrell the gardener. A few quick jerks of my wrist and a bit of careful timing to make sure I got caught and we'd be twenty thousand up and Mickey Jarett wouldn't be laughing any more. It was easy for him to say – he didn't have to toss off a dirty old man. Anyway, Myers would think it was hilarious.

If anything I'd rather have done it to Icarus, which I suppose goes to show that Mickey Jarett wasn't as stupid as he looked. Not that it was worth the trouble, at ten to one, not to mention the stigma of getting seen doing it, which would have to happen if it was to count.

That was how bad it was. I spent most of the day thinking about the rival merits of the various filthy suggestions they'd made. I couldn't face Worrell, nor the consequences of doing Icarus. Pebble the dog might even have been OK if they hadn't outlawed what he was always trying to do to people's legs; anything else was out. Annie wouldn't have gone for it. Daddy would have shot Mickey Jarett. In any case, it kept coming back to the same old stumbling block: what to do about Myers?

I needed to think, and I also needed to get away from being constantly propositioned. If I hadn't known about the bet I would have taken one of them up on it, probably Nigel, who was quieter than the others and had nice eyes. Having said that, I was fairly sure he'd put twenty on me going with Pebble, so I was pretty glad Anderson had tipped me off. All the male attention was working me up, though, and it was getting pretty hard to stay cool and detached.

What I needed was a ride, out on the heath with the cool wind in my hair and nobody else but me and Athelyna, which is the name of a Saxon ancestor of mine and not silly at all. Obviously I'd noticed the huge size of Icarus's cock before, and I suppose it's impossible for any red-blooded girl to see a thing like that and not be at least a little affected. I'd never really thought about it, though, not the way they'd suggested. As I saddled Athelyna up it was impossible not to keep glancing at Icarus and the great meaty black thing that hung from his belly. It goes stiff sometimes, for no apparent reason, and it started to as I mounted up. The thought immediately came to me of just how difficult it would be to take it in my fanny, and what it would feel like.

I've never left the stable yard so fast. My cheeks were blazing, and must have been crimson. I've done some rude things in my time – I've even greased another girl's bottom hole with butter so she could be buggered – but not that, never ever. It was hard to get it out of my head, and as I rode up towards the high ground I was alternately thinking of how it would feel and cursing Austin Myers.

I actually wanted to come, but I didn't trust my own feelings. I really quite like to be taken charge of during sex, and there were two ways my fantasies would go if I tried

193

to do it. It's very easy for real humiliation to turn into sexual humiliation in my head, and one way was to imagine myself giving in to Myers. The other was to think of Icarus.

My favourite thing is a spanking. There's something about being punished that makes my inhibitions slip away, and nothing makes me feel so sexual and so open. Unfortunately there was nobody on the heath who was going to smack my bottom for me, and the only person I'd have trusted to do it, Anderson, was with the others.

In fact I couldn't do anything, not anything that ended in my partner coming anyway. Well, that wasn't strictly true, because I might not get found out, but that would mean going with a stranger and I've never had the courage, or stupidity, to just let myself get picked up. All I could do was play with myself, and after all my dirty thoughts, made worse by riding, I was getting desperate. I did try, but if I hadn't needed a pee I might even have resisted. As it was I had to stop, and that was it.

I reined Athelyna in on a lonely bit of heath by a big stand of pines, feeling naughty and guilty all at the some time. I popped my jodhpurs and knicks down to my ankles in the shelter of a clump of bracken and let go. It does feel naughty peeing in the open, fanny and bottom bare to the air in a thoroughly embarrassing position, and a pretty helpless one as long as the pee is running.

There's always the temptation to have a sneaky rub, and now it was impossible to resist. I dried myself with a tissue and moved a little away from my wet patch, shaking my head with my need and at my own inability to resist it. Squatting is a good position, both because it's rude and because I don't get my clothes dirty. It's also the position that'd I'd have been in if I'd had to see to Icarus's cock, but I pushed that firmly back in my mind.

Instead I concentrated on spanking, thinking of how nice it feels to lie helpless over a lover's lap, maybe with just my knickers down, maybe naked, always with my bottom bare. Always with the one who's doing the spanking fully clothed, though, to bring home my exposure to me. It's afterwards that the cocks come out, and go in my mouth or up my fanny, with my bottom all red and tingly as I say thank you for the spanking.

Anderson was good, I'd heard how good, and I could just imagine being across his knee. He'd take my jodhpurs down, slowly, peeling them off my bum. My knickers would come with them, leaving me all bare and ready, my bottom sticking up high, showing to everyone as I was prepared for my spanking, showing it, showing my fanny, knickers down with my bottom on show and eighteen cocks being readied for my hole . . .

I stopped, breathing hard. The fantasy had been going the wrong way, towards the humiliation of being punished in front of the shooting party, then fucked, undoubtedly by Myers. I know myself too well to think it would have gone any other way.

Closing my eyes, I tried to concentrate. Anderson might have come with me, had he not been playing host. Then I could have had my spanking in peace, out here in the woods where I could be punished privately, with only the horses to know. He'd find a stump to sit on, or maybe a fallen tree. Over I'd go, bottom up, hands on the ground. My jodhpurs would come down, my knickers too, and I'd be bare and ready. He'd spank me, firmly, telling me off as I was punished, my boots kicking up and down as I struggled under the smacks. Icarus would be watching, his huge cock growing . . .

It was no good; my mind would betray me every time. My legs were growing sore from squatting so long, and the worry of somebody coming was growing. That was it, it would be someone from the Forestry Commission, a woman, a big, fat woman with legs like tree trunks and huge red arms. She wouldn't be the sort to stand any nonsense, not from anybody, certainly not from some dirty little brat like me. She'd be outraged at seeing me playing with myself, grabbing me by the ear. I'd be thrown over the bonnet of her Landrover, knocking the breath out of me. Before I could recover my arm would have been twisted into the small of my back. My jodhpurs would come down, jerked off my bottom despite my squeaks and protests. I'd beg for my knickers to stay up but she wouldn't even bother to answer, just grabbing them and wrenching them so hard they tore. Then I'd be spanked, hard, so hard. I don't break easily during spanking, but she'd make me, smacking away with her huge hand until I was squealing and begging, kicking and cursing, snivelling and blubbering . . .

I came, crying out softly as I thought of how badly I needed it, and as I came the solution came to me, pure and simple, fully formed in my head.

The table stretched away in front of me, ten men on one side, nine on the other, Daddy at the far end, separated from me by so much glass and silver that I could barely see him. Myers had managed to get the place on my left, Davey Sams was to my right. All evening Myers had been giving me everything he'd got, with talk of money and cars mixed with remarks on how much more beautiful country girls were and how he'd always liked red hair. Davey's conversation was very different, all in the past really, about things he'd done and the people he'd known in the Sixties. Not that I caught much of it, because with Myers' smooth manner and easy flattery I wasn't really paying attention.

I'd decided I couldn't wait any longer. I've never been good at holding back. Tonight was the night, and I'd had Anderson put down a couple of bets for me to make sure that whatever happened I didn't lose out completely. I was getting drunk quickly too, drowning my nervousness in champagne, Mosel and Claret as one course followed another.

I was actually beginning to enjoy it, and finding the obvious envy of those further down the table amusing. They could see me and Myers, even overhear us, and they must have realised that our conversation was getting increasingly intimate. Certainly they must have seen that I was getting increasingly giggly.

Myers knew he was onto a good thing. He also knew he'd have to make his move soon. Once the pudding was finished we'd move through into the smoking room and he wouldn't be able to monopolise me any more. He only needed his moment, and it came as Goldsmith poured me a glass of Barsac. I was blocked from Davey by the bulk of the butler, and Myers leaned close, his hand sliding down around my waist.

'We'll have to retire to the smoking room soon, but let's finish this conversation over a bottle of champagne later . . . in your room.'

'I'm not in my room. I'm sleeping up in the servants' passage; that way I don't get pestered. Third door on the left from the stairs. Don't say anything when you come. Just slip in: I'm a bit shy.'

'Ideal.'

He gave me his best smile and moved back, his hand dropping to follow the contours of my lower back. Goldsmith moved on. I ate pudding in silence, hardly aware of the conversation around me. It was the same in the smoking room, with everybody chatting blithely away while to me it all seemed to come through a haze. I excused myself as soon as Daddy had left, gave Myers a coy smile and made for the servants' stairs.

The room I had chosen was about a quarter the size of my own room, barely furnished with a view out to the parapet and a piece of sky. Somehow it seemed perfect for sordid liaisons, and I was feeling more and more excited as I undressed and put on a short robe, over nothing. I knew I'd have to wait, and sat on the bare mattress, listening and toying with my nipples to arouse myself. It wasn't too long, and then I heard the door go across the passage. My heart was right up in my mouth as I crossed the landing, knocked quickly on the door and pushed in without waiting for an answer. Goldsmith was sitting in a chair, still in uniform, his big hands folded placidly across his belly.

I couldn't speak, but I knew there was no time to mess about. He was looking at me, a man I'd known since childhood, a big, paternal figure, always there, heavy and silent in the background. I stepped forwards, feeling so uncertain. He nodded and patted his lap, an affectionate

197

gesture, not threatening or pushy at all. I didn't sit, though, I laid myself down, closing my eyes as I settled myself over his knee. He never said a word, but he understood, gently lifting the tail of my robe to bare my bottom.

His arm closed around my waist, not hard, but heavy and somehow forceful. My toes were on the floor and I lifted my bottom, pushing up, offering myself. His palm touched me, covering most of both cheeks. He pushed, gently, lifted it and brought it down with a firm swat, full across my bottom. I cried out, not loud, and as much from pure emotion as pain.

Goldsmith spanked me well, swat after swat across my bare bottom, never saying a word, but giving me the punishment I wanted. I took it in silence, panting gently to the stinging slaps, feeling my bottom warm and the sexy, wanton emotions in my head grow until at last they had pushed out all the embarrassment and shame and I knew I could do it. I didn't stop him, though, but let him have his fill, enjoying my bare bottom and the sight of my open cheeks and wet fanny.

He must have known I was ready, and there was no need to speak as he finally stopped and allowed me to slide to the floor. I crawled around, pushing out my warm red bottom so that he could see what he had done if he wanted to. He already had his fly down, wide open beneath his belly, and as I got into position he pulled out his balls and cock. I'd meant to do it in my hand, a quick flurry of tugs, keeping contact to a minimum. I'd been spanked, though, and it seemed so ungrateful to show distaste for my task.

As he allowed his body to slip forwards on the chair I was already opening my mouth. I took it in, all of it, the full, fleshy mass of his manhood, cock and balls as well. He tasted strongly male, also of talc, and I knew that he'd had the decency to wash and prepare for me. It was so typical of him, seeking to please even when he knew it would be me who was the servant.

My sucking was eager, genuine, driven by friendliness as much as the fact that I was thanking a man who'd given me a spanking. He soon began to grow, his cock stiffening until his balls slipped from my mouth. The head came out, poking from the meaty foreskin, red and glistening as I pulled back to watch, taking him briefly in my hand. I hadn't expected to be so turned on, not nearly, and before I went back to sucking I shrugged off my robe to leave myself nude, nude and kneeling between his knees, my smacked bottom stuck out behind, his cock rearing proud in front of me.

I took it back in my mouth, enjoying the firm, meaty feel. It was lovely, and I didn't want to hurry, but I knew I had to. I began to mouth his cock, sucking my cheeks in and moving my tongue on the underside. He gave the softest of moans, deep in his throat. It was too good to waste, and I let my hand slip back, between my thighs, finding the wet flesh of my fanny, open and sensitive, my bump a hard point in the middle. As I began to masturbate he started to stroke my hair, soothing me as I sucked, making me feel so wanted. It was perfect, spanked and sucking the cock of the man who had punished me and finding that he didn't gloat, or try to push me further, but stroked and comforted. I came like that, whimpering a little in my throat as my muscles squeezed, really revelling in the cock in my mouth.

He was nearly there, breathing hard and pushing up into my mouth. I took his balls in hand, rolling them over my fingers. Pulling back quickly, I pursed my lips and rocked forwards again, letting his cock penetrate the tight bud of my mouth. He came at that, his cock jerking as I took it in, deep so that he came in my throat. I swallowed dutifully, gulping down his slimy, salty come.

Even as I pulled back from his cock I heard the noise and realised that I'd taken too long. Goldsmith heard it too, hastily putting his cock away as a door slammed somewhere down the corridor. A voice sounded, female and angry, followed by a bleating protest from a man.

'You should perhaps stay here, Miss Caroline,' Goldsmith remarked as he made for the door.

I wiped my lips and reached for my robe, pulling it on as Goldsmith closed the door behind him. His voice was adding to the noise outside, demanding to know what was going on. I waited, listening, until Croom's voice joined in, along with another.

At that I stepped into the passage. The scene was wonderful to see. Annie was at the centre, clad in a huge, frilly nightie, one bare red arm extended to the neck of Austin Myers' dressing gown, which she was obviously not going to let go of in a hurry. Goldsmith stood by, looking like thunder, Croom by him, stern and reproachful. Mickey Jarett was there too, and as I emerged from the same door which Goldsmith had come out of, my bare legs showing beneath a robe that hardly covered my fanny, his eyes flicked quickly to me, then to Goldsmith's fly, which was still undone.

'It looks like the butler did it after all,' Croom quipped. 'What was it, five hundred to one?'

Revenge is sweet, and sexual revenge sweeter still. Generally that sort of situation arises out of bad luck, and it is a drawback of being attractive that you are always seen in sexual terms. On the other hand, some people are quite capable of getting into awkward sexual situations without any help at all. The next story, is from Ella, who we met in Bad Penny, *a student of mine. She is petite, delicate and somewhat fey, and also a confirmed believer in all things supernatural . . .*

Black Shuck – Ella Daniels

The track ended abruptly at a gate. Beyond was a field, beyond that reeds, with two brownish red sails visible on what must have been either a broad or a stretch of river. It was the third dead-end I'd come to and I had to admit that I was completely lost. To pull off the main roads so that I could get a proper feel for the countryside had seemed a great idea at the time. Now I wasn't so sure, although I couldn't deny the feel was there.

I'd wanted to catch the atmosphere that inspired M R James and Conan Doyle to set gruesome tales in East Anglia. It was there in plenty, from the great flint churches, some in ruins, to the cliff edge villages crumbling slowly into the sea. True, it was hard to find anything sinister about the hot, flat land I was driving through, nor the placid cows and slowly moving sails within my range of vision. Rationalists will always try to say that it's all in the mind anyway, but that's not my experience. The present scene was pleasantly rural, Dunwich had been creepy, and it wasn't just because I knew the history and the stories.

It took another hour to find the cottage, a bungalow of decaying red brick and flint at the end of a track no different from the others I had followed. I unpacked and bathed, then put on a light summer dress that promised the most comfort for what promised to be a warm, close evening. There was a pub about half a mile from the cottage, at a crossroads, and it seemed an ideal place to start my researches, also to have supper. I decided to walk, partly so that I could enjoy a drink with my meal and partly for the sake of the atmosphere.

The lane was lonely, a narrow dirt track between high hedges, with only the farm that owned my cottage on its whole length. I am very sensitive to the supernatural, and it did feel eerie, perhaps unnaturally quiet. More than once I found myself looking back over my shoulder, half-dreading, half-expectant of what I might see. There was nothing, and I reached the pub with the familiar mixture of relief and regret.

I was actually quite nervous about going into the pub. Some people are still funny about women going into bars alone, even now, and I wasn't at all sure what sort of welcome I would get. As it was I needn't have worried. There were only two other customers, a pair of weather-beaten men in rough work clothes who ignored me completely. The landlady was friendly, and agreed to do me egg and chips even though they didn't usually serve food midweek. I had a couple of glasses of white wine with my meal, then ordered a gin and orange while I decided how best to get into a conversation about local hauntings and apparitions. In the past I've always found that you need to gain people's confidence before they'll really open up, and now was no exception.

Two more people had come in while I was eating, farm workers by the look of it, big, sturdy men with red faces and callused hands. One I recognised from when I'd picked the key up at the farm, which gave me my introduction and after that it was easy. I stood a couple of rounds and soon had them talking. I learned about how the old railway line to Walberswick had cut through a Viking burial ground and the eerie feelings and sounds walkers had experienced in the now abandoned cutting. That was really exciting, and I determined to visit there the next day. Next they began to talk about the ghostly black dog that was supposed to haunt both Norfolk and Suffolk. This caused quite a discussion, with each of them having a different opinion. The landlady argued that the dog was a manifestation of the devil, to which the farmer replied that he was supposed to be Odin's black dog and that the legends went right back to the time when the Vikings had raided along the coast. One of the labourers was more sceptical, saying he had read that the story had been invented by eighteenth-century smugglers to discourage interest in their activities. All the others believed in the legend, but slightly different versions. They called the dog different names too, Black Shuck, and the Galleytrot, both of which sent a shiver down my spine. The only thing they could agree on was that if you heard his footsteps coming up behind you the last thing to do was run.

I was thrilled, and was desperately scribbling notes as they talked. After another round of drinks one claimed to have actually seen the dog. It had come towards him down a lane one chilly winter evening back in the Fifties. He'd thought it was just a large black mongrel until he'd seen the red of its eyes, which left him too terrified to move, but when the dog passed he had looked back and it had gone. That triggered an admission by the oldest of the labourers. During the war he had been watching an aerial combat with an American serviceman in one of the lanes when the dog had leaped out from the hedge, red eyes blazing and jaws gaping wide. He had known what it was and held his ground. The American had run, right into the path of a burning Heinkel as it crashed into the ground. He even offered to show me the crater as proof.

By closing time I was shaking with excitement, and very drunk. It was a wonderfully rich mine of stories, but as the men left one by one I found myself facing the prospect of the walk back to the cottage with rising trepidation. In the end I had to leave, and as the pub door closed behind me I was left in absolute silence, suddenly broken by the call of a bird. The moon was bright, near full, casting long shadows on the crossroads. I was shivering and biting my lip, as scared as I'd ever been during my ghost hunting, but deep down hoping it would happen.

The lane was in blackness, only the hedges and the occasional patch of moonlight showing my way. After a couple of hundred yards I realised that I ought to have made a visit to the loo before leaving the pub. I needed to go, badly, so after a moment to listen in case anybody came, I whipped down my panties and squatted in the lane. It was all too easy to imagine a car coming and catching me in my embarrassing position, so I pushed hard and finished quickly, only to realise that I'd peed my panties. I couldn't very well pull them up again, so I took them off completely, reasoning that it wouldn't show under my dress and that nobody was going to see anyway.

It was still embarrassing to be walking along with a pair of dripping panties dangling from my hand, and I was praying that the people in the farm had all gone to bed. I hurried past the farm gate, knowing that only my cottage lay beyond. The feeling of being bare under my dress was odd too, and a little naughty, which pushed thoughts of phantom dogs to the back of my mind. At least it did until I heard the noise behind me.

My heart leaped straight into my mouth, and if I hadn't just peed I would have wet myself then and there. The noise was the padding of paws, a dog's paws, coming up behind me at a trot. It took all my will power not to break into a blind run, but I remembered what the men had said: never run, never ever run. I walked on, shaking hard and listening to the gentle thuds of the beast's paws. It was Black Shuck, it had to be, doubtless summoned by our conversation. Speak of the Devil and he's sure to come, and now he had.

I looked back, I had to, but I could see nothing, only to stop dead as the moon moved out from behind a cloud and two glowing eyes appeared, no more than ten yards behind me. As I turned I stumbled, going down on my knees in shock and fear. I tried to rise, only to stop as something touched my leg. He was behind me, touching me, and suddenly I couldn't have moved if I'd wanted to. I could hear his breathing, a deep, rasping sound like nothing I'd ever heard from a mortal dog.

My head was spinning with drink and I felt detached, not in the real world at all. Maybe I wasn't, but I felt everything, his huge muzzle touching the bare skin of my

legs, pushing up under my skirt, sniffing. A little pee had
run out and I could feel it, warm and wet as it ran down
the inside of my thigh. His tongue touched me, lapping at
the salty pee, then higher, up my skirt, lifting it. My sex
was bare and his tongue was on it, flicking, lapping, his
thick saliva running down my flesh.

I was being prepared for sex, by a spirit, maybe by the
Devil himself if the landlady was right. My vagina seemed
to open and swell, welcoming it despite my terror. Coming
wide to accept what I knew would be put in it, and what
my mind was struggling to accept. His licking was becoming firmer, deeper, up the full length of my crease, anus
included, as if to cleanse me for his use. My mouth had
come open, gaping wide in helpless response and I found
myself reaching back, pulling up my dress, displaying
myself naked from waist to feet. In answer his tongue
burrowed into my vagina, deep, filling me until I was
moaning.

His tongue left my vagina. It was going to happen, I did
not doubt it. I felt I should be nude; somehow it was
proper. Quickly I pulled my dress over my head, my bra
following, baring myself in sublime surrender to what was
about to be done. I looked back and now I could see him,
a huge, black creature, dim in moonlight, Black Shuck
himself, about to take me and fuck me. I moved onto all
fours to get more comfortable for mounting, my head
swimming with wonder and ecstasy. He came forwards
behind me, his paws scrapping on my haunches, his thick
belly fur rubbing on my buttocks. His legs came down
around my middle, trapping me, even as I felt the hot, hard
tip of his penis bump against my sex.

He tried to enter me but missed, rutting between my
cheeks and prodding at my anus, panting all the while. I
cocked my bottom up, raising my hole, and in it went, deep
up me with one, long, smooth motion. As he began to
hump on my bottom I was transported, undergoing the
strongest emotions of my life – fear, yes, but also
sublime, religious ecstasy. It was wonderful, I was kneeling
and the Devil's cock was inside me, mating me, maybe

making me pregnant, and I realised that it was what I'd longed for all my life.

I was groaning as he fucked me, mumbling through open lips, only to be set panting as he gave a sudden flurry of hard pushes. His cock went further in me, to the hilt, so that his hair was tickling my anus. I could feel his balls slapping on my sex as he rode me, hard and rough, the coarse hairs tickling my clitoris. He was going to make me come, I knew it, and then something began to swell in the mouth of my vagina. It was incredible, like nothing else, his penis swelling at the base, filling my hole and stretching it until I was plugged full, my skin straining on his cock. He kept moving, fucking and fucking, the knot of meat moving in my hole, his balls smacking my sex, teasing my clitoris, his belly pushing over and over onto my upraised bottom . . .

So I came, the most beautiful, longest orgasm of my life, cried out to the night with my body mounted and filled, clasped in hairy arms, a moment of perfect, absolute ecstasy. It seemed to go on for ever, one long, long peak with little ones, higher still, each time his balls nudged my sex. I collapsed as it happened, my face to the ground, my mouth full of soil, my hands on my breasts, squeezing my hard nipples between my fingers. There was come in me, I knew it, and that was the thought I held as I came, fucked by the Devil and made pregnant. Caught and mounted, but not raped, taken willingly, deep, deep up my hole.

I must have fainted, because the next thing I remember I was lying in the lane, nude and soiled, with warm fluid trickling from my vagina and my mouth full of dirt. Of Black Shuck there was no sign; he had vanished as suddenly as he had arrived. My head was still swimming, and if it hadn't been for the state of my vagina I'd have thought it was all a hallucination. The uncertainty grew as I half-walked, half-ran back to the cottage. I was still nude, clutching my dress and undies in my hands. Inside I turned all the lights on and made a thorough job of locking up, despite my ecstasy.

At last I felt secure enough, and I made an inspection of my body in the bathroom mirror. All doubts left me. There

207

were red marks on my ribs and the sides of my breasts, little scratches where his claws had caught me. My vagina was full of sperm and sore, and with a mixture of fear and hope I wondered if I really was pregnant. I washed and cleaned my clothes, but I didn't douche, and after a period staring out at the moonlit fields I fell asleep.

In the morning I felt more rational and tried to put my experience down on paper. I had met Black Shuck, that I was sure of, and he had mated me. Whether he was the devil, a Norse deity or some spectral form I didn't know. He had taken me in solid form, so unless I had been transported to some para-reality he had physical identity, or at least could assume it at will. All that fitted with the legends, which spoke of claw marks and tooth marks. None spoke of him having sex with women – but then, who would have admitted it?

I had arranged to meet the old labourer at the pub so that he could take me to see the crater made by the crashing Heinkel. That meant that I would be able to ask him further questions, although I wasn't going to tell him what had happened to me in a hurry. I set off down the lane, now brightly lit in the morning sun. I couldn't find the site of my experience, which added a new facet to the mystery. Possibly the lane in which I had met and been mated by Black Shuck was not the lane that I was on at all.

The farm gate had been there, I remembered passing it, and as I reached it I paused. It was slightly open, and there, dozing in the sun, was the largest, shaggiest black mongrel dog I had ever seen, his eyes raised to mine in a hopeful, even thankful expression.

Silly girl. Still, if it had been me I'd have treated the whole thing rationally and missed out on the experience, real or otherwise.

Some experiences are best not real, particularly fantasies that involve being sexually forced, even raped. This is always difficult ground, and while the fantasy of being forced to do something dirty can be compelling, it is important to understand that it is exactly that, a fantasy, and not the desire for the reality.

My last essay explores my fantasies about being in situations over which I have no control. These vary, and do not so much involve me actually being forced against my will, but rather being made to do things regardless of my will . . .

Damsels in Distress – Penny Birch

Being female and sexually submissive is very much against the grain of modern society. We're always told we should be strong, empowered, in control. That's as may be, but no amount of preaching can alter the fact that many women's sexuality revolves around exactly the opposite. Sure, it may be hard, even impossible, to translate fantasy into reality, but that doesn't alter the basic desire. In reality I always make the choice, even if it is the choice to surrender myself completely, subject only to a stop word. Fantasy is different; I let my imagination run wild.

At the simplest level a woman, or a man for that matter, may enjoy fantasising about something they don't really want, most often forced sex. This very definitely does not mean they want it to happen in reality, not in any way, shape or form. The psychology behind this is complicated, but one aspect of it comes from the way old-fashioned social values deny a female her sexuality, or stigmatise a woman who expresses it. Thus it may be more acceptable to say 'he got me drunk and we ended up in bed before I really knew what I was doing', than 'he was so fine I went down on him in the cinema and we ended up in bed'. Things are changing and girls are bolder, but if you think it's no longer true, try friends' reactions to, 'The bastard tied me up and squirted a pint of milk up my bum with a turkey baster' and, 'It was great, I asked him to put me in

bondage and give me a milk enema, and he did it, with a
turkey baster!'

I was brought up to believe that sex is dirty. I know,
rationally, that it isn't, but I still get a kick out of the
feeling that something is being done to me, or that I've
been made to do it, or that I can't help it, rather than that
I'm doing it by my own choice. Being in distress thrills me,
and the dirtier, the more shameful the distress, the better.
Other emotions work for other people; fear, for instance,
and helplessness. Two friends, who've never met, both have
fantasies about being tied helpless to a railway line. I can
see the power in it, but it doesn't work for me. Shame does.

For me, much of the thrill of exhibitionism comes from
the shame I feel. Others feel differently, and the last thing
they want is humiliation. This is even true of being a
pony-girl. For some it is a very elaborate form of sexual
display, for others an exquisite erotic humiliation. Some
girls even get a sexy thrill out of being spanked without any
of the burning shame that brings me most of my pleasure.

One special thrill comes from the idea of people being
indifferent to my feelings, perhaps regarding my distress
not as exciting, but as silly, a nuisance, a childish affecta-
tion . . .

The nurse hands me the surgery gown without a word and
bustles out, clearly too busy to worry herself with my
concerns. I look round, realising that I am going to have
to undress in front of everybody. It would have been bad
enough in front of women, but more than half the other
patients are male. None show an open interest, but they
can all see me. I'd expected bed curtains, especially as the
ward is mixed, but there aren't any. I stand there, vaguely
wondering what to do and going slowly red.

'Do hurry along, Miss Birch, we have a schedule to
keep,' the nurse snaps, turning briefly from the form she is
filling in.

I feel stupid and small as I put my hands to the buttons
of my blouse. After all, I am in for my own good, and I
am being treated for free. That doesn't make having to

strip in front of half a dozen leering old men any better. I am going to have to take my blouse off to get the gown on. After that I can finish under the protection of the gown, even though it will still be embarrassing.

It is, horribly embarrassing. Even just standing there in my bra I know I am crimson in the face, but when I put the gown on it just gets worse. It is tiny, obviously designed for a child and not a grown woman at all. In front it barely comes down to my pussy, and at the back the ties leave a wide gap that I just know will show the whole of my bottom crease. Not that it makes much difference, because my cheeks are going to be peeping out from under the hem anyway. I glance at the nurse, wondering if I dare demand an adult gown, but the hard, impatient look on her face as she scribbles on the forms tells me what the answer will be.

I am shivering as I undress. My bra comes off easily enough, but I have to close my eyes when I take my jeans down, to shut out my surroundings. It feels awful with my panties showing. I know full well that I am supposed to take them off, but I just can't make myself do it. Instead I stand there dithering and biting my lip. Finally the nurse notices.

'Come on, Miss Birch, pants off. Do you think I haven't seen a naked woman before?' she demands.

It makes me feel so silly, and before I really know what I am doing my thumbs are in the waistband of my panties. Down they come, and off, showing my bare bum to the whole ward, maybe even a peek of my pussy as I bend to pull them off one ankle. As I turn I catch a sly little smile on one of the men's faces, just for an instant before he turns back to the book he is pretending to read. The nurse pays me no attention whatsoever.

I scramble into bed, blushing furiously. I've been told to hurry, but for the next half hour nothing happens. Finally the Sister comes in, a big, strapping woman with huge red arms and a no-nonsense expression on her face. I'd found the nurse daunting, but she is worse.

'Turn over,' she commands as she approaches me, her tone making it very clear that I should have known what to do without having to be told.

She is pulling the bedclothes down even as I turn. My gown is whisked up, and to my horror I find my bare bottom on show to the whole room. She leaves me like that as she pulls on gloves, then takes a thermometer from her pocket. I open my mouth helpfully and she gives me a look that tells me immediately that I am being both stupid and foolishly coy. It also tells me where that thermometer is going.

I shut my eyes as her hand goes to my bum. My cheeks are opened and the cold glass of the thermometer touches my anus, letting me know that it is showing to everyone. The Sister gives a little tut, as if to suggest that I hadn't wiped properly, and prods the thing at my hole. In it goes, up my bum, and my cheeks are released, holding it in place.

For three minutes I lie there, trying to hold back my sobs of humiliation. Three minutes, but it seems like three hours, with ten pairs of eyes feasting on my bare pink bottom, the men lecherous, the women amused. At last it is over, the thermometer pulled out with a quick jerk. The Sister reads it and grunts, not troubling to give me the result.

'Sample, please, Miss Birch,' she announces, dropping the thermometer into a dish of antiseptic.

She is holding out a bed pan. I can only stare in horror, not really believing that she could expect me to fill it in front of other people, but knowing that that is exactly what she expects. Her expression changes from cold efficiency to the sort of look I might expect if I were a particularly obtuse dog.

'Come, come, we don't have all day,' she chides, shaking the pan at me.

'I . . . I can't,' I stammer. 'Not here.'

'There's no such word as can't,' she snaps. 'Now will you do it, or do we have to catheterise you?'

'I'll do it,' I answer, aware of the sullen tone in my own voice but unable to keep it out.

I pull the sheet up, concealing myself, an act that provokes a testy sigh from Sister. I can tell what she thinks of me, that I'm a spoiled, prissy little brat who's just slowing her job down for her. I don't care; I'm not showing my bare pussy to the room, especially while I pee. It's not easy, but I manage to do it, and as my pee squirts into the pan it sounds like a waterfall. Halfway through she hands me the specimen bottle, which I manage to fill. One of the men makes a remark to another, finding my efforts to keep the sheet covering my pussy comical in the extreme. I don't answer, but I feel my face go redder still. At last I'm done and Sister hands the pan to the nurse. Again, as I extract the thing from under my now damp bottom, I make an effort not to show anything.

'I can't think why you're being so bashful,' the nurse remarks. 'Everybody will see it when you're shaved, anyway.'

'Shaved?' I demand, but she is already lifting a stirrup and clipping it into place.

I look on in horror, my mouth open and my cheeks flaming red as the stirrups are prepared. There is a weird, crawling feeling in my pussy and I can do nothing as the bedsheet is pulled unceremoniously down. My gown is tweaked high, right up over my belly.

'Come, come, do try and be helpful,' Sister chides.

My feet come up as if of their own accord, numb with shock. Into the stirrups they go, spreading my pussy. Two of the men are now leering openly, and the women are watching too, obviously enjoying my distress. I am wide open, showing every detail of my sex. Sister gives a look of disapproval and a click of her tongue as she sees how hairy I am, another nuisance. The nurse is preparing the razor, an evil-looking cut-throat like something Sweeney Todd might have used. Sister has taken a bar of carbolic soap, coarse and green.

I watch as the soap is worked into a lather, wishing they would hurry up so that I can cover up my sex again. Not only my cheeks are red with my blushes, but my whole face, my neck too. It is really obvious, but no more obvious than my nipples, which have gone hard and are poking the thin cotton of my gown up into two little humps.